THE HELL WHAT BROKE LOOSE WHEN CHARLIE CAME

SENJA SUUTARI

Boilerplate Books, llc | Maine

For information contact us at www.boilerplatebooks.com
Book and Cover design by Boilerplate Books, LLC
ISBN: 9781734793406

10 9 8 7 6 5 4 3 2 1

CONTENTS

CHAPTER 1

NIKKI LEINO had been crying and unpacking for two days. She had walked out of a five-year relationship, bought a mobile home for seven thousand dollars—practically her life's savings—and moved into it. For the first couple of days all she'd done was weep as she unpacked one cardboard box after another. She was free now, wasn't she, so why did she feel so wretched? She situated books, files, clothing, her few household items, her portable TV, her desk, and her prized possessions: her computer and printer. As an act of liberation, she set her art table in the largest part of the house—the living room, the front room overlooking the lake. There, after she'd taken down the awful brown curtains and yellowed Venetian blinds, she had a full view of lake and mountains. No longer did Nikki have to keep her work out of sight, sealed into the tiniest upstairs cubicle.

Nikki had never been entirely on her own before. As a child she had lived with her family. As a young adult, she'd shared apartments and rents with various roommates while they all dealt with the *angst* of making it in "the real world," waiting to become rich and famous.

Nikki would write and illustrate children's books, and, once successful, she would do Good Works and make the world a better place. All that had changed when she met Phil.

Well, Phil Lowry was history now! Nikki needed a new life, and she'd have to start from scratch. During their five years on Vancouver Island, she had made no friends, at least no close ones. The people she knew had been Phil's friends, at least that was how Nikki thought of them—actually Phil's business associates—whom Nikki had been expected to entertain at a moment's notice. *(These people are important to my career, Nikki. I need you to help me. You can do your drawing anytime. It's not as though your job even pays enough to support you.)*

Phil had been right about one thing. Her dream of becoming a writer of children's books *hadn't* paid off. Still, dammit, she wasn't ready to toss it aside like a gum wrapper either. She took a day job at a book store with the idea of developing markets as a freelancer in her spare time. She soon discovered that any free time she had was entirely at Phil's disposal, and if Phil hadn't done so much traveling, Nikki probably would not have made the career move that her mate found so galling.

At the time, it had been almost accidental. Nikki enjoyed working crossword puzzles. One day, instead of solving the puzzle in a magazine, she had used the blank grid to design one of her own. To her surprise, she found she had a talent for it. Why not try it? Phil was away at a convention on the mainland. Nikki spent the weekend designing four 15x15 crosswords, drew grids and inked them in, typed up sets of clues and sent them to the editors of a puzzle magazine. It had been a fun mental exercise, and, anyway, what did she have to lose? If she sold a few puzzles, she could use the money for art supplies. A few weeks later she had received a note of acceptance and a check. Phil had thought it was cute—then.

Four years later, Nikki was producing enough puzzles a year to be able to quit the book shop job and work full time at home. Phil affected a pose of amused tolerance: "Oh, she's still cranking out her little puzzles. I keep telling her she should get a *real* job, but she seems to enjoy it, and *somebody* has to do it, I suppose."

It was sobering, now, to Nikki, that after five years of living with Phil, her "little job" with its paraphernalia was really all she had. Her decision to leave, fraught with anguish though not hastily made, subsumed that she wanted nothing from the relationship and was willing to forfeit everything. *Leaping empty handed into the void.* The void turned out to be Eagle Lake Park, owned by the Moons.

The Moon family owned a hundred hectares of land along the edge of the lake; operated a campground, a small convenience store (open only in summer months) and exercised absolute authority over who was permitted to live in their domain. Nikki had somehow managed to pass muster with Adelaide Moon, her husband, George, as well as Hector and Ida Moon, George's elderly parents. Whether Adelaide's maternal instincts had been aroused by Nikki's obvious misery, or whether the aging vacant mobile was becoming a liability, Adelaide had okayed the sale, and Nikki was in.

Nikki's unit was one of eight, lined up side by side, a little unevenly, like pigs at a trough with their snouts facing the water. The trailers stood on a ledge carved out of a mountainside, with a steep slope rising behind them and a precipitous drop in front. A narrow nameless gravel road gave access to parking spaces between the units, spaces just big enough to accommodate two vehicles parked one behind the other. Towering Douglas fir trees on the hillside behind them offered some shade, but rooms facing the lake got the full brunt of the afternoon sun. Nikki thought that the light would be good for her artwork.

Her unit was ten years old—a single, with two bedrooms, one bath, and a living area separated from the kitchen only by a counter partition. It had been lived in by heavy smokers; the walls, ceiling tiles, and every surface was overlaid with a wash of nicotine yellow (burnt sienna with a touch of cadmium, Nikki, the artist, noted) and the place reeked of stale cigarette smoke. She knew she would have to repair and remodel, and, although Nikki had walked out of a house filled with furniture, her own possessions were so meager that she had needed to buy a table and chairs as well as a mattress to replace the moldering hulk that had come with the place. But the pad rent (which included water and garbage pickup) was only a hundred a month. If her markets held, she'd be able to scrape by. She had piled her belongings into her six-year-old Mazda truck—a truck just a little older than the relationship she was leaving—and moved into her new dwelling. Its smallness suited Nikki's desire to curl up in a hole and die.

CHAPTER 2

THE TEAKETTLE was whistling on the gas range. Nikki had showered and dressed. This living alone was *weird*. You could get up whenever you wanted. You could go to work in your pajamas if you wanted. Nikki had realized that no longer would she have to get up at six o'clock in the morning, in winter, to shovel out the driveway if it snowed, because Phil, who had a bad back, had to get to work. Okay, maybe her life at the moment lacked structure, but living alone, you'd never have to explain why you rented *Attack of the Killer Tomatoes*, nor would you have to relinquish *Coronation Street* for a political debate.

Nikki, an unabashed Anglophile, loved the long-running British soap opera that centered around a pub in England. She adored *Monty Python's Flying Circus*, never missed a *Masterpiece Theatre*, and howled with laughter at *Black Adder*. Phil could never understand what she saw in them, particularly when most of them were old reruns.

Nikki made herself a cup of coffee. She'd taken to skipping breakfast. Nikki never really wanted breakfast, and now that she was alone, she no longer had to eat it—regardless of what conventional wisdom (and Phil) had to say about it being the most important meal of the day. She picked up her cup and took it outdoors, out onto the deck that some previous owner had added to the mobile home. The deck was one of the things that had charmed Nikki—a 12x14 raised platform that overlooked the best view in the trailer park. The floor was covered with green indoor-outdoor carpeting that tended, alternately, to shrink and to bubble in dry and wet weather, but was wonderfully forgiving to bare feet. Nikki would have to buy a deck table and chairs, but for now a folding webbed chair that had been left behind would do very nicely.

It was a glorious morning! The lake was quiet and glassy as a mirror, reflecting perfectly the range of mountains across it, as well as the few clouds that hung motionless in the blue. To Nikki's surprise—and delight—the grassy area between the deck and the drop-off to the lake was inhabited by dozens of *rabbits!* Nikki had seen them, of course; they were hard to miss; but she hadn't really focused on them. The rabbits of Eagle Lake Park were, in their own way, famous. Nikki wondered how they came to be—possibly tame rabbits gone feral—but there were, incredibly, hundreds of them. They seemed to be of many breeds—some black, some white, some white with brown ears and noses, some speckled—quite unlike the small wild brown rabbits that were native to the island. They also seemed to have total dominion over the area; the grass was nibbled to a nub (no one would ever have to mow the lawn here!) and the ground was riddled with holes, not burrows, but scooped out depressions. Apparently the rabbits had dug them—some deep, some shallow; some were occupied by the animals themselves, wallowing in bare earth. Nikki, who had never seen anything like it, sat fascinated as she sipped her coffee. The view also included an island that looked to be uninhabited. Small and overgrown with Douglas firs, it lay some distance from the shore, looking rather untidy with its ragged vegetation.

"Howdy, neighbor."

Nikki started. Absorbed in the view, she hadn't noticed that she had neighbors within a few feet, on both sides. Nikki turned and saw, in a screened enclosure, a woman on the deck of the mobile home on her right. The woman was wearing a bathrobe and carrying a cup. "Oh, hi," Nikki said, rather lamely.

"Welcome to Shangri-La." The woman gave a laugh. Nikki saw that she was about her own age.

"Yeah, thanks." The nearness of the neighbor's porch and the screen made Nikki think of a confessional.

"I'm Marj. Marj Kuusisto." The woman waited to see if that would have any impact.

"Kuusisto? That's Finnish, isn't it?"

"Yep. As much as Leino is, right?"

"Well, hail countrywoman! Yes, of course. My parents are Finnish too—sort of. My dad's a mix."

"Yeah, I knew it from the name. Mine is really Marjatta. Named after a grandmother. It's from the *Kalevala*."

"So's mine. Nikki. It's Annikki. *Also* named after a grandmother." If it hadn't been for the screen, they'd have been hitting "high fives."

"So how did you wind up as one of the inmates?"

"Inmates?"

"Oka-a-ay, so you haven't been through orientation."

"Orientation?"

"Oh, don't mind me. I'm one of those people who has a thing about authority."

"Yes, I guess," was all Nikki could think of to say.

"So are you all settled in or could you use some help?"

Nikki realized that it was exactly what she *did* want. More than anything in the world, she could really use someone to relate to, someone to *talk* to. "God, Marj, I'd love it!"

"Okay, wait till I put my clothes on."

Nikki had already finished unpacking, but the mobile home still looked shabby with its smoke-grimed ceiling and its dirty gold kitchen wallpaper, on which someone had mounted over the sink—of all things—stick-on panes of veined mirror. They, too, were so filmed with gunk that they reflected only blurred shapes. It was hard to tell whether the low-pile industrial type carpeting in the kitchen had once been blue or brown; a dirt path marked the hall runner and, in the living area, gave way to stained and faded gold shag wall-to-wall with a smell that conjured up bygone household pets.

Now, in front of Marj, Nikki looked around and felt like crying—again. What had she done? Why had she bought this dreadful place? Hadn't she seen how hideous it was? "It's awful, isn't it?"

"Hey, look at this." Marj, in picking at a dog-eared corner of the wallpaper, had loosened a strip. "You're not going to believe this, but I think somebody wallpapered over wood paneling!"

Nikki worked loose an edge with her fingernail and gave it a tug. The paper, an adhesive-backed vinyl, pulled off easily without tearing. The surface beneath revealed itself to be floor-to-ceiling panels in a dark brown wood. "Why would anyone cover that up with crappy wallpaper?"

Marj yanked off another strip. "I don't know. Maybe we'll find a big hole in the wall or maybe some part of the place has been gutted by fire. You want to chance it?"

"Sure. I can always spackle and paint. I *hate* wallpaper."

They set to work, and by noon they had transformed the walls of the kitchen. The veined mirrors were gone, and there seemed to be nothing wrong with the paneling except its dark color.

"Now it looks like a cave in here," Marj said. "It makes the place awfully dark. Probably why someone papered it."

"Never mind. It's kind of cozy. It just needs a good go with Murphy's Oil Soap or Liquid Gold."

"Ooh, you sound like my mother, peace be on her. She used to speak TV commercial."

"Listen, you don't spend five years taking care of a two-storey colonial without learning something about household products."

"Were you married?"

"In a manner of speaking."

"Living together?"

"If you can call it living."

"Hey, I'm sorry. None of my business. Look, it's lunch time, your kitchen's a mess. Come over to my place and I'll make us a sandwich. We can pick up this trash later."

"That sounds great, but you must have something better to do than spend your day ripping off my wallpaper."

"In other words, do I have a life? No. Not at the moment. I'm jobless."

"You live alone?"

"Don't I wish! Come on, I'll introduce you to my crazoid."

Marj's companion turned out to be a large white cat that was lying, as if posed, in a shaft of sunlight. The animal had the long hair of a Persian without the pugnacious look, and appeared almost ethereal as he gazed upward with an air of serene detachment. "He's *gorgeous*. He looks like that cat in the fancy cat food commercials." Nikki reached out a hand to pat.

"I *strongly* advise you not to do that." Nikki pulled her hand back. "The cat is beautiful but he has lightning reflexes and the patience of Satan. So unless you have a death wish, I suggest you just ignore him. The telephone repairman? I'm sure there's still some of his DNA under Casimir's claws."

Nikki grinned. "Casimir, huh? Seems to suit him. How long have you had him?"

"Seven years . . . six months . . . three days . . . for my sins."

"He's *so* beautiful. Is he a Persian? He must be strictly a house cat."

"His mother was a long-haired Silver Tabby Maine Coon who had a brief but passionate affair with a white sea-going tom, and if you mean, do I ever get a break from him, no I don't. Are you kidding? With all the rabbits at Eagle Lake, I wouldn't dare let him out of the house. Adelaide Moon would kill me. He almost got me barred from the park."

Marj busied herself in her little kitchen. Her mobile home was about the same size as Nikki's but cheerier, sunnier, and full of house-plants. A planter with a string-of-pearls hung in front of the kitchen window and a philodendron twined up the post of the room divider. The top of the TV console by the view window was crowded with pots. The porch rail inside the screened enclosure was studded with containers of greenery, with hanging baskets suspended from hooks above.

"How long have you lived here?"

"Eight months. Long enough to hope for parole."

"Why? What's wrong with Eagle Lake Park? Am I going to find out I've moved into a community of vampires?"

"You may live to see the day when you wish that was all!"

"Oh, come on, tell me, tell me, tell me."

"You'll find out soon enough. I take it you haven't been to one of Adelaide's *salons* yet. I didn't see you there Sunday night."

"No. I was too busy crying and baying at the moon."

"God, Nikki, I'm sorry. Breaking up can be hell. I know. That's why I'm here too."

"You're divorced?"

"Yes. My husband—my *ex*-husband, the English professor, had trouble with the verbs 'lay' and 'lie.' He managed to lay every woman he could get his hands on and then lie about it."

"The infernal triangle."

"In his case it was more like a pentagram. What about you? Was it another woman?"

"Oh yes. Indeed it was. At least that was part of it. A former lover. *Susan*."

"Don't tell me, let me guess. She was always the big love of his life, the all-consuming passion that never really burned out—the torch he'd carried for years. And when she came back, nothing else mattered."

"You're *good*. Except you'd have to say *her* life. My ex is a woman. Phil, short for Phillida."

Marj put down the bread knife and stared, open-mouthed. "Uh, do you like tuna fish?"

"Tuna's fine."

Suddenly Marj laughed.

"What's so funny?"

"Oh, I was just picturing Adelaide Moon's face if she knew she'd let a lesbian into the park. She turned down one single young man because he had a tattoo, and Adelaide knew that meant he must be a drug addict. And she nixed one woman because she bleached her hair and Adelaide said that a single woman with that shade of hair had to be a prostitute."

"Well thanks for including *me* in that category."

"I'm sorry, Nikki. Obviously I'm an idiot. You just took me by surprise. I have to confess I don't know much about the gay community."

"We're just people like everyone else. I like to think of us as being a little more gentle and tolerant than most civilians."

"I didn't mean to be offensive. But really, if you plan on staying here, I don't think I'd wear a sign around Adelaide. The woman's a bitch. She treats this place like it was her private kingdom and expects us all to grovel. Her Sunday night coffee parties are her way of controlling what goes on here, keeping her nicotine-stained finger on the pulse of her subjects. She likes to play games—pit people against each other. If she finds out we're friends, you can bet she'll try to cause trouble. Divide and conquer. That's Adelaide. She sometimes acts like she's a poor little victimized waif, but don't you believe it. She runs this place like Mussolini ran Italy. The rents are always on time. By the way, when you take in your rent check, watch out for

Prince, the dog. You want a beer with your tuna?"

"I think I'm going to need one."

CHAPTER 3

By the end of the month Nikki was beginning to feel more at home. She and Marj had found the wood paneling uniform throughout the mobile, and had ripped off the wallpaper in all the rooms but one, the spare bedroom that Nikki planned to use as an office. It was done in a cheery red and yellow floral on white background that lightened and brightened the tiny cubicle, so Nikki decided to leave it alone until she had time to either paint or repanel. Then Nikki had gone into what she called her Merry Maid Mode, applying cleansers and elbow grease to walls, windows, surfaces and floor. There wasn't much she could do about the carpeting until she could afford to have it replaced. She *had* thrown out the curtains—packed them up for the Salvation Army—voluminous stretches of heavy dark fabric, mounted on rods that were much too long for the windows. She had then splurged on having a department store install vertical blinds that could be angled to block out the glare of the late afternoon sun. Nikki had left the view window to the lake uncovered except for a pair of draw drapes—although, so far, she had never bothered to close them.

It had been exciting to fix up a place that was her very own. All the decisions had been hers. No one was there to tell her that the small birchwood dining set would never be adequate—or that she needed a proper couch and coffee table in the front room. Phil had been a traditionalist. Phil would not like Nikki's present décor. *Wha' a shayme,* Nikki thought, in her best *Monty Python* British accent. Of course, Phil hadn't liked *Monty Python* either. And if Nikki decided to carpet the place in plaid and paint the ceiling hot pink, no one could stop her!

Nikki had also met some of her other neighbors. On her left lived a young couple who appeared to be newlyweds going through their first adjustment period. They seemed to be obsessed with each other, alternating embarrassing public displays of affection with noisy fights. Fortunately they both had jobs in town and were gone all day. So far Nikki only knew them as Janet and Bob.

Next door to the young couple, the last mobile in the park belonged to an elderly husband and wife. The woman, who had stopped on her way to the mailbox to introduce herself as Paulette Crushill, seemed a motherly sort. She used a cane, explained at length that her doctor had advised her to walk in order to improve her oxygen intake and her arthritis, and that her husband, Fred, recently retired, suffered from high blood pressure, and also hiked every morning at six o'clock, rain or shine. They had a yappy little poodle that incessantly barked at rabbits through their porch screen.

The mobile home next to Marj's was larger, not a double wide, but on which an addition had been built to add more living area, so that the unit took up two spaces. Nikki had yet to meet the owners. So far, she'd seen no signs of life, although a large camper stood in the parking space, and Nikki idly wondered if the occupants might be away on vacation. Beyond it stood three more units whose inhabitants Nikki would meet later.

Barkell Road was the only road in and out of Eagle Lake Park. It bisected the Moon property, separating the commercial campground from the mobile homes, and formed a "T" with the nameless road to Nikki's place. On the other side of it lay the campground, and, behind that, a forest crisscrossed by hiking trails and dotted with numbered camp sites.

Thus far, Nikki had avoided the camp area, although she enjoyed walking down Barkell Road to the two-lane highway to pick up her mail, even on drizzly days, like this one. It gave her a break from her desk, and a chance to enjoy the beauty of the place: the various views of the lake, the huge western red cedars and Douglas firs, and the ubiquitous bunny rabbits.

Nikki unlocked her compartment in what she called the "mailbox condo," took out the contents without looking through them and slipped them into a plastic bag to protect them from rain, then headed back at a brisk pace. As she passed under the arched sign that proclaimed: Eagle Lake Park: Boating, Swimming, Camping; she fancied that she was entering another country—a small kingdom with its *Alice in Wonderland* queen. There was no shortage of white rabbits, and the place did strike her as being just a little mad. It was almost like a biosphere. It had its own shop; the water supply came from the lake; sewage was piped into a common septic tank; and the park even had its own garbage dump in a clearing in the woods, a dump that was periodically set on fire by the Moons. There were, at least according to Marj, strict rules for living, and unabashed discrimination as to who could get in.

Apart from the summer campers, boaters, and water-skiers who paid their money and used the camp area, there seemed to be no children living in any of the mobile homes. Nikki wondered if that was one of Adelaide's rules, and felt that it would have been a good one. With the steep drop-off—more of a cliff than a hill—the terrain would have been dangerous to children. There was enough vegetation clinging to the slope to perhaps break a fall, but a tumble could easily result in severe bruises and broken bones. And if one hurtled with enough force, one could go crashing down on the rocky beach below. It made Nikki, who was not overly fond of heights, a bit uneasy, but man, what a view!

Nikki had an unobstructed panorama of Eagle Lake, and she never tired of its changing moods—rosy with pink clouds at sunset, slate gray and dented by raindrops, ruffled by wind, and always inhabited by something—a beaver leaving a V-wake as it crossed from shore to island, flocks of ducks moving as if on conveyor belts, Canada geese, great blue herons, and always a bald eagle or two perched in a tree. Paulette Crushill had told her to watch for a flock of trumpeter swans that would be arriving in the fall. She would see them, exhausted by their migration, floating, their heads tucked under their wings, like huge marshmallows on the water. At night, a couple of owls, soundlessly as shadows, would fly from the ragged little island to the cedars on the hillside behind Nikki's mobile. When she lay in bed she could hear their ghostly hooting as they called to each other.

Nikki loved the sounds and sights of nature, and usually kept her windows open at night to catch the cool air. She was not fond of the sounds of living so close to her neighbors, particularly Janet and Bob, who were not only given to yelling at each other, but to noisy weekend parties with their friends. They had invited Nikki, but so far she had passed up the get-togethers that mercifully wound up a little before twelve. (Adelaide didn't 'low no geetar playin' after midnight!) and ended with sounds of loud laughter, shouted parting witticisms, and the slamming of what Nikki thought of as the car with eight doors, directly beneath her bedroom window.

Marj, of course, was a delightful neighbor. Nikki didn't know what she would have done without her—maybe ended up opening her veins with a ginsu knife or Cuisinarting herself a puree of sleeping pills. As it was, Marj had seen her through the worst of it. She'd lent her hands and her heart and her humor. Nikki couldn't possibly repay that, but she could invite her over for a really nice dinner. *Stuffed mushrooms. Pickled quail eggs. Fresh sockeye salmon basted with wine and baked in parchment. Tossed green salad garnished with fresh herb dressing. Veggie? Tiny new potatoes—from the organic farm that provided such things even late in the season—boiled in their skins, sprinkled with chopped fresh chives and stirred with just enough thick cream to form a sauce. Yes. And a bottle of Chardonnay—no, make that champagne. Mumms Cordon Rouge. Or maybe even Veuve Clicquot Ponsardin brut. Marj deserves champagne.*

Nikki was planning her dinner for two as she headed back from the mailbox. She had another errand as well. It was the first of the month, and she had to drop off the pad rent check at the Moons'. The Moon house was also a mobile home, but had been added to several times so that it had become a rambling rancher, festooned with hanging baskets of cascading petunia and verbena. Guarded by a six-foot chain link fence with a gate to contain the dog and bar the rabbits, flowers in beds bloomed unravaged and the only stretch of lawn in Eagle Lake Park was neatly clipped. The place was somewhat dwarfed by George's garage which stood at the end of the driveway outside the fence—a huge metal Quonset big enough to drive an 18-wheeler into.

Watch out for the dog, Marj had said. To her relief, Nikki saw no sign of Prince, the Moon canine. The garage doors were closed, and Nikki hoped that the dog was inside. George, who ran a construction firm, was nowhere in sight, probably out on a job. Nikki opened and shut the gate, went to the front door and rang the bell. No response. She looked around and noticed small sign on a side door that said "Office." *Ah!* She knocked. No reply. She turned the knob. The door opened and Nikki called out, "Hello the house! Anybody home?"

She saw that the room could hardly be called an office. It was a utility room with a washer and dryer; indeed, an ironing board stood waiting with a basket of laundry and the iron plugged in, though not turned on. Another door, open, led into the house interior. "Yoo-hoo.

It's me. Nikki Leino. I'm here to pay my rent."

Nikki had no intention of entering the house itself. She wondered if she should leave the check on the ironing board, but that seemed a bit iffy. She heard movement from inside. "Mrs. Moon? It's me, Nikki." There was the click of nails on tile and Nikki found herself almost eye to eye not with Adelaide Moon, but with a huge Great Dane. The dog regarded her suspiciously.

"Oh, hi, Prince. Nice doggy. Is your mother at home?"

The animal took a step forward and gave a low growl. *Oh Christ. Cujo on duty.* She and Prince stood locked in eye contact. Slowly, very slowly, Nikki laid the check on the ironing board, then picked up the iron and placed it on top to anchor it. Slowly, carefully, she backed toward the door, and as soon as she had hold of the knob, opened it, darted outside, and slammed it behind her. *From now on, Mrs. Moon, you get your checks in the mail.*

She was just going out through the gate when Adelaide Moon, herself, came over the hill. "Hi, Nikki, is there something I can do for you?" Adelaide was a woman in her late forties, but looked older. She smoked incessantly, was anorexically thin, with nicotine-stained fingers and teeth, stringy hair, and dark circles under her eyes.

"Yes, Mrs. Moon. I just left my pad rent on your ironing board."

"Thank you, Nikki. I hope Prince didn't scare you. He's big, but he's just a big softie. Wouldn't hurt anybody."

"I don't think I'd care to test that, Mrs. Moon."

"Call me Adelaide. Everybody does. I hear you're gettin' nicely settled in, Nikki. You'll have to come over for coffee Sunday night and meet everybody. We're just one big family here. Drop in about eight. We're all very casual."

"Thank you, Mrs. M—Adelaide. I'll try."

"Oh, no-no-no. None of this 'try' business. You *be* there. I want to show you off to the crowd." She grinned. "You're lookin' a lot better. Eagle Lake Park must agree with you. But you need to get out more.

You need to meet people. Livin' alone, you never know when you're gonna need friends."

"Yes, Mrs.—uh—Adelaide."

"So you just be here Sunday night, you hear? You wouldn't want people saying you think you're too good for the rest of us."

"No, Adelaide. Okay, Adelaide." *Pushy old broad.*

Sunday would take care of itself. Right now she was planning a dinner for Saturday night. It had been a while since Nikki had done any entertaining. Living with Phil, she'd had to do a lot of it. Phil wasn't much of a cook, and had left it to Nikki to plan and execute dinner menus, and even the *hors d'oeuvres* for occasions that Nikki wouldn't be allowed to attend. *(You know I hate it as much as you do, but these are conservative middle-class people with traditional values and wouldn't understand our situation.)* As result, Nikki had become somewhat of a gourmet chef, adventurous and eclectic, though constrained by Phil's requirements that nothing be too *outré*. She sometimes wondered what Phil's meals were like now. Diet TV dinners, most likely, unless, of course, *Susan* was a whiz in the kitchen.

Nikki had never met Susan, wouldn't be able to pick her out in an *identity parade,* as the English would say, although she had seen a bad photo of her once, accidentally, when Phil had asked her to go get her manicure kit from her vanity drawer. Nikki had opened it to see a head shot of a smiling woman with a gap between her two front teeth. She'd wondered, idly, who it could be, and had turned the snapshot over and read, "Love you, Susan." *Hmm.* She knew, of course, of Phil's earlier relationship, but only in a general way. Phil never discussed it, and when Nikki had asked, Phil had made it clear that her past was none of Nikki's business, as if Nikki had been a child inquiring about grownup things. Now she wondered idly how long it had been going on, and for the first time, it occurred to Nikki that maybe Phil's decision to work for the Institute for the Developmentally Challenged hadn't been entirely job related. Had their cross-country move to Vancouver Island been because *Susan* lived here? Had they been seeing each other all along? Nikki felt that she'd been played—suckered. What had she been to Phil—a younger woman to punish Susan with? Make Susan jealous?

Back at her desk, Nikki checked the mail: a couple of catalogs, a grocery store flyer. There was a check from her puzzle publishers and the return of an illustrated story she'd submitted to a children's magazine. *Oh hell, why do I even bother?* Nikki felt that by now she should be professional enough to handle rejection slips, but her ego still shriveled at the sight of an envelope addressed to her in her own hand—the inevitable SASE—containing material she had buoyantly sent off in hope of acceptance, now returned, violated, gang-raped (she visualized) by a savage pack of howling apes. She opened the envelope that had been forwarded from her previous address. The manuscript was bent from being in the mailbox but otherwise clean, not stained with human excrement, semen, or even coffee. The rejection was the publisher's equivalent of a "Dear John," thanking her for her interest, but regretting that the material did not meet their needs, and signed, anonymously, "The Editors." *I wonder if they even read it.* There was one more piece of mail that fluttered to the floor. *Too early for my VISA statement or phone bill.* Nikki picked it up, turned it over, and once again recognized, with a pang, the handwriting. It was from Phil.

Nikki had not seen Phil since they'd had that awful scene in the kitchen. Now the sight of her own name scrawled, as if angrily, on the envelope brought it all back—just when she had almost, *almost* begun to think that she might be able to get past Phil and all things Phil. She stared at the envelope, wondering whether she should take a match to it. It had been mailed from—Seattle? What was Phil doing in Seattle? Maybe she was at a seminar—or a retreat. Phil was big on retreats. That's why she hadn't called. Now she wanted something. Phil *always* wanted something. With insight born of her new freedom,

Nikki realized that Phil had never sought her out unless she wanted something. What was it going to be? A curt note saying Nikki had forgotten some item of property and would she please go get it out of the garage—or attic—or basement? She still had her house key. Or would the note be from the *other* Phil—the neurotic, needy Phil—the Phil who suffered from clinical depression—the Phil of stormy scenes, sepulchral moods, and chilling threats of suicide? Nikki ripped open the envelope. Two lines on hotel stationery: "I'll be back next week. We have to talk." *Oh, sweet Jesus!* Nikki crumpled the note and tossed it in the waste basket. That was the *other* thing about Phil: Phil could never let go of anything. Fortunately, she didn't have time to dwell on the meeting with Phil. She had a dinner to plan.

...

Saturday night Marj arrived bearing a plant. "I can't get over what you've done to this place! It even smells clean! Here's a bit of green. It's oxalis, but I call it shamrocks. It looked a lot better this morning before Casimir got into it. I'm sure it'll recover in your care."

"Thanks, Marj, but I don't know. Plants don't grow for me. I suspect a mom curse. She can make a broomstick sprout, but any plant I bring home self-destructs. It's like they take one look at me and lose their will to live."

Marj looked at the champagne on ice and the tray of hors d'oeuvres. "My *god*, Nikki. Remind me never to cook for *you*. I was expecting something on the order of Kraft dinner and beer! I haven't seen anything like this since the last time I was seduced."

"Not to worry. I never try to seduce anyone who's straight. It's too exhausting. Have a seat on my new beige futon couch—or maybe you'd prefer the new charcoal black fabric sling chair. I'm afraid it's a bit too cool for the new table and deck chairs outside."

"Oh, *très chic.* Is that what the delivery truck brought yesterday?

Nice choices for the room. Comfortable, casual, and defies tradition all to hell."

"*I* like it. Have a quail egg?"

"Now, where on earth—?"

"That new little Chinese shop in Harbour Park Mall. I pickled them myself."

Nikki expertly opened the champagne and filled two flutes. "To the good ship Independence and all who sail in her—and to dear old friends newly met."

Nikki had served her dinner, grateful that nothing in the unfamiliar oven had scorched or dried. The fish had been moist and flaky, the salad crisp, flavored with Nikki's own formula dressing, the raised yeast rolls (that she had decided upon only that afternoon) so light they fairly floated, and the dessert a delicious concoction of fresh berries topped with sour cream and sprinkled with cinnamon.

"Okay, you've made your point. Nikki can cook. You realize, of course, that we'll have to diet for a week to work this off."

"Not at all. Remember that I spent five years living with a woman who would threaten to slash her wrists if she gained an ounce! Fish is low in calories. Nothing was fried. The little bit of whipping cream in the potatoes and the sour cream on the berries doesn't amount to much. No sugar in the dessert either. We're legal. Not that *you'll* ever have anything to worry about."

"Well, let's do the dishes. What do you want to do with this leftover fish?"

"I'll put it in the refrigerator. Be lunch tomorrow. You want to take a piece of it to Casimir? I'll take the bones out and give them to that other cat that comes through here."

"There's a cat?"

"I don't know whose it is, unless Paulette and Fred have one. It came by yesterday. A big orange tom. I gave it a bit of leftover cutlet."

"It must've come from the farm in the valley. Nobody here has a cat except me, and Casimir, on pain of death—*mine*—never goes out."

While Nikki and Marj cleaned the kitchen, Nikki's coffee maker produced a pot of fragrant brew.

"Perfect ending to a perfect meal. I'm totally intimidated."

"You had it coming. Don't you know no good deed ever goes unpunished?"

"It was worth it. Just look at this place!"

"It still needs a lot of work, but I can't afford to do everything all at once."

"You know what would really look good in here? Some artwork on the walls. That dark wood would be a perfect background for colorful paintings. You're an artist. Why don't you paint something?"

"Oh, Marj, art is something that *happens*. You don't just set out to paint a bunch of stuff for your walls. You have to be inspired."

"Then get some plants. You need more plants."

"I told you, for me, they die. Some swiftly, some slowly, but they always die. I might be able to grow herbs in a window box or out in the garden, but the minute I bring anything indoors it croaks. It's like the Springfield cemetery on *The Simpsons*, except the stones would read: *Shasta Daisy, Christmas Cactus, Impatiens, African Violet.*"

"What you need is a plant that's self-sustaining. Something fool-proof—you should pardon that—something *invincible* like the rubber tree my mother used to have, or maybe a Boston fern. Sure, a big, frondy Boston fern would look *great* in here."

"Oh, I don't know, Marj."

"Tell you what. There's a new nursery on the Island Highway I've been wanting to check out. Why don't we take a drive out there tomorrow and see what they've got. I hear they have all kinds of exotic herbs."

"Herbs?" Nikki had never met an herb she didn't like. "Maybe I could put some in a planter on the deck."

"Great. We'll go tomorrow afternoon. Nurseries are always open on Sundays." Marj yawned. "All that champagne. I'm going to sleep like I've been clubbed."

Marj left, bearing salmon wrapped in tinfoil for Casimir. Nikki took the plate of fish bones outdoors and placed it on the ground by the deck steps. It was a beautiful night. The stars were blazing, the milky way a highway of light in the heavens. Nights were growing cooler. She walked a little way toward the lake, being careful not to step in any of the rabbit holes, and took a seat at a weathered wooden picnic table. Every mobile in Eagle Lake Park had one of those tables. She sat on the plank seat and looked back at her new home. The unit bore the brand name, *Villager*. It was white with blue trim and stood out in the darkness against the other mobiles. Hers was the only one that had an unscreened deck, surrounded only by a railing, and the new molded white plastic table and chairs under a big blue and white striped umbrella made it look festive, like an outdoor café. Inside, with the lights on, her place looked cozy and inviting. Through the window she could see her living room filled with symbols of her new life. Her drawing board was now the most prominent, and there seemed to be no real division between her working life and her home life. But except for Marj's oxalis on the art table, there was no sign of any living thing. Maybe she *did* need more plants.

CHAPTER 4

NIKKI SPENT Sunday morning checking out her outdoor surroundings. At the end of her parking space, across from the kitchen door, stood two metal storage sheds. They'd been padlocked, but now she went in search of a key and found one hanging on a hook in the hall. One of them, she found, housed a clothes dryer that could be plugged into a kitchen socket by use of a long extension cord. Inside, in the hall, next to the heater, Nikki had found a tiny washing machine. She'd never seen a washer so small and wondered if it could handle sheets and bath towels, even if washed singly. Now here was the dryer to match. She didn't have much faith in either, but maybe in an emergency. . . .

Other than that, the sheds were empty—a good place to stack her deck chairs and umbrella come winter. There was also a storage area underneath the deck that could be accessed by opening a hinged panel of skirting. Inside she found leftover building materials—a number of cinder blocks, a couple of two-by-fours and a few planks. There was also a length of garden hose, a couple of clay as well as plastic flower pots, and a wooden planter that might do nicely for herbs.

Nikki came in and surveyed the living room. The large picture window was flanked by narrow louvered windows that reached from floor to ceiling. There were also large windows on the side walls. Houseplants would get plenty of light, but she needed something to set them upon. No problem. Using cinder blocks and one of the planks from the storage area, it only took Nikki a few minutes to fashion a long low shelf next to the window sill. She placed Marj's oxalis on it. The plant did look a bit battered, as if it had been in a fight, but Marj had assured her it would heal. Nikki also made mental note of a metal hook in the ceiling. No doubt some past inhabitant had used it to suspend a hanging plant in the window. Maybe she could use that—but that would kill the view. No, she'd get something for the shelf—something to keep the oxalis company. She began making a mental list of things she might need: soil, fertilizer, maybe more pots. What was it her mother always used? Peat moss? Vermiculite? Greensand and blood meal? Well, no need to get that involved. Simple potting soil should do.

"Maybe we'd better take my truck," Nikki told Marj as they were getting ready to leave. "I think I'm going to need garden stuff."

"In that case we'll need to bring big plastic bags to put the plants in so they won't get windburned on the drive back."

"You're going to have to point this place out to me," Nikki said as she drove down the Island Highway. "I don't think I've ever seen it."

"It's on the right, about ten kilometers. You have to turn off onto a dirt road. It's called Gary's Greenery. There should be a sign."

"Gary's must be a tax write-off or a some kind of a front." The truck was bumping along a dirt road. "How does he expect to compete with other nurseries way out here? How'd you ever hear of him anyway?"

"I don't remember who told me. Maybe it was Adelaide. Anyway, we're here—I *guess*."

The road had ended in a small gravel parking lot, defined by the cedar and fir logs that frame West Coast parking lots and pile high on every ocean beach. For a plant nursery, the place looked untidy. Potted plants, trees and shrubs stood in disarray, the whole stretching off into a wooded area so that it was hard to tell where the nursery ended. In the middle of it all stood a ramshackle building with a moss-covered roof—more of a lean-to, as the front was open to the elements. It appeared to be unattended.

Nikki looked around. On a rough plank table, pots were crowded so close together that the plants had all grown into one mass of greenery with tiny blue flowers. The effect was charming, but Nikki wondered how anyone could detach any of them.

"*Lithospermum*—or *lithodora*—one or the other. Hard to tell them apart," Marj said.

"Hard to *pull* them apart too, I'll bet. I wonder where the proprietor is." The property clearly extended for several acres, and probably included other buildings, but the rampant vegetation obscured the view.

"Good afternoon, ladies. And might I be of service to you?"

A bit startled, Nikki and Marj turned to face the voice behind them. They saw a short, rotund man with a gray beard. He was dressed in baggy trousers, gray shirt and suspenders, and was wheeling a barrowful of compost.

"You'll have to excuse look of the place. As you see, I'm not sorted out yet. Used to be cow barn. Needs a good go."

Nikki grinned. Cute, she thought. Like a little Santa Claus with a British accent. "Are you Gary?"

The man laughed. "No, Luv. Gary were me dad, rest his soul. His sign were the only thing left of family business. Kept it in his memory—and never had to pay for another. Now, was there something you fancy? Or, maybe you'd like a bit of a wander. Follow any path. They meander a bit, but they all lead back here. Garden supplies inside—tools, peat moss, soil and the like. I'm Bert. Bert at your service."

"Thank you, Bert. We're looking for kitchen herbs," Nikki said.

"And houseplants," Marj added.

"And we'll probably need potting soil for a window box."

"Ah, well, you'll find what's left of herbs on table over there. Bit late in season, so if you're going to plant window box, you'll need hardy perennials. Nice Greek oregano over there, and thyme, rosemary, sage and the like. Things aren't labeled yet, and they're a bit jammed in, but give us a shout if you need help. Houseplants inside." Bert picked up his barrow and wheeled away.

"I think I'd like oregano and thyme. And parsley. Oh yes, and chives, of course—and maybe this rosemary, in case I want to make focaccia bread – oh, and some sage and dill. And mint. Gotta have mint for mint sauce!"

"You'll need a box." Marj found a cardboard flat. "Look, he still has pineapple sage!" She rubbed a leaf. "Smells heavenly, but it won't survive the winter unless you bring it inside. Maybe we should take one to Adelaide. Make a good impression on the old bat."

"Adelaide! I'd forgotten about her."

"Would that we could!"

They had rounded up herbs, a hand trowel, garden shears, peat moss, vermiculite, a bag of potting soil, another of sand, two kinds of fertilizer—granular for outdoor use; water-soluble for indoor plants. Nikki was enjoying herself. Now they were inside, contemplating an array of potted greenery that included jade plant, aloe vera, hoya, spider plant and fern.

"The variegated spider plants are nice, but you have to hang them. Do you have a place to put a hook?"

"There's one in front of the window, but I hate to have anything that blocks my view of the lake."

"Then I still say the Boston fern is your best bet. They're all beautiful—nice and full. This one's already in a hanging basket in case you decide you want to put it up after all." Marj picked it up by the hook. The plant, freed of its companions, allowed its fronds to arch in graceful sprays of green."

"I like it," Nikki said. "I'll get one of those footed plastic urns to raise it high enough so the fronds can hang free but not high enough to ruin the view. Of course it'll probably be dead in a week!"

Bert was at the cash register. "Can I put that on my VISA?" Nikki asked.

"That you can, luv. Let's see, that was herbs, pots, garden supplies—and Boston Charlie, here. He *is* a lovely plant. Likes a bit of sun. Don't overwater Boston Charlie, and, contrary to some, don't mist him in this climate unless it gets really dry in summer."

"Boston Charlie? That's a good name."

"Wonderful companions, the Charlies. Very popular. Don't take much looking after, do they? And they're good conversationalists, folks tell me—them what talks to plants." Bert grinned and gave a sly wink.

"Boston Charlie's going to have to travel blindfolded," Marj said, as she took out a large lawn and leaf bag. Bert helped them secure the plants under plastic in the bed of the truck, and Nikki and Marj headed back to Eagle Lake.

The trip had been a bit of an adventure, and the women were in high spirits as they pulled into Nikki's parking space, where they unloaded *flora* and supplies, joking that Nikki had bought enough to handle a small truck farm. Nikki left her flat of potted herbs on the deck table, then took Boston Charlie inside and settled the plant, pot and all, into the raised urn. Charlie looked beautiful on the shelf by the window, his delicate but profuse fronds arching downward like a fountain, his green mass forming a pleasing transition to the eye between indoors and out.

"There you go, Charlie. Enjoy the view. Live long and prosper. You'd probably look better without the hanging hook and wires, but I'll leave them for now."

"You have room for a few more plants on that shelf. Maybe we should've picked up something that blooms—an impatiens or a cyclamen—although it might be too warm for it there in the sun."

"How do you know so much about plants?"

"I grew up on a farm and my mom was a plant nut. Whenever my brother and I misbehaved, she'd make us work in the greenhouse or go weed. And I had a summer job in a nursery when I was fifteen."

"Maybe you should get a job with Bert. He looks like he could use an assistant."

Marj sighed. "Well I'm obviously going to have to get a job someplace. I can't live on my divorce settlement forever."

"Hey, if you need to make up a resumé, my Mac and I are at your disposal. We can do an impressive presentation and run off as many copies as you like."

"I'm afraid there wouldn't be much to it. I never went to college, and after I graduated high school I took a job waitressing. I met Jonah and we got married. He didn't want me to work because he wanted us to be free to travel during the summers and sabbaticals."

"Sounds like a life most people would kill for."

"Yeah, it did to me too. But I never fit into it. They say there's no class system in North America but don't believe it. Nobody snobbier than a bunch of educators! When they heard about my school background—or lack of it—they just ceased to see me. I could actually see their eyes glaze over."

"You could've gone back to school. You *still* can go back to school."

"I suppose. But that wasn't all. See, what they don't tell you about being a faculty wife is that you're also expected to turn a blind eye to your husband's affairs—and that your husband is virtually expected to *have* affairs! I was just the resident bimbo—the one Jonah never should have married. I think he only married me because I was young."

"And beautiful."

"Oh, he liked me to get all dressed up in sexy clothes so he could show me off like a trophy."

"You didn't have any kids?"

"Jonah didn't want children. They'd have cramped his style as a satyr."

"I'm sorry it didn't work out."

"Yes, well, now all I have is Casimir. I got custody—and I'd better go see what he's destroyed in my absence."

"I guess I'll see you later at Adelaide's."

"Come by my place. We'll walk over together."

Nikki walked out with Marj, then decided she might as well plant the herbs. The sun was shining; there was a bit of a breeze from the lake; rabbits hopped leisurely across the cropped lawn. Nikki could hear shouting and splashing from the water below as a group of boys swam and played on a wooden raft offshore. She hummed to herself as she dragged out the wooden planter. It might have originally been a window box, but there was no way to attach it. Perhaps she might balance it on the deck rail, or, better yet, she could make an outdoor shelf in front of the window to match the one she'd made inside. More cinder blocks, another plank and it was done. She set the planter on top and filled it with a mix of soil, peat moss, and vermiculite, adding just a bit of fertilizer. Marj had said not to over-fertilize herbs but to give them lots of sunlight.

Nikki did her planting, situating the mint in its own clay pot. Marj had warned her that it was an invasive plant that would run rough-shod over less aggressive herbs. She gave everything a good drink of water and stood back. Working with plants was fun! Maybe she could even devise a proper garden—but how? Rabbits would surely destroy it. As it was, she hoped it wouldn't occur to them to climb up on deck and dig up the stuff in the planter—which would have been easy enough for them to do. Nikki had seen rabbits lounging on *top* of the park picnic tables. Still, numerous as they were, they seemed to be shy enough of people so that Nikki had never been able to lay a hand on one. "Just keep your distance, guys, unless you want to end up as *hasenpfeffer.*"

Satisfied, Nikki finished up her horticultural afternoon by putting away her tools, then came inside and watered her indoor plants as well, noticing how the herbs outdoors at the same level as her indoor shelf made it look like one wide planted bed. She showered and changed, made a meal of leftover salmon, and, by ten minutes to eight, was at Marj's door.

"I see you brought the pineapple sage. That should mollify Her Nibs. Her nose has been out of joint because you've been here three weeks without attending her little soirees."

"I'm not looking forward to this one. I *hate* being thrown into a roomful of strangers."

'I know. I remember the first of Jonah's faculty cocktail parties. I guess the best way to prepare you is to tell you to be prepared for anything. Sometimes they're just dull. Sometimes there's a power demonstration or a call to arms. There's usually gossip, but the biggest thing is *control*, and as a newcomer, I suggest that no matter what you hear or no matter what anyone says, just try to ignore it. If Adelaide picks on someone, don't try to defend them. If she picks on you, just plead ignorance and apologize. Later I can clue you in on what was *really* going on."

"Jesus!"

"Amen!"

CHAPTER 5

"Marj! Nikki! Come on in. Don't mind Prince. Hey, George, come and put the dog in the garage. The big dummy's gettin' in everyone's way. Come in and sit down."

Not really knowing what to say, Nikki handed Adelaide the potted herb. Marj segued in with "Nikki found you a pineapple sage, I didn't think you already had one. They have a wonderful fragrance."

"Aw, isn't that sweet?" Adelaide rubbed a leaf and sniffed. "Did you go to Bert's?"

"Yes. Nikki wanted herbs and a plant for her front room."

"Oh good. Gettin' settled in. I'm glad to see you went to Bert's. He's had a hard time of it, trying to get that place runnin' single-handed. He used to live here in Eagle Lake Park, years ago, he and his wife. His dad ran a nursery, and when he died, Bert took it over. But when the city expanded, he had to move. Needed more acreage, so he bought that farm. We all told him it was too far off the highway, but no, he wouldn't listen. His wife died not long ago, and I expect he's still having it rough, although there are some who say he wasn't *too* sorry at her passing. I mean she'd been sick a while, and a man gets restless, if you know what I mean. Well, Nikki, we're glad you finally made it to one of our coffees. You know, we're just one big happy family in Eagle Lake Park. Come on in and meet everybody."

Nikki edged into the living room and found a seat on the couch. Prince, the dog, still unconfined, followed her and stretched out next to her feet under the coffee table. Marj settled into a kitchen chair that had been brought in for the occasion.

"You already know Paulette and Fred," Adelaide said, "and George's parents—and Janet and Bob Lindsay. This hippie with the long hair is my son, Clark." Clark rolled his eyes and grinned. "And here we have Emily and Justin Laderheim. They live in the unit next to Marj's, and just got back from a month in Spain. I hope you brought lots of slides, Emily, to show us poor folks who can't afford to travel. And this handsome fellow is Raymond Cantwell." Adelaide indicated a pudgy middle-aged man with pink skin who squirmed and gave an embarrassed laugh. "Raymond is the man I can't live without, but don't tell George." She patted his balding head, and Nikki realized that this must be some sort of a running gag. She gave Raymond a sympathetic smile.

"Now that we all know each other, let's have coffee and some of my pineapple upside-down friendship cake."

The conversation took off in low key. Emily and Justin answered polite questions about their trip, and explained that their slides hadn't come back yet. Janet and Bob said little, but Nikki noticed that Janet was trying to keep a straight face while Bob sat beside her, arms folded, but with one extended finger surreptitiously stroking her left breast. Marj sat, sphinx like, listening to Paulette go on, at length, about her daughter who had married a man who wasn't nearly good enough for her. Hector Moon looked as though he was about to nod off. Ida, his white-haired wife was speaking in slow measured cadences to Raymond Cantwell about the proper way to plant petunias in hanging baskets. Raymond, in turn, was nodding and appeared to be listening intently to every word. George seemed to have nothing to say, and after a few minutes, without apology or explanation, got up and left the room. Prince elbowed his way from under the coffee table and followed him. Neither returned. For some reason, the scene struck Nikki as being funny until Adelaide, who had been leaning back in her chair, smoking a cigarette and narrowly watching everyone through the haze, cleared her throat with a hawking smoker's cough.

All conversation stopped and all eyes turned to Adelaide who smiled and said, "You know, this is *nice*. We're all here together, just like a happy family. And that's what I like about our little Eagle Lake Park. We're not grand. We're not fancy. But we're all family." (Did Nikki imagine it or was everyone beginning to squirm?)

"While you're all here, I thought I should mention that George and I are real proud of how nice the park looks, and we appreciate the way you all keep your areas lookin' so good. There is one little tiny thing. Justin, now that you're back, would you mind parking your camper down by the lake instead of in your driveway. It sits up so high that it blocks Raymond's window, what with these spaces bein' so small. A car is low enough so you can see over it, but all the time you've been gone, Raymond has had the light to his living room cut off. I'm sure George can find a spot down by the lake for you." Justin Laderheim looked annoyed but nodded in resignation.

"And Fred. I know you like to do your woodworking since you retired, but maybe you could store your materials somewhere out of sight. There's a shed in the utility area that George could rent you for a few dollars a month."

The room had gone quiet. Then, to Nikki's astonishment, Adelaide turned to *her*. "And Nikki, I know you're new here, so you couldn't have known, but Marj tells us that you've been feeding stray cats in your area. With all the bunnies around, we don't want to encourage any cats in the park, so would you please not leave any food for them."

Dumbly, Nikki nodded and shot Marj a look. Marj gave an almost imperceptible shrug and resumed her impassive face.

Embarrassed at being singled out, Nikki gulped down her coffee and, at the first opportunity, stammered something about having to get back because she was expecting a call from her mother. Marj immediately got up. "I'll walk back with you. I forgot to feed Casimir."

"Aw, what a shame you both have to rush off. Next time, plan to stay awhile. I think Emily and Justin will have their slides back, and George can set up the projector."

Making their way back, Nikki was fuming. "If I ever go to another one of Adelaide's parties, I'll bring *my* camera so I can get a nice picture of Hell freezing over."

"It *was* brutal tonight. I want to apologize for the cat thing. No, I didn't go blabbing to Adelaide, and it wasn't the way it sounded. It was Paulette I talked to. She'd seen the orange cat, and we wondered whose it might be. Paulette said that if Adelaide found out, she'd get George to shoot it. I said if we all gave it a few scraps, like you did, it probably wouldn't bother the rabbits. I should've known better. Paulette is a hot line to Adelaide."

"Doesn't matter. Maybe Adelaide is right. But she might have mentioned it to me in private rather than point a finger in front of everybody."

"That's Adelaide's way. She likes to make examples. Now nobody else will feed a stray cat, or dare leave building materials around—or park large vehicles between the units. One swat kills a lot of flies. Usually, though, she waits till you've been there a few times before she squashes you under her thumb." Marj giggled. "She busted me for using pink toilet paper."

"It's *verboten?*"

"*Ja wohl.* It was hysterical. The septic system backed up, and Adelaide found pink toilet paper in the plug that clogged it. She went around to all the units like the prince with the glass slipper, looking for Cinderella. I was guilty, and promised to use nothing but biodegradable white in future, but she made it sound as though in the two weeks I'd been here, I had single-handedly stuffed enough pink tissue into the pipe to clog up all of Eagle Lake Park!"

"This place is a minefield."

"You'll learn to appreciate the subtleties. Like tonight. Why did Adelaide hit on you your first night? Punishment. Punishment for ignoring her klatches for three weeks. Why make it sound as though I ratted on you? She knows we're friends. As I told you, divide and conquer."

"I think we both need a gin and tonic. You don't really have to feed Casimir, do you?"

"Are you kidding? Do you think I'd dare leave the house without serving His Majesty his gourmet cat food? He loved the fish, by the way. You're not expecting a call from your mother either, are you?"

"Are you kidding? My mother should call long-distance? Only when someone dies! Otherwise she waits for *me* to call *her*. And I *do*. Every two weeks."

"Where *are* your parents?"

"They're still on the East Coast and still fighting the battle of the sexes. It's incredible that they've actually stayed together. My brother and I were convinced they'd get divorced as soon as we left home."

"At least they still have lives."

"You've heard the saying, you can't go home again? In my case it's true. My parents keep moving. It wasn't that long ago that they built their dream house, and my mom had beautiful raised garden beds constructed. Now my dad wants to sell out and move to the city. He feels he's too young to bury himself in the country. He craves excitement. He's always had this youth thing."

"How old a man is he?"

"Chronologically he's fifty-six, but he brags about having the body of a twenty-year-old—to which my mother says that the twenty-year-old just called and left a message that he wants it *back*. He went through a crazy midlife crisis, dyeing his hair and his moustache and wearing tight jeans and cowboy boots and a bandanna. It came to an end when he found he was being hit on by every gay man in town. He had to shave off the moustache when the smell of the dye kept making him nauseated."

Marj was laughing. "They sound like a hoot."

"Oh yeah, they're both very funny, but better at a safe distance! They have one of those marriages. My mother does a standup routine on how they had a very small wedding, held in a phone booth in Halifax, and how instead of the vows, she was read her Miranda rights . . . 'you have the right to remain silent.' She said she would have kept her maiden name, except it didn't matter, because henceforth she's be known only as *that poor woman*.

"I think I'd love your mother."

"My dad is like ball lighting. You can't ignore it but you'd better not get too close. He's very talented, and he loves to be outrageous. And he gets away with it because everyone thinks he's joking. The man is obsessed with his appearance and his health, and goes around claiming that his great-grandmother was a Romanian gypsy, and that he's a direct descendant of Vlad the Impaler."

"Dracula?"

"They're a strange pair. I think of my mother as Helga Bloodax in a Viking helmet, and my dad as Vlad the Nitwit, dancing in front of a shrouded mirror, singing 'I Feel Pretty.'"

"Do you see them often?"

"I promised . . . and I'll live to regret it, I know . . . but I promised I'd positively visit next summer, no matter where they end up. Mom insisted on it when she's heard Phil and I are no longer together. Then, of course, she told me that she *never* liked Phil, and that I should move back East where I belong. Dad said that since I like writing stories for children, but clearly don't have any talent, I should consider becoming a nanny."

"What does your dad do?"

"He's a commercial artist. He has a sign shop and also does illustrations for action comics."

"And your mom?"

"She's does a newspaper column on wild mushrooms and she's had a couple of cookbooks published. Now she's working on a book on gardening."

"Then you come by your talents honestly. Do you have brothers and sisters?"

"Like you, I have one brother. He married a woman who inherited land and they're out in country with their horses and dogs. As a family, we don't see much of each other, but if there's trouble, all the phone lines light up."

As if in illustration, the phone rang. Nikki picked it up. "Oh . . . hi, Phil." She saw Marj give her a look that asked if she should leave. Nikki shook her head, then watched Marj open the door of the refrigerator, look inside, take out ice, tonic water and gin, and proceed to mix two drinks. Marj left one at Nikki's elbow, then took a seat in the front room and turned on the TV, just loud enough so she could pretend not to overhear the conversation. Nikki talked briefly, then put the phone down, picked up her drink and joined Marj.

Marj turned off *Murder, She Wrote*. "I see you keep your gin in the refrigerator."

"Old habits die hard. Phil liked an ice cold martini after work, so I always kept the gin and vermouth in the fridge. I guess I'm still doing it."

"As if Phil might drop by. *Is* she going to drop by?"

"Not tonight. I do have to see her, but we're going to meet in neutral territory."

"Will it be awful?"

"Probably. I don't know. I don't think I want to go."

"Then *don't*. You don't have to see her if you don't want to. How come she even has your phone number?"

"When you're in a minority group, there's really no such thing as divorce—any more than you can divorce a sister. The only way I could *not* see Phil again would be for one of us to move to Omsk. If neither of us wants to move away, and if we ever want to take part in any social life in the gay community, we're going to have to put a good face on our parting, and appear as friends. Therefore, if we have any residual anger or angst or, as Phil just said, 'lack of closure,' we're going to have to duke it out privately."

"I thought she was into another relationship."

"So did I."

"You think she's having second thoughts? Would you *want* her to have second thoughts?"

"No, certainly not! At first all I wanted was out. Then when I left, I thought, oh my god, what have I done? But now, I feel I'm beginning to get my life back."

"I know how that is. When I walked out on Jonah, I was angry. Then I was devastated. I'd never been so alone in my life. I think if Jonah had made some move, I'd have run right back to him. Then I went into a depression. Didn't want to see anybody or go anywhere. I holed up here at Eagle Lake, and I guess I can thank Adelaide for a lot of things. The woman is pushy, manipulating, and annoying, but you can't ignore her, and in their own purgatorial way, the people around here brought me back into the world. I see this place as a sort of a post-relationship *Twilight Zone*. And when we're ready, we'll bust out of this joint."

"Not a bad analogy. I know how much help *you've* been to *me*. When Phil and I split up, I found I really didn't have any friends of my own. We moved here as a couple, and everyone knew us as a couple. Phil was always the dominant one, so they're all more her friends than mine. I sometimes felt like the batty wife in *Jane Eyre*.

I was more of a dogsbody, and got treated like one. When I moved out I left everything."

"Same here. When I married Professor Henry Higgins, I left my old friends behind. When I left Jonah, his world hardly noticed, but when I tried to return to *my* old world, it had moved on. I found I was alone."

"Do you have family?"

"None that count. My mother died a few years back, peace be on her."

"Well, at least you have Casimir. I don't have so much as a Mexican jumping bean."

"Don't forget Boston Charlie." Marj and Nikki raised their glasses. "To Charlie!" Marj got up and walked to the plant shelf. "Charlie looks good there, and I see you put your herbs on the other side. It must be a great spot for plants. Even my oxalis seems to be looking better already. That's amazing."

Nikki took a look. Marj was right. The oxalis looked as if it had grown new leaves since the night before, and the ones torn by Casimir were hardly noticeable. "Do they grow that fast?"

"Not usually. Not that I've noticed. They must really like this spot."

Nikki yawned. It was early, but the drink had made her sleepy.

"It's my fault," Marj said. When I heard you were on the phone with your ex, I added an extra shot of gin. Thought you might need it."

Nikki laughed, "Thanks a lot! I think I'll go to bed early. Tomorrow I have to design a bunch of crossword puzzles and try to figure out where next to send my latest rejected story. It hasn't been rejected enough times yet for me to trash it."

"I don't think I could handle that. I mean, you slave over a story or spend years on a book—and they send it back with a 'sorry, we don't want it.' I don't think my ego could take a shot like that."

"Mine's not thrilled about it either, but it comes with the territory if you're going to freelance."

Marj got up. "I'm gonna go home and watch *Mystery*, and spend a little time with Casimir. He sulks if he's ignored. I'll see you some time tomorrow. Good night, Nikki. Good night Charlie."

Nikki washed the two glasses, dried them and put them away. *I could've left them in the sink—or in the middle of the floor!* Phil had hated to see dishes unwashed or a bed unmade or a surface undusted, and somehow it had always been Nikki's job to see that she never did.

Nikki stretched out on her futon couch but didn't turn on the TV. *Phil. Phillida Lowry.* Would there ever be a time when Phil wouldn't be structuring Nikki's life? She wondered just what Phil was going to ask of her. The woman on the phone hadn't been the gothic Phil or the dictatorial Phil. It had been, if possible, the charming Phil. The old Phil. The woman Nikki had adored. She remembered how much fun Phil had been in the beginning—the two of them running hand in hand along a beach; lobster dinners at the Dunes; drives through the countryside, searching for antiques; making love in an inn four-poster bed, laughing at how scandalized the original owners would've been—unless they, too, had been lesbians. And the talks—talks that lasted deep into the night, over wine, about all the things they were going to do together. Nikki felt tears sting her eyes. *Closure.* "Nikki, I think our relationship is suffering from a lack of closure." What the blazes did that mean? Weren't all the tears and screaming fights closure enough? The day Phil had slammed out of the house and left Nikki to pack her belongings and clear out—how much more closure could you have than that? Nikki considered making herself another gin and tonic but rejected the idea. She'd need a clear head tomorrow, and she should get up and get ready for bed.

Nikki closed her eyes for just a moment, then opened them again with a start. *What the hell—?* There was a rustling noise—very loud and very close. Nikki sat up, sprang from the couch, then backed away, stupefied by what she was seeing. It was the fern! Boson Charlie! It was moving, agitated as if by a strong wind. The fronds were waving, shuddering, as if the stalks were being vigorously shaken. So violent was the movement, that Nikki's first thought was *earthquake*. However, nothing else in the room was affected. It only lasted a few seconds while Nikki watched, her eyes wide, her mouth frozen open.

The shaking stopped. Nikki took a cautious step toward the plant. *Okay, there has to be a logical explanation. Something's in the fern. A bird? A mouse? A bat?* Without taking her eyes off the plant, Nikki backed into her kitchen area, opened a drawer, and pulled out the first thing her hand touched: a large wooden spoon. Slowly, she advanced on the plant. As she came closer, she saw that the floor was littered with bits of broken-off leaves and stems. *I didn't dream it unless I'm still dreaming.* Carefully she touched the fern with the spoon. Nothing happened. She prodded the spoon into the base of the plant, expecting to see something run or fly out, but again she got no response. *This is crazy.* She grabbed the spoon by the bowl and stabbed at the mass with the handle, poking it through the fluff of greenery. Nothing. Gaining courage, she put the spoon down and gently parted the fronds with her hands, like a school nurse looking for head lice. The plant looked perfectly normal. Nikki noticed that her own hands were shaking.

What to do? Find the logical explanation. Wind? Impossible. The windows were tightly shut. She found herself wishing Marj were still there. She *could* call Marj. Yeah, that would be thing to do all right. She pictured the call: "Uh, Marj, this is your new friend, Nikki. My Boston fern just went ballistic and scared me. Can you come over?"

Whatever else, Nikki was not sleepy anymore. It was possible that whatever had inhabited the fern was now loose in her house. True, she hadn't seen anything, but that didn't mean that some lightning fast varmint hadn't landed on her rug and taken off for wherever. It could be waiting for her under the couch or in the bathroom or in her bed, for that matter—a thought that made Nikki's blood run cold. The fern had just come from the nursery. It was possible that some little creature might still be in residence in the soil, in the root ball.

Maybe she should put the fern outdoors for the night, and tomorrow repot the thing and search out any interloping critter.

I could have Marj stand by with a stun gun and net!

The initial scare over, Nikki was beginning to see the humor—almost. Thankful that she'd left the wires and hook in place, Nikki gingerly picked up the plant and carried it out on deck and set it down next to the herb planter. "Good night, Boston Charlie. Tomorrow you and I are going to have a close encounter."

CHAPTER 6

Nikki awakened late. She had not slept well. After putting Charlie out for the night, she had thoroughly searched the house. Finally, satisfied that nothing was lying in wait for her, she had gone to bed, but had lain awake, half expecting some leathery, feathery or chitinous creature to run across her body at any moment. When she finally had drifted off, her sleep had been troubled by dreams of being pursued by a giant iguana, that then somehow turned into her high school math teacher, who kept chalking algebraic equations on a blackboard and screaming at her to find "x."

Nikki showered and dressed, feeling a bit guilty at her late start. She made herself a cup of coffee, then surveyed the fern bits and pieces still on the carpet. She should vacuum. But no, the scattered specks of greenery were solid evidence that what had happened last night really *had happened*. She hadn't dreamt it.

It was a clear sunny morning and the lake was calm. Nikki took her coffee on deck. There she saw that one of the rabbits—a large, burly white bunny with one black spot between its eyes—had climbed up onto it, and was hopping around on the carpeting, depositing little piles of "pellets." Nikki grinned. *Gives fresh meaning to the term poop deck.* She went back inside and came out with a couple of slices of bread. "Hey, Bruno, continental breakfast is being served at the *bottom* of the steps." She tossed down the slices. Bruno stared at her blankly. "Shoo!" Nikki advanced upon the rabbit who merely side-stepped with a couple of hops. Nikki clapped her hands. "Go on, scat!" Finally Bruno found his way to the steps, descended, located a piece of the bread and settled down to eat it—only to be immediately joined by three other rabbits who made off with the rest.

Nikki checked her plants. They were looking good. They were looking *better* than good. The herbs she'd planted only the day before, looked as though they'd been growing for a month. She had certainly picked some fine specimens—larger and more vigorous than she remembered. *Maybe I've inherited my mother's green thumb after all.* As for Boston Charlie, he seemed none the worse for his night out. Here, in the clear light of morning, last night's incident was beginning to seem silly. There had to be an explanation for what had happened, and Nikki was going to try to find it. She picked up the plant and carried it down to the picnic table. Carefully she began untwisting the wires that attached the planter to the hook.

"I see you're liberating Boston Charlie from his hanging wires." It was Marj.

"Sort of. What I'm trying to do is get him out of his pot so I can see if anything is living in the soil."

Marj raised an eyebrow, but merely said, "Okay. You turn the pot over, and I'll hold the plant."

With two pairs of hands, it was easy to slip the fern out of its container. Nikki found nothing unusual—no holes by which anything could enter or leave. The soil was packed evenly, molded into the dish shape of the planter, and looked to be undisturbed. Nikki situated the pot back on the root ball. They turned the fern over, and Nikki re-attached the wires.

"So how come Charlie's being strip searched?"

Nikki looked at her friend, wondering if she should tell her what had happened. Marj would probably think she . . . but still. . . . "You're a plant person, Marj. Have you ever known of a Boston fern moving by itself?" She described what had happened, ending with "Is there some natural cause that might make it do that?"

Marj had been listening carefully. "I've never heard of anything like that. Are you sure it wasn't the wind?"

"The only window open was the one in the bedroom, and the bedroom door was shut."

"And you're sure you didn't dream it."

"I have fern fallout on my rug I'll be glad to show you."

"That *is* weird. The only thing I can think of is that Charlie has been in Bert's nursery, jammed up against a lot of other plants—you know how he keeps the place. Is it possible that the fronds could've been under tension—like a Christmas tree when it's baled for shipping? When you put it on the shelf, the fronds relaxed and sprang free?"

"Marj, that plant was moved several times. It made the trip home over a bumpy road in the back of my truck. I carried it in and put it in the urn. It got bounced and jounced enough to loosen any tension there might have been. I swear I watched that thing thrash around and scatter bits and pieces of itself for several seconds. It wasn't a single jerk, like a spring going off."

Marj regarded Nikki thoughtfully. "Okay, Nancy Drew, we're going to get to the bottom of this one way or another, but there *is* one other possibility. It's a reach, but we can't entirely dismiss it either. You *have* been under a lot of stress lately." Nikki opened her mouth. "No, just hear me out. I do *not* believe in the medical practice of calling everything they can't diagnose 'stress.' Still, you *did* have a drink last night—a rather strong one, thanks to me. You did say you lay down on the couch and closed your eyes. Could you have fallen asleep, *gotten up and walked in your sleep?* Could you have dreamt the episode with the fern and maybe, in your sleep, could you have *shaken the fern yourself?* Is that possible?"

Nikki sighed. "Anything's possible, I suppose. But not probable. Not to me. Something shook the hell out of Boston Charlie. Either some animal or Charlie himself. I watched it happen."

"Well, next time I go to the library I'm going to see if I can find something on Boston ferns. Plants move all the time. Most of them move so slowly we can't detect it, but they do move. They grow, they turn toward the sun, they scatter seeds, they twine around things, they react to being touched. I've never heard of one doing the cha-cha, but maybe there's something in a book someplace. I'd go today, but the library's closed."

"You're certainly taking this well. I was afraid you'd think me a nut—and you probably *do*, but you're too polite to say so."

"Let's just say I love a mystery. What are you going to do today? I'm heading up island. You want to come?" There was a tentative, almost pleading note to Marj's question, but Nikki failed to pick up on it.

"I'd better not. I have a deadline and I'm nowhere near it."

"In that case I'll leave you to labor on Labor Day. I'll see you later, and if Charlie does another dance, let me know. If this becomes a regular thing, we can rent a camcorder and try to get it on tape."

...

Despite the late start, Nikki ended up having a good day. She put Charlie back in his spot next to the shamrocks (she'd left the wires in place in case she had to move him again), then settled in to design her September batch of thematic crosswords. This particular batch was composed of show business themes, and Nikki worked quickly and well, almost as if her mind had already executed the puzzles, and all she was doing was copying them to grids. Even the sounds and smells of Labor Day observance—kids in the park, shrieks and shouts and splashing; the smell of wood smoke and meat being cooked on open fires; the raucous revelry of a horseshoes game—didn't disturb her concentration. By early afternoon she had a dozen puzzles designed and clued—certainly more than her usual output. Her brain had worked with lightning speed, connecting words easily and surely, with little time spent searching for words that fit. *Wish I could do this all the time!*

Nikki was so pleased with her output that she decided to quit early. She went out for a breath of air and saw that Marj's parking space was still empty. Nikki thought of walking down to the park, hiking the trail, but then decided against it. Too many people out there today, and she didn't feel like connecting with anyone—certainly not with Adelaide. She went back inside. Then she had an idea. Marj had mentioned that she should paint pictures to hang on her walls. That could be fun! Nikki hadn't done any real painting in a long time. Most of her artwork, with Phil, had been posters and banners advertising various fund-raising projects for IDC.

Now Nikki realized that while she had plenty of markers and a set of watercolors, she didn't have any oils—at least none that hadn't dried out. *Darn! and the art shop's closed.* Never mind, she could use the watercolors for now. She retrieved her easel from her office and set it up in the living room, next to her drawing table. *The place is starting to look like a warehouse. No wonder Phil made me keep my stuff out of sight!* She set up her paints and a large watercolor canvas board which she preferred to paper. *Okay, now, what will be my subject?* Without further planning, she made a sweeping stroke across her canvas, and then, as if her hand and arm had had a life of their own, proceeded to work swiftly and surely.

...

"Knock knock!"

"Huh?"

"You're supposed to say, 'Who's there?'"

Nikki peered through the screen door. "Mr. Cantwell?"

"You're supposed to say 'Who's there?'"

"Okay, who's there?"

"It's me. Raymond."

"Raymond who?"

"I told you, it's me, *Raymond.*"

And indeed it was Raymond Cantwell, the pink-faced, balding man Nikki had met at Adelaide's. Nikki also realized with a bit of a chill that Raymond, whoever he might be, had the mental age of a child. "Well, what can I do for you, Raymond?"

"Adelaide says for you to come to the barbecue."

"Oh, thank you, Raymond but I don't think—"

"*Adelaide says for you to come to the barbecue.*"

"Oo-kay. Where *is* the barbecue, Raymond?"

Raymond smiled like a delighted child. "Down by the lake. Everybody's there. They're cooking chicken. Adelaide says for you to come to the barbecue."

"Well thank you very much for inviting me, Raymond. Maybe I'll come down a little later, would that be all right?"

Raymond smiled and nodded. "Lots of good things to eat at the barbecue. All kinds of colors—and they all sing. I'll tell Adelaide you're coming to the barbecue."

"Thank you, Raymond. I'll see you later."

"Down at the barbecue. Adelaide says—"

"—to come to the barbecue. Yes. Thank you. Good-bye, Raymond."

Nikki returned to her easel and pondered Raymond Cantwell. Who was he? Obviously the man was deficient to some degree. He seemed to be an ally (or was it familiar?) of Adelaide's. Someone to do her bidding. Nikki regarded the work on her easel. She'd been working on a watercolor of a scene, but now the sight of it surprised her. She took a few steps back and looked at it. *What, exactly, could I have been visualizing here?*

The scene looked to be of a garden—or a nursery. There were plants, all rather crowded together, but all very beautiful. Nikki was taken aback and quite impressed by her own choice of colors and her method of execution. The plants were depicted in many hues and shades, with a much better rendering of light and shadow than Nikki would have expected of herself. Usually the final painting fell short of the picture in her mind. This time the picture was so much better than anything she'd ever done, that Nikki was a bit dumbfounded. One jarring feature was the sky. It gave the impression of being circular, or dome-like. It seemed to press down, enclose—and there was something a bit sinister—claustrophobic—about that sky. Well, enough for today. Maybe she could fix it tomorrow. She stared at the painting thoughtfully. Did It look familiar or was it just evocative? (Nifty puzzle word.) It wasn't Bert's nursery, but there was something vaguely similar about it. Or maybe not. Something half-remembered. Maybe it would come to her later.

Nikki realized that she was hungry. She hadn't eaten anything all day, and now she was ravenous. She thought of making herself a salad, but her taste buds, tantalized all afternoon by the smells of barbecues, rejected the idea. *So Adelaide says I should go to the barbecue? Well, why not? I think Adelaide owes me—and maybe I'll learn more about this strange place and the people who live here.*

CHAPTER 7

NIKKI, IN shorts and oversized sweat shirt, strolled down to Barkell Road and turned left, past the cleared area studded with barbecue pits and campers. There, for park patrons, also stood a building with showers and laundry facilities, and a couple of storage sheds that housed camp gear.

Behind the campground stood a forest of magnificent cedars, firs, alders and arbutus trees. In order to use the beach or to camp in the woods, one had to pass through a gate and check in at the convenience store. At night the gate was closed to keep out unauthorized vehicles, although it didn't stop pedestrians who simply walked around it. But if anyone wanted to drive in or out of the campground at night, the Moons would have to be notified and the gate opened. It effectively barred carloads of kids looking for a place to party on the lake.

Eagle Lake Park was alive with activity. Everyone seemed to be outdoors, enjoying the last big weekend of the season. The island climate was mild enough for campers to use the park year round, but from now till spring there would not be as many of them. In winter, instead of water-skiers and swimmers, the lake might host fishermen or (Marj had warned Nikki) duck hunters. Today there seemed to be little gatherings everywhere: families making a day of it— playing games, picnicking, cooking on grills—and feeding the park rabbits who were having a field day of their own. They hung about in groups, waiting for someone to throw bread or raw vegetables, then attacked the food in a pack, the quickest making off with the largest, with the rest in pursuit. Nikki noted that they were energetic but not particularly bright. They often ignored smaller pieces of bread in order to chase the rabbit that had grabbed the big one and, in their haste, lost the smaller scraps as well to newcomers.

Nikki walked over the hill toward the lake, past the home of Hector and Ida Moon, down through the open gate and on toward the shore. She looked around for Adelaide but saw only strangers—people gathered in private groupings to enjoy the outdoors.

"Yoo-hoo, Nikki. We're up here. Come on through." It was Adelaide Moon. Nikki looked up. The barbecue wasn't down by the lake after all. It was in Hector and Ida's back yard, *overlooking* the lake. Nikki retraced her steps, went in through a small garden gate and walked around to the back of the house.

Except for Marj, they were all there—the Moons, the Laderheims, Janet and Bob, Paulette and Fred, Raymond—and a couple of people Nikki hadn't met. George Moon, a tall, beefy man with a face that could have been carved on a totem pole, was wearing a soaring chef's hat and an apron that said "Kiss the Cook" as he tended chicken pieces on a large grill.

Adelaide, cigarette in hand, met Nikki. "I'm glad you could make it. George is makin' his special barbecue. We only decided to do this last night. You left so early we didn't have a chance to tell you."

"Maybe I should've brought something."

"No, no, no, Nikki. We've got *tons* of food and beer. Barbecue and coleslaw and beer. Nothin' fancy. It was a last-minute thing, like

I said, but there's lots of it, and I just want you to help yourself. Get a plate and get George to serve you up his specialty. I was hopin' Marj would be coming with you, but Raymond tells me she's not home."

"Marj left this morning. She said something about going up island."

Adelaide gave Nikki a knowing look. "Oh, I guess she went to see *him* then."

"Him?" Nikki couldn't keep from asking.

"Her father. He lives up near Fanny Bay."

"Marj never mentioned that she had family on the island. I thought her parents were both dead."

"She and her dad don't get along too well. I don't think she sees him very often. Some family trouble, I guess. Marj doesn't like to talk about him. Hey, Raymond, go find Nikki a plate and utensils—and get her some beer too." Raymond, who had been hanging within earshot, dashed off like a spaniel after a stick.

"I hope Raymond didn't make a nuisance of himself when I sent him to fetch you. He's like a kid, but he's harmless, and he's very handy. He helps take care of things in the park." Raymond returned with a paper plate, plastic knife and fork, paper napkin and a Styrofoam cup brimming with beer. "Now you just get George to serve you a nice big piece of chicken. Salad's on the table," Adelaide said to Nikki. Then, to Raymond, "I'd like you to keep an eye out for Marj's car. If you see her, I want you to go up and tell her to come to the barbecue."

"I'll say 'Adelaide says you should come to the barbecue.'"

Adelaide hesitated. "No, you tell Marj that *Nikki* says she's to come to the barbecue. You got that, Raymond? If you see Marj, you say that *Nikki* says she's to come." Seeing Nikki's questioning look, Adelaide smiled. "It'll tell Marj you're already here. Otherwise she'll go over to your place first. Raymond can only keep one thing in his mind at a time."

Nikki found a place at the picnic table and began wolfing down chicken. She abandoned the all but useless knife and fork and picked up the meat with her fingers. It was *delicious*. George had marinated it in some wonderful sauce that gave it not only the piquancy of vinegar but a touch of sweet and an herb flavor that Nikki couldn't easily identify. *I wonder who I'd have to sleep with to get the recipe—George or Adelaide?* She had accepted a drumstick and thigh, but now, shamelessly, went back for seconds. "George, the chicken is fabulous. What do you put on it?"

George compressed his lips in what might have been, for him, a smile, and wordlessly plopped a breast with wing attached on her outstretched plate. *A man of few words. A man of no words. I don't think I've ever heard him say anything.*

"That sauce is so secret he doesn't even tell *me* what's in it." Adelaide had come up behind Nikki and laughed her wheezy laugh.

"Well, I've never tasted chicken this good. I didn't know your husband was a gourmet chef."

"He used to be a volunteer fireman when we lived in the States," Adelaide said, as if that explained everything—and, in a way, it *did*. Firemen's groups all over America were known for their annual barbecues. "There's lots of chicken, so be sure to take some home with you later. But right now I want you to meet the Hatches—Walter and Louise. They were out on Gabriola Island last night, visiting their daughter. They live in the unit next to Raymond."

Walter Hatch was a bluff, booming man in his sixties. "Glad to see more good-looking single women in this park. Used to be Eagle Lake was a place only for the newlywed and the nearly dead! Ha-ha-ha!"

Louise, his wife, an elegant little woman with neatly coiffed gray hair and a pair of glasses on a chain around her neck, smiled politely. "So good to meet you, my dear." Her manner was a gentle as her husband's was hearty. She made Nikki think of floral china cups and tea cozies.

Nikki also saw that Clark Moon, George and Adelaide's son, had joined the party. He had a pretty young girl with him, and two were obviously an item. Nikki learned that her name was Shelley, and that they planned to be married in the spring.

"They're awfully young," Adelaide whispered to Nikki, "But what are you gonna to do? We're fixin' up Unit One for them so they can have a place of their own. At least they'll be where we can keep an eye on them, and maybe Clark will finish school. If they can just keep from gettin' pregnant for a while!"

Nikki, replete with chicken and sipping her second—or was it her third—beer, was feeling mellow. Eagle Lake Park was, after all, pretty neat. *Pret-ty neat indeed!* It was a beautiful place—an *interesting* place, what with all the bunny rabbits. Nikki giggled. I mean, where can you live surrounded by bunny rabbits? And the people? They weren't so bad. Nah, they were okay. Even Adelaide. Adelaide was okay. Adelaide was, in some ways, a bit like Nikki's mother. No, she wasn't *anything* like Nikki's mother; she didn't *look* like her mother. But she did like to run things, like her mother, and she did like to keep track of you, like her mother. And what Adelaide wanted, she got. And *that* was a lot like her mother. And that was also a lot like Phil. *Phil* had been a lot like her mother. But enough of mothers. Nikki shouldn't be sitting alone thinking of mothers. She should be *mingling*. When you go to a party, you don't sit waiting to be entertained. You're supposed to *contribute*. Nikki's mother had said that. A good guest contributes to the party.

Nikki noticed that Ida Moon was sitting alone in a lawn chair. Okay, Nikki, go over and *contribute*. Find something nice to say and strike up a conversation. She picked up her beer and took it with her. "Mrs. Moon, I've been admiring your hanging baskets. They're very beautiful."

Ida Moon looked pleased. "Thank you, Nikki. I make them up myself. I find that the cascading petunia works very well, but it needs a sunny location."

"I tried a basket once but everything died."

"They need a lot of water. I water mine with a weak solution of liquid fertilizer, and I line the baskets with plastic bags—with just a couple of holes for drainage. You can't see the bags because I put in a nest of moss first. This year I put in some of those moisture crystals that absorb water and gradually release it."

"You know a lot about plants, Mrs. Moon."

"Been growing them all my life."

"I don't suppose you've ever had a Boston fern go—no, never mind. Can I get you some more chicken or anything?"

"Oh, no thank you, dear. I think we're all going to have coffee and cake for dessert. I've got to go find Hector and remind him to take his pills. Oh, there's your neighbor, Marj."

Marj had, indeed, joined the group. She was chatting with Janet (of Janet and Bob) and seemed to be listening to, or telling, a funny story, as the two of them were laughing. Nikki felt a pang. Excluded. She could have gone with Marj "up island" and maybe learned more about her friend's family. Her instincts as an artist and writer made Nikki curious about people. She tended to watch them, noticing the way they stood and moved. She listened to the way they talked—as if someday she might have to give testimony in court—or write a description. Nikki also loved to unravel mysteries about people. Marj, for instance. Marj seemed to be very up front, but she hadn't said anything about her father. Marj claimed to only have a high school education, but she seemed to be heavily into books and research—and she certainly did not *sound* uneducated. Was that because she'd felt inadequate with her former husband's friends? Had she launched into a self-improvement program? And, if so, was that before or after her divorce?

Or was Marj, like Nikki herself, a woman who had spent her childhood in a world of her own—a world of books—because she never really seemed to fit in, and was often lonely and unhappy and afraid? Nikki stopped. She was treading on thin ice here. *Her* life had not been like that. Nikki's childhood had been quite normal. Her family had been—well, a typical family. Okay, so they weren't the Brady Bunch, but no family was. Her parents had fought, but nobody had beaten anyone with tire chains or stuck a knife in anyone's ribs. It had all been, more than anything, head games. They had all been experts at head games, specially her father: The Honcho of Head Games.

"I see you made it to another of Adelaide's parties after all." Marj interrupted Nikki's reverie. She sat down in the chair vacated by Ida.

Nikki grinned. "The spirit was willing but the flesh couldn't resist the smell of barbecue."

"Isn't it heaven? Glad I got back in time."

"Adelaide said you went to see you father."

"Yes, what's left of him.'

"Is he ill?"

"Alzheimer's."

"Oh, god! I'm so sorry."

"Yeah. Well, I thought I'd put in an appearance, but it's time for me to head back home. I'm not going to be good company tonight."

"Wait, I'll come with you."

Nikki, feeling a bit light-headed, found Adelaide and thanked her warmly, saying that she and Marj would be heading back now. Adelaide nodded. "Take care of Marj. She's always upset when she's been to see her father. We'll see you both Sunday night."

Back at their own mobile homes, Nikki said, "We missed the coffee at the barbecue, but I can make us a fresh pot. You don't want to be alone right now, do you?"

"No. I guess I don't. I'll just check on Casimir and then come over."

Nikki set coffee to perk, and Marj arrived within minutes. "Casimir has destroyed my emperor phlox. It had just come into bloom. Now there are flowers strewn all over the living room. Hey, I see you've been painting."

"Trying to."

"That's really *good*. Where is this place? I mean, what was your inspiration?"

"I really don't know. I just had an urge to paint, and this is what came out. I've been trying to figure out what it is myself."

"Looks like the Garden of Eden, doesn't it—or a corner of it."

"There's something wrong with the sky. It looks . . . oppressive. I don't know what to do with it."

"Yes, but it's interesting. Seems to say that there's a slightly sinister quality to all that beauty. I think I'd leave it alone."

"Maybe you're right. I'll give it another shot another time. Easier to do a new painting than to fix up an old one. You want anything with your coffee?"

"No thanks, but you're about to have company."

"Knock knock."

"Who's there? Come on in, Raymond."

Raymond Cantwell entered. "Adelaide says you forgot the chicken, and she sent you a piece of cake too." Raymond placed a basket on the kitchen counter. He stopped, transfixed, to look at Nikki's painting. "Ooh," he said. "Ooh!" Then, as if listening to an inaudible voice, he nodded, walked over to Nikki's plant shelf. He stood there, as if again listening to instructions, then turned to face Nikki, his eyes wide. "It sings," he said. "It sings all colors. It sings home."

"Uh, Raymond," Nikki said. "What do you mean it sings? *Who* sings?"

"*It* sings. It sings all colors. It sings *home*."

Marj spoke: "Raymond, *how* does it sing? Do you hear something?"

"It *sings*. It sings all colors. Red is rough. Blue is slippery. It sings all colors. It sings *home*."

"*What* sings, Raymond? The painting? The plant?" Marj asked.

"Everything. Everything sings colors. Everything feels. Everything *tastes* colors. Red is rough. Blue is slippery. Black is death. Oh, I don't like to hear it sing death." Raymond covered his ears.

"Okay, okay, Raymond. Everything's all right. Take it easy, it's just a painting."

Raymond looked distressed. "Not the painting." Raymond turned and pointed at Boston Charlie. "*He* sings death. I have to go now." Raymond turned and went out the screen door, leaving it to close behind him.

"What do you make of that?" Nikki asked.

"I don't know. You realize, of course, that Raymond is mentally retarded, but he's not insane—although he certainly seemed to be babbling today! I don't know what he was trying to tell us, but he was obviously upset by something. And it seemed to have something to do with Boston Charlie!"

Nikki and Marj both turned to look at the fern, half expecting—they didn't know what. But Charlie stood quietly in his pot without so much as a twitch. A houseplant. Just a houseplant. But wait, wasn't there something a little different about Charlie? Nikki was the one who noticed it. "He's grown," she said. "Yesterday his fronds only reached the shelf. Today, notice how they overhang it." And indeed, Charlie's green fronds hung gracefully almost to the floor.

"God, that's a beautiful plant," Marj said.

"Yes," Nikki said thoughtfully—and shivered.

"Goose walk over your grave?"

CHAPTER 8

TUESDAY MORNING found Nikki hard at work and, again, pleased by her own output. *Maybe I'm getting better at this and that's why I'm able to work so fast.* By eleven she had designed half a dozen new puzzles and was ready for a break. At the rate she was going, she would get her September batch done in half the time it usually took. She made herself a cup of tea and took it to her deck table, noticing how well her herbs were doing. Parsley was a spreading mound of green, chives speared upwards in a dense clump, thyme was already creeping over the edge of the planter and oregano formed a mass of rich foliage. Before long she'd be able to start harvesting. Even the rosemary, originally the smallest, was forming a compact little shrub. *Never had this kind of luck with plants before!*

Nikki sat facing her favorite view—that of the lake. A light breeze etched ripples in the water, distorting the reflection of sky and mountains, then puffed up to ruffle Nikki's hair. A great blue heron, neck folded in flight, crossed from the island to a Douglas fir on the lake's edge, and a flock of small ducks traveled in a convoy in the distance.

On the ground, rabbits were doing rabbit things. She recognized Bruno lounging under the picnic table. Nikki checked her deck carpeting, but saw no signs of visitation. She hadn't noticed that there were so many flowers. Marj's fuchsia, in a hanging basket on her porch, fairly glowed with red-purple blossoms, even through the screen. Bob and Janet's trailer had a climbing clematis vine that was covered with large flat pink blooms.

After her bizarre encounter with Boston Charlie, Nikki had found herself looking at plants differently. She was noticing that along the edge of the drop-off to the lake, in a tangle of grasses, wildflowers bloomed—brown-eyed Susans, daisies, Queen Anne's lace and yarrow. Why had the rabbits had left them alone? Was the terrain too steep, or was the vegetation simply too coarse? Did they prefer nibbling on emerging blades of grass? Did the flowers know this when they seeded themselves? Was there some sort of cooperation between plant and animal so that there would always be flowers as well as rabbits?

Nikki mused that she lived—they *all* lived—surrounded and supported by vegetation, but what did they really know about it? As Marj had said, plants move all the time, but their activity flies under our radar. Trees, for instance, go through all kinds of changes during any given year. Broadleaf maples were just beginning to display a few yellow leaves. Later they would become spectacular to behold.

Douglas firs, straight as ramrods, soared to the sky, their tops encrusted with cones that were just turning brown. Cedars had decorated themselves in a mottle of green and rust, as they selectively turned some their foliage the color of russet and allowed it to fall, a form of self-pruning for the evergreens. And then there were the arbutus trees that never managed to grow quite straight. Their red bark was always peeling like a sunburn to reveal an avocado green underlayer that felt cool and velvety to the touch. Nikki found them delightful and wanted to do a painting of the Pacific madrone one day.

Nikki mused that the trees had a life span much greater than her own. How old *were* these giants? What wisdom might be coded within them? Could we learn something from them if we didn't treat them merely as lumber? An old growth Douglas fir might have lived for hundreds of years but was vulnerable to any guy with a chainsaw.

Could we live without trees? What about insects and other species? The natural world was exuberant, rambunctious, bursting with vitality. Even the rabbits were sleek and glossy, glowing with good health. Nikki had read somewhere about a plague that wipes them out every seven years, and idly wondered if that would happen here. But certainly not today! Nikki closed her eyes and allowed her other senses to take over, feeling the soft breeze and the heat of the sun on her skin, hearing the sounds of birds—the shrill "police whistle" of a junco, and the rasp of ravens. She realized that the only sounds *were* those of birds. It was Tuesday. People were back at work. The park would be quiet during the day now. Nikki's mind went back to Adelaide's barbecue—and she opened her eyes with a start. What was that dream? God, that had been weird! Oh, if she could only remember it!

Last night she had actually dreamt of being at Adelaide's party, but there were . . . there were mathematical symbols! Yes, that was it. She was talking to Marj and a big plus sign kept flashing between them. Only Marj wasn't just Marj. She was also the number six. And Nikki was the number four, and when she and Marj were talking, a big number ten kept flashing above them. And when Nikki looked around, she could see that *all* the people were numbers, and, as they talked together, plus, minus and other math signs kept flashing between them with the result showing above their heads. She could see a big minus sign between Mr. Laderheim and Adelaide. Mr. Laderheim was a "seven" and Adelaide a "two"; and an equals sign with the resulting "five" above them. The signs were constantly shifting and changing, and so, it seemed, where the individual numbers. When Adelaide, a "two," turned to say something to Ida, she became a "three." She and Ida, who was also a "three," between them formed a plus sign, with a big blue "equals six" above them. There were other signs too: square roots and division signs—even fractions—as complicated mathematical calculations occurred with lightning speed at every human interaction, mirroring the intensity of each encounter. Nikki wished she could remember all of it. One thing she did recall: no matter how the group interacted, and no matter how the numbers kept constantly changing, the total number of the group was always forty-seven—a big glowing greenish forty-seven that floated high overhead!

It had been a strange dream—very exciting—and beautiful, with all the gorgeous colors of the math signs, like neon lights—only the colors had been much more vibrant than any Nikki had seen while awake. Remembering it all in a rush, she felt a bit out of breath. *What could it have meant?* There *had* to be some message in it, if only she could figure it out. Nikki realized her tea was getting cold and downed it in one gulp. *I should write it down before I forget it.*

But Nikki did not record the dream although she would have cause to ponder it later. Instead, in a burst of creativity, she went on to design another half-dozen puzzles, then went into her office and began printing up final drafts. She used templates she had designed in QuarkXPress software to set up the grids, a table cells format in Microsoft Word to execute clues, then printed them both on her Personal LaserWriter. She didn't stop for lunch, and, indeed, lost all track of the hours until she heard a knock on her door and Marj call, "Quitting time?"

"Come in, Marj. What time *is* it?"

"Quarter to five. Are you hungry?"

"Well, yes, I guess I am. I was on such a roll I just kept working. Why don't I fix us some of the chicken Raymond brought. We can finish that."

"My turn to cook tonight! Of course I can't compete with Nikki 'Julia Child' Leino, but in my humble way, I have a repast prepared.

So, milady, if you will repair to yon chalet, we shall dine—if Casimir hasn't demolished dinner."

Casimir lay inert, a puddle of white plush on Marj's couch, his eyes closed in sleep, just the tip of his pink tongue protruding. So relaxed was he that he didn't even stir when they entered. Dinner turned out to be newspaper-wrapped fish and chips from Ben's. "I realize it ain't what you're used to, milady. Plain food but palatable. White wine or Toby?"

"Toby. And I *love* fish and chips. They're so *British*. You know, when I was a kid, I went around for weeks talking with a British accent. It drove my family bonkers."

"Well, *I* always loved *Monty Python*. I went around saying, 'Now for something completely different.'"

"Oh Marj, I'd marry you if you weren't a heterosexual."

"Stick around, I might just rather switch than fight. I had a call from my ex today."

"Jonah? What did *he* want?"

"I don't know. It was on my answering machine when I got home. He wants to see me. *Now* he wants to see me. We split up, I went through hell with never a word from him, and now that I'm finally over him—at least I think I am—he wants to come tangoing back into my life."

"Usually they come waltzing back."

"Not Jonah. He tangos. With a rose in his teeth."

"Are you going to see him?"

"Probably. Amazing how that man can still make me jump when he snaps his fingers."

"I call that 'snapping to grid.'"

"Excuse me?"

"It's a computer term. There's a command on my Mac called 'snap to grid' which means to align immediately with an established reference point. I'm doing it too. I'm seeing Phil tomorrow night. It's a little like, 'good-bye forever—but yes, I'll still pick up your laundry.'"

"We women are such wimps."

"A qualified amen to that!"

"Let's change the subject. You know where I've been most of the day?"

"Is this a trick question?"

"I have been at the library, reading up on Boston ferns."

"And you found that once every hundred years they do a fertility dance that scares the shit out anyone who owns one?"

"Nope. Actually I found nothing. I gather the Boston fern is such a dull plant that nobody's written anything much about it—at least according to our local library. It was a favorite of Victorians, thrives even in low light conditions, and has spent most of its productive years adorning drawing rooms and the lobbies of hotels and stuffy men's clubs. According to my research, there's *nothing* demonic, controversial or even interesting about a Boston fern. It would qualify for the Boring Plant of the Month award."

"Don't tell Charlie."

"Anyroad, as our friend, Bert would say, there you are. If I were a fortune teller, I'd predict that your life with Charlie will be totally devoid of excitement."

But that was before the earthquake.

CHAPTER 9

Nikki was jolted awake at two in the morning. Dazed by sleep and disoriented, she didn't at first realize what was happening. Vancouver Island lies on a fault line, and whenever there was any sort of earth tremor anywhere, news reports made much of the fact that the Big One could occur at any moment.

Nikki had never experienced an earthquake, and while the feel of her bed shaking in the middle of the night was terrifying, it was quickly over. Cautiously, Nikki reached over and turned on the light. She got out of bed and looked around, half expecting to be jolted off her feet at any second, and made her way down the hall into her office where she saw that her computer seemed to be intact. In the living room, the lightweight plastic pot of oxalis next to Charlie had fallen off the shelf, spilling earth on the rug. Nothing serious. Nikki picked it up and replaced it. She would vacuum the rug later. A couple of books had tumbled to the floor and her easel had tipped over.

Nikki sat down on the couch, waiting, wondering if more would follow. If she planned to continue living on the West Coast, she really should prepare for earthquakes. Her mind ticked off possible ways. According to a pamphlet she had read recently, she should have food and water stored for emergencies, a first-aid kit, slide bolts on kitchen cabinets to keep contents from flying out, some cash on hand in case of whatever. And *oh, I don't know. How in god's name do you prepare for something like that?* She got up and went out on deck. Eagle Lake Park was quiet and dark. The sky was clear and starry. How could that be? *Am I the only one who felt the tremor? Did everyone else for chrissake* sleep *through it?* The lights were out at Marj's—and every other mobile as far as Nikki could see. *Am I going to find out that I dreamt all this?* With no answers forthcoming, Nikki went back to bed and slept soundly.

She dreamt that she was in a garden in which the plants were so tall that they towered over her. She realized then that they were all watching her, instructing her, while she tried to play a musical instrument that was like a xylophone. As she hit each key, it emitted not only a musical note but also a wave of color that rose up in the shimmering shape of a number. The teacher plants were telling her that, in between each key, there existed also a non-visible key that was part of the musical scale, the existence of which made the musical notes possible. It was important for Nikki to understand that these *non*-notes were an important part of any musical composition; and that a musical note existed only in relation to the tones that could not be heard. It was all making sense to Nikki in her dream, and she experienced an exalted moment of intellectual breakthrough at having grasped this fundamental principle of Universal Law—until she woke and tried to reconstruct her experience.

Nikki often had colorful dreams, and it wasn't the first time she'd awakened, sure that she had discovered the meaning of life—only to realize that what she'd been brandishing in her dream as the fount of all enlightenment had been a coat hanger or an ice cream scoop. The unusual thing about her recent dreams, however, was their math content. It was intriguing.

Nikki lay looking at the ceiling and walls. Everything looked normal. She should go see Marj and see if there had been any damage. She got up, dressed hastily, then saw that Marj's car was gone. She made a cup of coffee, looked through her rooms for any other signs of last night's tremor, then cleaned up the soil on the carpet.

At any rate, Nikki, herself, should go into town today. She had a check from her puzzle publisher to deposit and laundry to do. She had not tried using the mini-washer in the hall. Marj had told her not to wash anything white. The Eagle Lake water, though processed to be potable, had a brown tint that left streaks. As result, Nikki opted to take her clothes to the laundromat and buy bottled water for drinking.

Taking stock of her larder, Nikki saw that she needed eggs, milk and bread from the grocery store. She might even go to the art shop and pick up oil paints which she preferred to watercolors. She'd also need canvases in different sizes, and primer. Nikki didn't normally shop midweek, preferring to treat her self-employment as a "real job" by sticking to a nine to four schedule, and putting in extra hours when needed. This week, though, she'd made such good time that she felt she could treat herself to a day in town. It would be fun. Then, with a grimace of irritation, Nikki remembered she had promised to have dinner with Phil that night. *It has to happen sooner or later. Might as well get it over with. Maybe I should work this morning and just leave early enough to get my errands done in one trip—but I don't think I want the groceries and laundry sitting in the truck while Phil and I seek "closure."*

She gathered her wash into a plastic bag, set it in a wicker basket along with detergent, and put the basket into the front seat of the Mazda, scattering a few rabbits as she went. To her surprise, she found the orange tomcat boldly sitting on the lid of her garbage can and gave the animal a quick pat. "Run for your life, kitty. These are perilous times." The cat leapt off the can and vanished around a corner. Nikki paused to ponder. Somewhere she had read that animals leave an area before a quake hits. The rabbits obviously had *not*; neither had the cat. *Maybe they left and came back—or maybe that only applies in big earthquakes. Do animals have a way of measuring the magnitude in advance?*

...

As with everything that week, Nikki got her errands done in record time. She went to the bank which was almost empty, so that she didn't have to wait in line; then to the laundromat where there were plenty of machines available; on to the grocery store where she bought extra water and canned goods, "exqueezing" her way through a crowd of non-hurried shoppers. She stopped at the art shop, then pressed on to Home Hardware for batteries, a couple of battery lamps, a flashlight and a transistor radio; and finally to Pharmasave for first aid supplies.

"Preparing for an emergency?" the clerk asked, looking at Nikki's purchases. When Nikki mentioned the tremor, the clerk looked surprised. "Didn't hear about that. I'll have to watch the six o'clock news."

On the way home, she assessed her situation. She had a gas stove with a propane tank, which was better than natural gas in an emergency. Gas would be turned off, as would power, but if *her* part of the earth didn't move *too* much, if her own connection didn't sustain damage, she might still be able to use the stove for cooking and heat. *But am I the only person in Nanaimo who felt the quake? I thought everybody would be out buying supplies today.*

Nikki pulled into her parking space to see Marj. "Wow, looks like you've been doing industrial-strength shopping. Can I give you a hand?"

Marj helped Nikki unload the truck. "What are you going to do, hole up with all this food and do some serious painting? Put up a big Do Not Disturb sign?"

"I just thought it would be a good idea to be a bit more prepared in case we get another quake."

"Quake? What's got you thinking about a quake?"

"Oh, Marj. Not you too! Don't tell me you slept through the one last night! My bed was shaking like that scene in *The Exorcist*. It knocked over your shamrocks, and a few other things. I don't know how you could've missed it."

"Me neither. Casimir lands on my chest if there's even a hint of any disturbance. By the way, I saw the orange tom. He walked by my porch. Casimir saw him too. I thought he was going to claw right through the screen."

"Yeah, I saw him myself this morning. I thought animals left an area before a quake."

"I don't know. I slept through the night like a baby—and as far as I know, so did Casimir."

"I slept too. Didn't think I would. You were up early this morning."

"I had some errands in town and I went to the library."

"Still checking on Boston ferns?"

"No, I gave up on that. But I'm tracking down something else— something interesting that might apply to our friend Raymond Cantwell."

"Oh? What's that?"

"I'm not sure yet, but—oh, I'll have to tell you later; there goes my phone."

...

Nikki watched Marj run off to her unit, then went inside and finished putting away her purchases. She decided to create a survival shelf in the hall closet, stacking it with bottled water, radio, lamp, flashlight, batteries, first-aid kit, and an item she'd come across in the hardware store: a Swedish FireSteel. She took it out of its bubble wrap—a four-inch rod with a wooden knob through which was threaded a cord with a flat metal striker. Made for the Swedish military, it promised to be good for twelve thousand strikes, and that it would start a fire in any weather, even when wet. Following instructions, she took it to the sink and removed the black paint from the rod by rubbing it with the striker, laid a piece of crumpled paper towel in the sink, then pulled the striker "slowly and firmly" down the length of the rod. Sparks flew; the paper charred, then flamed. *Wow! Okay, earthquake or zombie invasion, I'm ready! I can make fire!* There was something primordial about that, something mystical and *vulcan* that stirred the soul of her inner goddess, and she stood, for a while, feeling triumphant, empowered and a little awed.

I guess I should also pack a bag with extra clothing in case we have to evacuate in a hurry. She found an old nylon airline carry-on and put in a pair of sneakers, jeans, sweater, an old jacket, underwear and socks—and the FireSteel. What else? There would be things you *had* to have—like toilet paper! That would be bulky. Maybe just a box of tissues—without the box. Then something occurred to her, and she nipped into the bathroom and came back with a handful of tampons and tucked them in as well. She'd have to give it more thought later, but now her actions were beginning to make her feel spooked, as if she were readying for a battle of some sort—as if the very act of preparation was increasing the possibility of chaos entering her life. *What am I doing?* Nikki laughed, suddenly. *I'm hoping for the best and preparing for the worst.* It was one of Nikki's mother's favorite sayings. *I'm turning into my mother!*

It was still early in the day. *Carpe* what's left of the *diem*. Nikki unpacked her paints and canvases, put down an old shower curtain she used as a drop cloth, set up her easel, and began a project more to her liking—an oil painting.

By five o'clock she had produced another landscape and she viewed it critically. Again she had painted plants—and painted them well. Something about the painting paralleled her dream of the night before—the one of the tall "teacher plants." *But why do I keep painting that strange sky?* The sky did, again, look like a plastic bubble, and had the same sinister cast as if it imprisoned everything beneath it. She studied the rest of the picture. This time she had added other features. There was a small stream that looked to contain not only water plants but small fish. All around it grew rank jungle growth—shrubs, vines, flowers, ferns. Nikki was surprised at the wealth of her own detail, but also wondered if her plants belonged to any known species. The earlier painting was on her art table. Now she took the watercolor and propped it so she could view both pictures side by side.

Surprised, she saw that her oil painting was an overlap and a continuation of the watercolor. If she'd been able to extend the watercolor downward a bit and to the right, she would have come to the stream. There were other subtleties that puzzled Nikki, who had produced both paintings by working furiously without having made preliminary sketches. It had something to do with the attitude of the plants. *Attitude of plants?* For example, a shrub that was blossoming next to a tree in the watercolor, now, in the oil, was taller, thinner and seemed to almost mimic the tree—as if the shrub were trying to *become* a tree, as if the paintings were not only a continuation of the scene but also a continuation in time itself. And there was a feeling of . . . of *emotion* involved. A yearning? A sense of *passion.* Everything in her painting seemed infused with movement and intent. Normally a landscape captures the present mood, but this one seemed to be in a hurry. Everything was in the act of becoming. Nothing was static. Everything was poised for change and already straining toward it, as if the plants—and literally every object she'd painted—had consciousness . . . awareness . . . and desire. *Okay, that's it. I'm becoming obsessed. I don't know why they turned out that way. Probably some sort of therapy for my own neuroses. And speaking of neuroses*—Nikki glanced at the clock—*time to shower and go meet Phil.*

CHAPTER 10

THEY HAD agreed to meet at Kristina's, a restaurant that featured Greek cuisine. Nikki saw Phil's Volvo already parked in the lot. One-upmanship! Phil could convey that Nikki was late, and thereby imply that her feelings for Nikki were deeper and truer than those of Nikki for her, and that *hers* was the greater suffering. At any rate, Phil would have had a chance to choose a table, establish herself in a dominant spot and order a drink. Nikki *had* scored the opening gambit in choosing Kristina's. Phil would have preferred the atmosphere at the Mahle House, but Nikki had wanted a place that would be less intimate, more crowded, more public for this first encounter. Less chance of a scene, and since Nikki knew Phil's passion for Greek food, she felt that Phil would be less likely to throw a *moussaka* in her face than fresh halibut in saffron sauce.

The hostess showed Nikki to Phil's table. Phil had chosen it with care, next to a window, the last table in the row so that she could sit, as in the Old West saloons, with her back to the wall. This would place Nikki with her back to the room so that Phil would be her only point of focus. Nice staging. Of course Phil had always been a nice point of focus—a tall willowy woman with Demi Moore hair and Susan Sarandon eyes. Tonight she looked particularly beautiful in her smart forest green business suit. Nikki, in her blue blazer, felt a bit schoolgirlish.

"I ordered you a martini. I thought we might both need one."

"How've you been, Phil? How was Seattle?"

"Seattle was a seminar. And I guess I'm surviving." Phil lit a cigarette and Nikki saw her hand tremble. (Phil had gone back to smoking?) "And you? Settled in your new place?"

"That right, you haven't seen it yet."

"Oh, I can guess. Minimal amount of cheap furniture and your art stuff all over the living room."

Touché! "And how is Susan?"

"We have a few things to work out."

"You and Susan?"

"You and I."

Nikki took a careful sip of her drink. "What's left to work out? We were a disaster. It had to end."

"It's not that simple. You don't just walk out of a five-year relationship right into another. My analyst thinks I haven't come through the grieving process. I can't help feeling that if you'd only been a little more patient—if you'd only waited. You *knew* the hell I was going through, what with the board evaluations and all the infighting at IDC. You knew I hadn't been sleeping, and you knew how vulnerable I was, and yet you picked that time—the worst possible time—to abandon me."

"Phil—Phillida—dear heart, there was *never* such a thing as a *good* time. I just picked a time, that's all. I thought it was the best of times—because Susan was back. You weren't going to be alone. It wasn't easy for me either. I cried for days. I keened. I howled at the moon."

"I—I haven't been able to do that. Maybe that's what's wrong. It's as though I'm in limbo. I can't seem to move on with my life. Perhaps we should try it again. Maybe we just need to talk things through. Maybe we should see a counselor. Would you be willing to undergo counseling?"

Nikki, who had been afraid that Phil might make a scene, now had the wild urge to overturn the table and run screaming from the restaurant. *How could I put this so it doesn't sound unfeeling?* "Uh, Phil, I don't think that's a good idea. We'd only wind up back in the same place. I know we're both healing. We're just doing it in different ways."

Phil took a handkerchief out of her bag and dabbed delicately at her eyes. "I knew you wouldn't agree." She sat silent, a woman shattered. Nikki could almost feel herself "snapping to grid." The old Nikki, at this point, would be mentally rolling up her sleeves to tackle the job of Making Phil Happy. This had always been the bottom line. Phil would weep. Nikki would leap into the breech to solve whatever the problem was, do whatever needed to be done, kill whoever needed to be killed (herself?) to achieve Phil's Happiness which, like the Holy Grail, always eluded. Now, in her deepest recesses, Nikki realized that something had changed. She was not the old Nikki anymore. She might not be free of Phil entirely, but she had tasted freedom and was not inclined to give it up. Casually she picked up the menu. "The *souvlakia* looks good."

Phil shot her a look that said, "How can you think of food at a time like this?"

Nikki grinned blandly. "Order anything you want. I'm buying!"

Phil frowned, then picked up her menu. "Oh, I don't know. Maybe a Greek salad. I haven't really had my mind on food lately."

"Well, you look smashing. I think you've lost a couple of pounds." The minute the words were out of her mouth, Nikki regretted them. She braced herself for the inevitable "I wish I could say the same of *you*. You know, you could stand to lose a few pounds yourself." Phil had always felt free to make negative remarks about Nikki's weight, Nikki's clothes ("Are you really going to wear *that*?") and Nikki's mental capacities ("Well, if you had any brains at all you'd know that—"). Nikki steeled herself to deflect the cutting remark, but it never came. Instead, in spite of her anguish, Phil seemed absorbed in the bill of fare. Nikki mentally chalked up a point for Greek cuisine. This was going to be all right after all, at least for now. She realized, though, that ending her relationship with Phil—or, more accurately— modifying it so as to make it bearable, wasn't going to be quick or easy. It would take time. There would be recidivism—nifty puzzle word. Somehow she would have to try to be a friend to Phil, see her through the unhappiness that she, herself, may have caused—and at the same time deal with her own feelings and try to keep from being emotionally dragged back. *Like taking out my own appendix.*

...

Back home again, Nikki put on the tea kettle and went out to sit on deck. Nightfall was coming earlier. She could see lights across the lake—headlights of cars traveling the road next to the water, and lights from a farmhouse beyond it. There were also lights on in the units in Eagle Lake Park. Paulette and Fred were at home; so were Bob and Janet. Marj's place was dark, although her car was parked. Maybe she'd gone on foot to visit someone.

"Hey, girl, how'd it go?" The voice startled Nikki. Then she saw it was Marj, sitting on her porch.

"Marj! I didn't think you were home. What are you doing there in the dark?" Marj was barely visible in her screened enclosure. "Come on over. I'm making tea."

It was growing cool, so they chose to have their tea inside. Marj seemed strangely subdued. "Anything wrong?" Nikki asked. "Did you hear from Jonah?"

"Not yet. This time it's my dad. I don't know what I'm going to do about him. That phone call this morning? I'm going to have to make some sort of arrangements."

"He's not living alone, is he? Someone must be looking after him."

"There's woman he's been living with since my mother died. But she wants out. Says he's not her responsibility, and that she can't handle him anymore."

"What about your brother. Where is he?"

"Still living in Ontario. When my parents sold the farm and moved to B.C. he stayed behind. He's married with three small kids, and not in a position to take on dear old dad."

"No relatives closer?"

Marj shook her head. "I'll have to find a place for him. I may even have to go up there for a while. If I do, will you take care of Casimir while I'm gone?"

"Of course."

"Strange the way things turn out. I mostly remember my father as a hard man who yelled at us a lot. My brother and I used to hide when we heard him coming. After we grew up, he didn't get any nicer. That's why Eddie—my brother—stayed East. He wanted to live as far away as possible. I think I would have too, if it hadn't been for my mom. She'd have been left alone with him. All my father ever did was complain and criticize and yell. We were all *so* scared of him. Now all that's left is a skinny little man who doesn't recognize me half the time, just walks around looking blank. Mary—Mary's the woman he lives with—has to watch him so he doesn't just wander away."

"Who is she? Relationship or care giver?"

"It started out as a relationship. My dad was widowed. Mary was sympathetic, and I think she moved in and took over. I didn't get to know her all that well. Obviously she didn't know what she was getting into. I think by time they met he may have already had early signs of Alzheimer's, but maybe she didn't notice. Now she wants nothing more to do with him."

"If he's at that stage, you obviously can't take care of him either.

Alzheimer's is progressive and he'll need professional care. Maybe you can find a place here in town so you can visit him. I know these places usually have a waiting list, but maybe Phil could pull a few strings. As head of IDC, she has connections. I can call her tomorrow."

"Apparently, then, you're still speaking. How did the dinner go?"

"So-so. There was no violence. We remained civil."

"What did she want? Did she want to get back together?"

"I'm not sure. The theme song was "You Picked a Fine Time to Leave Me, Lucille. "She says her shrink tells her she hasn't progressed through the grieving process, and somehow I'm responsible and I should go with her to a counselor."

"Oh, *god!*"

"She made me feel like 'you broke it, you bought it.' I shattered her life so now I'm responsible for her forever."

"Excuse me, but isn't there a *Susan?*"

"Her only true and passionate love, yes. Somehow Phil had nothing to say about her."

"So whatever could've happened? Susan turned out to be a knuckle-dragger who's gained fifty pounds and quit shaving her legs?"

"No, I don't think so. I don't *know.*"

"Or maybe no lost love can ever live up to the fantasy. Now that you've dumped her, will *you* become Phil's one true lost love?"

"Oh, hell, I don't know. Phillida Lowry is like superglue. Even if you break free, you can't get it off your fingers." Nikki got up and stretched. "It's been quite a day. Earthquake last night that nobody else noticed. I spent the afternoon preparing for disaster. My mother would be so proud of me. Then I painted a picture that turned out to be like my *old* picture. And to top off the day, Phil and I revisited our Holy War of a relationship. I think of it as the *jihad.*"

"Come to think of it, mine was a more like the Irani death sentence—a *fatwa.*"

Nikki picked up her teacup. "Here's to our exes, Fatwa and Jihad."

CHAPTER 11

"I REALLY should talk to a physicist about these dreams I've been having," Nikki told Marj who had come over for morning coffee.

"Don't you mean *psychiatrist?*"

"No, I mean physicist. Someone like Stephen Hawking. I keep having dreams about mathematics, and I'm wondering if there might be something *to* them—but I don't know enough about math to be able to judge." Nikki was holding a cube twisted together from pipe cleaners and was attempting to collapse it inward to join two outermost points.

"What, exactly, is it you're trying to do?"

Nikki had had another of her teacher plant dreams but she didn't want to mention that part to Marj. "In my dream I was being shown that if the farthest points of a cube can be collapsed into and *through* each other, the resulting diamond shape would be ten times stronger and ten times more flexible than the original." She tried illustrating with her pipe-cleaner cube, but of course the structure fell apart. "Maybe it's something that would happen on a molecular level. Maybe it's the *atoms or molecules* that must be collapsed and drawn into diamond shapes in order to produce a stronger, more flexible metal, for instance."

"Whoa. You're talking a different language here. I didn't know you were a math major."

Nikki laughed. "Believe me, I'm *not*. Math was never my forte. That's the trouble, I don't know whether this is valid information or a pile of garbage." She pulled the pipe cleaners apart and put them back into her art box. "I've got to get a day's work done. I'll call Phil later and ask if she can suggest anything about your dad. How soon do you have to get him situated?"

"Mary's with him now, and I hope she'll stay on a bit longer if she knows I'm looking for a place. If worse comes to worst, I could even bring him here for a little while. I'll have to talk to Adelaide about it."

Marj left. Nikki regarded her stack of puzzle roughs. She planned to spend the morning in her office, typing clues and printing them up. Later, she'd return to her art board to design more. Nikki rather enjoyed the change of surroundings from drawing table to office and back. It seemed to physically symbolize the difference between the creative work of designing and the grunt work of typing and printing, and for whatever the reason, she always felt that her mind worked more quickly in her spot by the window in the living room.

First, she took time to water her plants. Charlie was looking full and green and lush. "You could be the centerfold in *Organic Gardening*." Marj's shamrocks, despite their spill, were blooming, the plant studded with pretty pink flowers. Outdoors, the herb garden thrived in the warm direct sunlight, each plant a perfect specimen. Oregano was spreading outward, threatening to invade neighboring herbs, and Nikki wondered if she should transplant it into pot of its own. The rabbits had left the plants alone although they did, quite often, come up on deck and leave their sign. It would have been easy for, say, Bruno to stand on his hind legs and nibble the greenery. *Maybe they don't like the strong taste of oregano and thyme.*

Nikki could see Bruno in his favorite wallow under the picnic table. She went inside and came out carrying a raw carrot. She sat down on the deck steps and held it out. A couple of other bunnies regarded her with a mixture of curiosity and suspicion. "Hey, Bruno, come and get it." Bruno stared blankly. Nikki wiggled the carrot. "Come on, Bruno. You know what this is, don't you?" She waited and watched as the animal seemed to make a mental connection between Nikki's hand and food. Slowly he began hopping in her direction. "That's right, Bruno. Come on, boy. Can I get you to eat out of my hand?" The rabbit came close, drew back, advanced a little, wiggled its nose, stretched its neck and delicately began to chew the end of the carrot. Charmed, Nikki held tightly to the other end while Bruno alternately chewed and tugged. "Don't pull so hard, Bruno. If you make me drop it, you'll only lose it to the cheering section." Indeed, several rabbits had ringed the area, ready to pounce. Nikki was again struck by the beauty of the animals. All had glossy coats and clear eyes. They all seemed to be adults. In her time at Eagle Lake Park, she didn't remember seeing any young, at least not babies. *They'd have to be breeding—well, like rabbits. I guess Mama Cottontails keep their little ones stashed away, safe from eagles.*

...

Nikki's day went well. She finished printing her puzzles by noon, then took an hour to do her Tai Chi, shower and change. *I know I'm getting back to normal when I start exercising again.* From one o'clock on, she sat at her drawing table, designing—again with lightning speed—more puzzles, and at four o'clock she called Phil.

Phil did what Phil did best: took charge. "Leave it to me, I'll look into it. I'll get back to you—but just who *is* this Marj person?" When Nikki explained it was her divorced (from a man) neighbor, Phil seemed satisfied, even a little pleased that Nikki would be turning to her for help and advice.

Marj arrived at five. Nikki had put together a salad made of George's leftover barbecued chicken, and set the deck table so they could have their meal outdoors. She poured them each a glass of lightly chilled Riesling. "I think you'll find this a dainty little wine," Nikki offered, with a tongue-in-cheek smile.

Marj took a sip and a judicious tone: "Umm. A bit self-effacing, almost to the point of shyness, but naively aristocratic."

"The product of a fine finishing school, but still an ingénue." Nikki grinned, then turned serious, "Phil says she'll call back when she's checked out what's available. It may take a few days."

"Thanks, Nikki. You've no idea how much of a relief that is. I really didn't know what to do, how to go about finding a place. You hear such horror stories about homes for the aged."

"Phil's in the system. I think we can trust her judgment. She and I may not get along, but she's smart and I trust her integrity. She knows all the rules, laws, bureaucratic pitfalls and how to suck up to the right people."

"But why should she go out of her way to help me? She doesn't even know me?"

"Good question. Three-part answer: One, Phil is a champion of the underdog. A fighter for human rights. Two, right now she's relieved that you're a heterosexual. If you were a lesbian, who knows? Three—and please do not let this make you feel guilty—it's a way of controlling *me*. By helping a friend of mine, she stays in my life to fulfill whatever her keeping-the-door-open agenda may be. We'll take advantage of it."

"I feel I should be sending her roses and a bottle of wine."

"You'll get your chance, I'm afraid. Phil keeps track of her favors and calls them in like bank loans. And what have you been up to all day?"

"I went to the library."

"Again? Why don't you just get a job there?"

"That's not a bad idea."

"What with all the time you spend surfing the stacks, it would be perfect."

"I don't have the training."

"Training you can get. Start out as an assistant, maybe, and go to night school. Or take some college courses at Malaspina."

"I've thought about it. I think I'd like it. Of course I can't do anything now until I see what happens with my dad. That's what I've been doing, by the way, reading up on Alzheimer's. I wish we had Internet, it would save a lot of running around."

"Do you have a computer?"

"No, but I'd get one. I need to learn everything I can about my dad's condition."

"Ah. Yes, of course. Must be hell."

"Yes. For the patient *and* for the family. It runs in families, you know. There's a chance I could end up that way."

"*Don't even think it*. That's *not* going to happen. For that matter, are you sure your dad even has it? Phil tells me that many symptoms in the aged are often misdiagnosed as Alzheimer's. Sometimes it's a reaction to medication. Sometimes it's just the shrinkage of the brain in old age. Your dad may not even *have* it."

"Yes, I came across that too in my reading. My dad's not all that old, but I really don't know."

"When it comes to the brain and the human mind, I don't think anyone does."

"That reminds me. You remember yesterday I started to tell you about something—something that might explain Raymond Cantwell."

"Right!"

"You're a puzzle person, have you ever heard the term, synesthesia?"

"Uh, maybe—but right off I couldn't tell you what it means."

"Apparently it's a condition in which the senses all blend together. Instead of just hearing a bell ring, a synesthete may also 'see' the sound as a color or shape. There are several kinds. *Photism* is seeing lights where no light normally is seen. *Phonism* is hearing sounds. You remember how Raymond talked about Boston Charlie 'singing.' He was hearing when he should've just been seeing. *Chromesthesia* is the hearing or feeling of colors. Raymond kept talking about colors being slippery or rough as if he could feel them. In a synesthete, all the senses run together. Maybe that's the case with Raymond."

"Raymond is also childlike."

"Yes, in his case that's true. Many synesthetes have high IQ's, but Raymond isn't one of them. One thing though, I thought was interesting. A high percentage of synesthetes are also psychic."

Nikki rolled her eyes. "I suppose that could be useful if we ever have to hold a séance. Speaking of that, are you planning to go to Adelaide's little do again on Sunday?"

"I have to. I may be hosting my father for awhile, and I'll have to stay on her good side."

"I'm sure she won't object to your looking after your dad."

"No, she won't. It'll appeal to her soap opera sense of drama. In fact, I already spoke with her and she was very supportive. Even offered to help me keep an eye on him. So, of course I'll be attending the Sunday coffee."

"Then so will I. Solidarity forever."

CHAPTER 12

NIKKI WOKE with a headache and realized that her monthly period had started. *And I just changed the sheets yesterday.* She got up, showered and dressed, remade the bed, put coffee on. She had slept fitfully—probably had a few menstrual cramps during the night. She had no memory of dreams, but did have the sense that she had been listening to something screaming—a bird? an animal? It occurred to her that outside her metal shell of a house, where Mother Nature's world was populated by predators and prey, sudden death must happen every night of the week.

Nikki padded to the window to look at the view—usually her first act after the routine of personal hygiene. There were clouds rising over the lake, dark ones, sullen and threatening, looking like an extra range of mountains. A flock of ravens had flown in and landed on the cropped grass, the picnic table, even on Nikki's porch railing. There were at least a couple dozen of them, and their cries must have been the screaming Nikki had heard; even now three were squabbling over bread crusts that someone had thrown to the rabbits who, in turn, were keeping a discreet distance from the birds.

Nikki looked at her plants and realized they needed water. The oxalis had folded up its leaves and its little stems were curving downward in a wilt. Boston Charlie felt light when she picked up the container. "Sorry, guys. Mama's been neglectful." *Sun probably got too hot yesterday. I'm going to have to water more often. Get your act together, Nikki. No wonder plants die in your hands!* She filled the dish detergent squeeze bottle that she had cleaned out for the purpose, added a few grains of Phostrogen—the stuff in the blue box that Bert had told her his mum always swore by—gave the bottle a shake and watered both oxalis and Charlie. She refilled the bottle and went out to water the herbs. It was then that she saw the dead rabbit.

Nikki assumed it *was* a dead rabbit. At first it was hard to tell. The poor thing had been badly mangled and left to lie on the ground a few inches from the foot of the deck steps. At least it wasn't Bruno; but it had been a large rabbit, a brown one. Nikki wondered what had killed it. An eagle? Wouldn't an eagle have carried it away and eaten it? Maybe not. *Something* had clearly been making a meal of it. A cat? The orange tom? Would a cat attack so large an animal? Could also have been a stray dog. Nikki wondered what other predators might lurk on the island. At any rate, she decided to quietly dispose of the body. If she raised a cry, Adelaide Moon would have George patrolling the grounds with his gun, shooting any stray cat or dog, innocent or guilty.

Nikki brought out a plastic bag and gingerly picked up the dead animal by the ears and dropped it inside. Now what? *I'll have to take it to the dump.* So as not to be seen carrying it through the compound, Nikki put the bag in her truck.

She drove to the edge of the woods and parked next to the dirt road that led to the dump area. There she picked up the bag and continued on foot, feeling upset, and wondering whether the cries she thought she'd heard had been those of the rabbit. *I hate it when stuff like this happens.*

The dump was deserted, and looked oddly macabre. Nikki realized that it had been recently burned over—a mass of charred debris, not burned to ashes but reduced to a blackened heap, presumably to keep down the smell and the flies. Nikki tossed the bag on the pile and left, relieved that no one had seen her.

Back home, she found herself unable to concentrate on work. The incident continued to nag her. *Rabbits die all the time. Rabbits are a dime a dozen—specially at Eagle Lake. Probably a dog. Might even have been Adelaide's dog if he managed to get out. Or it could've been a wild animal. Aren't there supposed to be wolves and cougars on the island?* She visualized gleaming cougar eyes peering at her from the darkness of the woods whenever she walked to the mailbox. Cougars were known to stalk people. But, again, wouldn't a cougar have carried away the rabbit? Nevertheless, the world of cute bunnies in the park had taken on a sinister quality, matched by the threatening sky—both skies—the sky outdoors and the one in Nikki's paintings. She studied the watercolor and the oil, and, in the gloom of the overcast morning, Nikki's painted sky looked even more suffocating in both pictures.

I should slap a coat of white on both of them and be done with it. Nikki might have acted on the impulse if Marj hadn't appeared at her door. Marj was carrying Casimir and a plastic bag and was obviously distraught. "I just got a call. I have to go pick up my father. May I leave Casimir with you? I should be back in two or three hours, but in case I'm not, it's better he's here. I brought cat food but you'll need his litter box. Here's my key."

"Of course, but I could've gone over and fed—"

"I don't know what I'm going to find. Mary called. She says she won't stay another day. I may have to spend the night. I just don't know—and anyway, it'll be better if Casimir isn't there if my dad comes home with me. He's always hated cats. *Please.* I don't know what else to do." Marj put the plastic bag on the table. "I brought lots of food just in case—he gets a tin of Kitty Gourmet in the morning along with some of the dry Crunchy Bits. And here are his favorite bowls. He gets a bowl of water too—make sure it's lukewarm." Marj pulled out a package of foil envelopes. "And this is for supper. I give him one envelope of Moist & Tasty—he particularly likes the tuna, and a fresh bowl of tepid water."

"Don't worry about Casimir. We'll get along just fine. But don't you want me—or somebody—to go with you? Can you handle this by yourself?"

"I don't know. Maybe I can get Mary to help. Maybe I won't need any help. I'll call you. And if I'm not back, will you tell Adelaide what's happening?"

"Yes, yes, of course I will. And I'll go get Casimir's litter box and whatever. You just go on. And drive safely. It'll be okay."

"You're an angel." Marj gently lowered Casimir onto the carpet. The magnificent animal reacted like a royal personage inspecting slums. He stood still for a moment, then examined the soiled carpet with a look of disbelief, sniffed it, and delicately picked at it with one claw. As if satisfied that its shoddiness did not merit his attention, he raised a majestic tail into a white question mark and began, slowly, to examine his surroundings, casting Marj a flashing glance that seemed to say, "You want *me* to stay *here?*"

"Thank you, Nikki, thank you, thank you! Oh, you may want to put Charlie on the hook and move the shamrocks into another room." Marj fled.

Nikki, staunch friend, stood in mild shock as she realized that she now had a cat—not just for a couple of hours but maybe for the duration. "Looks like it's you and me, Casimir. I'm not crazy about the arrangement either, but let's try to make the best of it." Casimir who had been pacing around Nikki's living room, now eased himself into the space under the futon couch.

Nikki glanced at the clock. If she hurried, she might be able to catch Phil at IDC before she went off on one of her power lunches. Luck was with her.

"I've made a few calls and it looks good, but I'll have to meet with your friend and find out just what her father's financial situation is. These things usually take time, but I think I can call in a couple of favors. Can she keep the old man with her for a few days? This is Friday and nothing ever happens on a weekend."

"Maybe. I don't know. I mean Marj doesn't know what he'll be like. It didn't sound good. She may not be able to handle him. Would there be such a thing as a temporary placement?"

"If the old guy turns out to be uncontrollable, we can have him removed to a temporary facility. I have a place in mind I think your friend will be happy with. Most retirement homes don't take people with Alzheimer's, and those that do usually keep them drugged and tied down. I know, I know. It's barbaric, but it's the real world. This is your friend's father, after all. Meanwhile, if he becomes unmanageable, call me."

Nikki could feel herself "snapping to grid." The scenario was all too familiar—Phil, powerful and decisive, taking charge. Nikki realized, with a feeling of discomfort, how much she *had* relied on Phil's judgment and direction, and how readily she had deferred to it whenever there was anything difficult or unpleasant to be faced. She had resented Phil's being in charge, but it had also been a safety net, hadn't it? Nikki had never needed to make any *big* decisions or face any *big* problems—financial or otherwise. She'd been like the protected wife of a corporate executive, indulged, patronized, pigeonholed and bullied—but well insulated from the rough real world.

Well, she would have to explore those insights later. Right now she had to go round up Casimir's paraphernalia. She looked for the cat, found him still under the couch. Her gaze made contact with Casimir's clear yellow eyes. The cat blinked slowly. "Stay where you are, Casimir. I'll be right back."

To her surprise, life with Casimir promised to be uneventful, possibly pleasant. Nikki was even getting work done. The house seemed cozy with the big cat sleeping on the floor and rain softly tattooing on the metal roof. Nikki was beginning to think it might be fun to have a cat of her own. She'd set up Casimir's litter box in a discreet corner behind the couch, not so much because it was unsightly, but to give the cat, who bore the name of a Polish king, the privacy she instinctively knew he would prefer. She had set out a bowl of clean water, and would, come evening, open Casimir a packet of the expensive cat food of his choice. Later, perhaps, they might even indulge in a game of "catch the kitty treat"—as she had seen Marj do, toss a tiny fish-flavored bit for Casimir to catch in mid-air and devour. In a flush of optimism, Nikki had even brought Casimir's brush and comb—just in case their relationship advanced to the point where Nikki could lay a hand on him. Right now it was still a standoff. While Nikki worked at her drawing table, the cat seemed to sleep soundly, but whenever she walked about the room, Casimir's gaze followed her. So far, he had made no move toward the houseplants, nor had Nikki changed their location. Nikki knew enough about animals not to force herself upon the cat. Rather, she pretended to ignore him. "I'll let *you* be the one to make the first move."

It was at about five-thirty, after she had fed Casimir—or rather after Casimir had refused to eat the food she set out—that Nikki heard a car pull into Marj's parking space. *Thank God!* Nikki went to the window but couldn't see anything as Marj's parking space was on the other side of her mobile home. Soon, however, she saw Marj, carrying a suitcase, walk around to the door of her porch. Nikki realized that she still had Marj's key, but then she saw Marj put down the bag and fumble in her purse for a key to the screen door. An elderly man was with her, and he certainly did not look threatening. Short and thin with sunken cheeks and a few white wisps of hair—more tanned than Nikki had expected—he was dressed in slacks and a knit shirt, and looked old and frail, as if he could have been Marj's grandfather rather than her dad. The man stood looking around as if bewildered, mouth slightly open, his hands clasping and unclasping. Marj picked up the bag, and gently steered the old man inside. *Daddy's home.*

Nikki would have liked to go over and offer help—and return the key to Marj's front door—but was fearful. *What do I know about Alzheimer's anyway? I know they don't remember things, and I might just confuse the old guy. I've heard people with Alzheimer's can be abusive and even violent. I sure wouldn't want to set him off.*

"Meanwhile, Casimir, why don't you eat some of that *nice* cat food? You know that there are cats in Ethiopia subsisting on a diet of sand and dust?" Casimir didn't even glance at it. Instead, the big white feline paraded himself across the living room to the window, stopped in front of the Boston fern and took a swipe with his paw at one of the hanging fronds. The frond swung back and forth, then came to rest. Diverted by this new game, Casimir batted it again. As the frond swung by, Casimir jumped up to catch it with his front paws, grabbed the greenery in his teeth, pulled off bits of leaf, then spat them onto the rug. Doing a little scuttling dance with his hind legs, Casimir struck out again and sent a frond flying. But this time it snapped back sharply and whacked him across the face. Casimir, startled, leapt backwards, and landed awkwardly on his haunches. Nikki couldn't help laughing. "You should've been here the other night, Casimir. You'd have *really* seen something."

But Casimir had had enough. Trying to regain his dignity, he got to his feet, backed away from the plant, then crawled under the couch.

It was evening. Darkness had come even earlier because of the rain, and now Nikki heard thunder. Thunderstorms were rare on the island, usually no more than a distant rumble. This time, however, the thunder was growing louder and seemed to be almost overhead. A sharp flash of lightning followed by a tumbling roll sent Nikki into her office to unplug her computer. She wondered how Marj was getting along but had heard that it was dangerous to use the phone during a storm. Nikki looked out her window and saw a blinding fork of lightning slice across the lake. The power blinked twice, then went off. Nikki was left in the dark to watch the pyrotechnics. Each flash was reflected in the lake, distorted by rough black water; rain was falling heavily, a deafening drumming on the roof.

As Nikki, sitting at her art table, watched the storm at full force, she realized that she was seeing something else too, something she could not at first quite understand or believe, but there it was, and she *was* seeing it. Astounded, Nikki realized that she was seeing *rabbits*—the rabbits of Eagle Lake Park. They had not sought shelter from the storm, but were out in the open. Illuminated by flashes of lightning, they seemed to be moving, dancing? No, fighting! Like boxing kangaroos. They were leaping at each other in a wild and frenzied ballet. The phrase "mad as a March hare," came to Nikki's mind. What on earth could they be doing? Was she really seeing what she saw? A low growl of thunder prowled the sky, then a sharp whipcrack of lightning—and Nikki nearly fell off her art stool as something thudded into her lap. Casimir! The cat clung, digging nails into her thighs. Gently, painfully, Nikki disengaged claws from flesh, then wrapped protective arms around the big soft beast and hugged him tight. "Any port in a storm, eh, Casimir?"

By 9:30 the storm had subsided to a steady rain. The phone rang. It was Marj. "How are you getting along? Is Casimir driving you up the wall?"

"Not at all. He's being a perfect gentleman. He didn't want to eat at first, but I think the storm left him a little shaken. Now he's polished off most of his Moist & Tasty tuna to calm his nerves."

"Looks like our power will be out for awhile."

"Yes, if it hadn't been for my quake preparation I'd be sitting here in the dark." Nikki had lit her two small battery lamps. "Do you have lights?"

"Yes, I'm okay with oil lamps."

"I saw you arrive with your dad but I was afraid to come over. I thought I might upset him."

"Just as well. I don't know yet, myself, how to take care of him. He's asleep now in the bedroom. I'll use the couch. I got him to eat a little soup before the power went out, but we sure didn't need this weather his first day here."

"How did he react? Did the storm frighten him?"

"Oddly enough, he didn't seem to mind it. He was watching TV when the power went off. When I lit the lamps, I saw him still just sitting there, staring at the blank screen. The only time he got upset was when I unpacked his things. I'd brought some stuff from home—photographs, his bed table clock—familiar things that would make him feel more at home. But they only seemed to get him agitated so I put them all away. I think he's confused, disoriented. Like a sleepwalker."

"Does he know who you are?"

"I'm not sure. He said my name several times, but I couldn't tell if he really remembers me."

"I talked to Phil. She says she'll have to meet with you about the financial arrangements, but she said there's a place she thinks would be right for your dad. But it's the weekend, and she asked if you'd be able to take care of him for a couple of days."

"I *guess* so. I mean, he hasn't been any real trouble so far. He sat quietly in the car for over an hour, just watching the scenery. Mary said he tries to slip out of the house and wander off, but I keep the doors locked. She says he goes into rages and breaks things, but so far he's been more like a zombie."

"Well, Phil says if he turns uncontrollable, she can have him removed to a temporary place."

"Let's just wait and see. Did you get a chance to talk to Adelaide?"

Oh shit. "I'm sorry, Marj. I forgot all about calling her."

"Just as well. I'll call her in the morning."

After Nikki hung up she realized she hadn't mentioned the rabbits. She wondered if Marj had seen them. Nikki decided to go to bed early. She was having cramps and felt she could use a good night's sleep. She left Casimir in the living room and, by light of her portable lamp, brushed her teeth and her hair, then crawled into bed and listened to the sound of rain. As she was about to drift off to sleep, she felt a movement, then soft sighing puffs of cat paws punching into goose down, then a pressure as a feline body settled next to hers. Nikki reached out her hand and felt soft fur. She patted whatever part of the cat her hand touched. "Good night, Casimir."

CHAPTER 13

It HAD not been a restful night. Nikki awoke with a headache and menstrual cramps. A hot shower would have been soothing, but the water was barely lukewarm. At least there *was* water, thanks to the emergency generator that kept the pump running—but Nikki, in throes of Day Two of her monthly period, was in no mood to count blessings. The power was still off so her hair dryer was useless, although she could still use her electric toothbrush. Nikki dried herself off, pulled on jeans and a sweater, and ran a comb through her damp hair. At least she had a propane stove; she would be able to make coffee. Tea would not do this morning; her system needed caffeine.

Casimir was nowhere in sight. *That's right, hide you little varmint if you know what's good for you.* The cat had not slept quietly. At some time during the night, Nikki had heard his feet hit the floor as he jumped off the bed. She had been just about to fall asleep again when she heard the sound of paws galloping down the hallway—repeatedly— *gobbity gobbity gobbity scr-r-rape*, then back again, *gobbity gobbity gobbity sli-i-ide bump.* Just when Nikki had gotten to the point of being able to ignore it, the noise changed to that of a cat on the prowl—the thud of cat feet jumping on—and off—whatever. Nikki wondered if she had left her office door open. She wondered if Casimir was shredding her houseplants. She knew the power was still off because the face of her digital clock was dark. She was having menstrual cramps and did not want to get out of her warm bed to see what the crazy cat was up to. Finally she dozed off, slept fitfully, her dreams chaotic.

The hall carpet runner was pushed into pleats—evidence of Casimir's midnight ride. Nikki kicked it back into place. Otherwise, the house looked normal. Her office door *was* closed, the plants were unsavaged, and Casimir lay curled up under the couch, seemingly asleep. *Oh no you don't!* Nikki opened a can of Kitty Gourmet trout treats with her manual can opener, and set out Casimir's breakfast. "Come and get it, hairball. Do your sleeping at night." She warmed a little water in a pan on the stove, poured the cat a bowlful, then removed and disposed of the solidified lump in the litter box, thinking, as she followed her new morning ritual, that having a cat had its down side.

Nikki put water on to boil. Mr. Coffeemaker was out of commission; she would have to do with instant. While waiting, she watered the oxalis and noticed that Charlie had a couple of fronds that seemed to be turning brown. The plant was "human" after all! Up until now Charlie had presented himself as such a flawless example of perfection that he could have been made of plastic. Nikki picked up the container. *Could use water.* She carried the fern outside and set it on the deck railing where she was able to snip off the dead fronds (and the one Casimir had shredded) without having the bits fall on the carpet. She gave the plant a good drenching and left it to drain. Inside, the kettle was beginning to sing. Nikki went in, made a cup of coffee and took it back out on deck.

The sky was cloudy and the water leaden, but otherwise Eagle Lake Park looked calm enough. Rabbits were hopping about as usual, nibbling grass or crusts of bread, wallowing in their shallow holes, with no hint of their night of wilding. Everything was quiet at Marj's, but Nikki could hear voices in the park. They seemed to be coming from the Crushills. She leaned over her deck rail and saw Paulette, Fred, and Adelaide Moon in heated conversation. Nikki strained to hear, but couldn't make out what Paulette was saying. Adelaide, replying, could be heard very clearly: "It wasn't Prince. Prince never gets out. It must've been some stray dog."

Intrigued, Nikki edged down the steps and strolled toward the commotion. She could hear Paulette now: "Well, something killed those rabbits. There were at least a dozen of them dead this morning all over the park. Fred found them when he went for his walk. He gathered them up so they wouldn't draw flies. They're all in a plastic bag if you want to see them."

More dead rabbits?

"I'll have Raymond come get them and take them to the dump. Must be some vicious dog runnin' loose. I'll get George to track it down." Adelaide turned and spotted Nikki. "Oh, Nikki. You haven't seen a stray dog around, have you? Fred found a bunch of dead rabbits this morning."

"No, Mrs. Moon." Nikki didn't mention the dead rabbit that she, herself, had found, nor the odd behavior of the rabbits in the rainstorm.

"I'll ask around. Maybe somebody else saw something." Adelaide started off in the direction of Marj's.

"Uh, Mrs. Moon. In case Marj hasn't had a chance to call you, she wanted you to know that she had to bring her father home yesterday. He's here now. He may still be asleep."

Adelaide glanced at her watch, then back at Nikki. "Oh, really? It's the first I've heard of it. How is he?"

"I didn't meet him, Mrs. Moon. I only saw him from a distance. Marj says he's a little disoriented, but otherwise he's okay. Marj is trying to get a permanent place for him. A friend of mine is helping her."

"Is that so? Well, isn't it *nice* that Marj has a helpful friend at a time like this." Something in Adelaide's tone conveyed just the opposite—the suggestion that Marj would have done very well without interference from a Johnny-come-lately neighbor who now, it seemed, knew more about what was going on in Eagle Lake Park than Adelaide, herself, did.

"I'm sure Marj appreciates *all* her friends here, Mrs. Moon. She's told me how helpful *you* were when she first moved in. She mentioned that you've been like a mother to her." *Lay it on thick, this broad will lap it up. Marj needs to stay on her good side—if she has one.*

"Marj is a sweet girl. You're both nice girls. And I've told you, call me Adelaide. And tell Marj that I'll drop by later to meet her father and see if there's anything I can do to help. And be sure to keep an eye out for any strange animals in the park."

...

"Is she gone?" Marj came out of her house. "I heard Adelaide out here but just couldn't face her first thing this morning. God, I scarcely slept at all."

"What kept you up, your dad?"

"No—yes. In a way. It's what being a mother must be like when you have a new baby. You keep listening for every sound. My dad's a restless sleeper. He snores. He mumbles in his sleep. He calls out for my mother. He got up a couple of times to go to the bathroom. Of course the power was out so I had to use a flashlight to take him to the can. I wish I had more experience with this sort of thing. How's Casimir?"

"Resting comfortably, I'd guess, after a night of fritzing out. I think he ran the Iditarod."

"Oh, I'm *sorry*. Must be because he's in a strange place. Did he break anything? Is he eating?"

"No, he didn't and yes, he is. The cat's fine. Don't worry about him. Where's your dad now?"

"Watching Saturday morning cartoons."

"You mean the power's back on?"

"As of a few minutes ago."

"Adelaide said she'd come by to meet him. I told her you were keeping him here until you find a permanent place."

"Did she seem okay with that?"

"Fine. Just fine. She offered to help if you need it."

...

What with the power back on, Nikki dumped the cup of instant coffee she had left on the deck rail and put on a pot of *real* coffee, taking time to grind the beans, then blow-dried her still-damp hair. She noticed that the rugs had a light frosting of white cat fur, and took out the vacuum cleaner. Yes, being a pet owner had certain drawbacks. Casimir was nowhere in sight, but when Nikki turned on the machine, he bolted from under the couch and streaked down the hall. Nikki laughed as she remembered how, as a child, their family dog had always been terrified of the vacuum cleaner, and she'd never seen an animal who could bear the sound of one. *If I ever had to trek through a jungle, I wouldn't need a rifle—just a Dustbuster.*

"The spirit to do comes with doing." It had been one of Nikki's mother's favorite sayings, usually in response to Nikki's moaning about having to clean her room. Nikki had thought of having it printed on a T-shirt and giving it to her mother for Mother's Day. It was right up there with "acquire a taste," a phrase Nikki had grown up thinking was all one word. "When the queen invites you to dinner and serves liver, are you going to make a fool of yourself by saying you don't *like* it?" Grudgingly, Nikki had to admit that her mothers culinary adventures had given her an eclectic palate that served as a basis for her own cooking skills, and that yes, once you start cleaning house, the work builds an impetus of its own. Vacuuming done, Nikki went on to scour the bathroom, scrub the kitchen counter, sinks, stove top; she even cleaned the refrigerator. Housecleaning had been her usual Saturday chore when she and Phil were together. Phil was rarely there. Phil usually had some seminar or project that kept her busy all day. Nikki would have the house clean and dinner ready when Phil arrived, and the only time Phil ever made any comment was the day Nikki moved the couch. "You've changed things around in my house!" *Well, it's her house now—and I wonder who gets the privilege of keeping it clean. One thing about my place now, it's small. Doesn't take long to pull it together.*

Her own house in order, Nikki went out to retrieve Boston Charlie. The sun was trying to come out and the sky was showing patches of blue. A light breeze riffled the fronds of the fern. *Yes, Charlie, you're one gorgeous hunk of greenitude.*

But something else seemed to be going on. In the distance, Nikki saw Raymond Cantwell talking to Paulette. He had a large lawn & leaf bag at his feet. *Full of dead rabbits, no doubt,* Nikki thought with a shudder of distaste. She turned away to see that someone was on Marj's deck. Through the screen Nikki saw that it was her father who was sitting in a chair and watching rabbits—live ones. The old man was smiling with delight, and Nikki saw him get up and try to open the screen door. It was locked. Einar Kuusisto gave the handle a twist, then another, but couldn't get it open. Finally he gave up and sat back down again. *Marj must have locked the door to keep him from wandering away. I wonder where Marj is.*

As if in reply, Nikki saw Adelaide Moon approaching Marj's deck. "Yoo-hoo, Marj. Are you there?" Adelaide shaded her eyes with her hand and looked through the screen. "Oh, you must be Marj's father. How *are* you? I'm Adelaide." She tried the door but found it locked.

"Marj, are you in there?"

"Be right there, Adelaide." Marj came out. "Sorry. I just got out of the shower and had to get my clothes on." She unlocked the door and let Adelaide in. "Adelaide, this is my dad, Einar." Then, taking him by the hand and talking a little more loudly and distinctly, "Dad, this is Adelaide Moon. She runs this park. She's come to visit you. Her name is Adelaide."

Einar got to his feet. "Do I know you?"

"No, Dad. You've never met Adelaide before." Einar nodded absently, sat back down and turned his attention back to the rabbits. "He's still trying to get used to his new surroundings."

"Oh, I know, Marj. And you can't really leave him alone, can you? Like when you have to go shopping. If you like, I could come stay with him."

"Thanks, Adelaide. I may have to take you up on that later."

They'd been talking over him, and Einar had retreated into his own world. Now Adelaide addressed him directly. "It's been nice meeting you, Einar." Then, to Marj, "I guess we'll be seeing you tomorrow night."

"At the coffee? Oh, I don't think I'll be able to make it what with Dad here."

"Bring him along."

"Are you serious?"

"Sure, bring him along. He'll be fine, won't you Einar? He can meet the people in the park, and they can meet him. That way everyone will know who he is, and we can all sort of look out for him. I'll get Raymond to keep an eye on him in case he needs to use the little boys' room or anything. Be a break for you to get out."

"Well, maybe. . . ."

"Sure, hey there's Raymond now. Yoo-hoo, Raymond. C'mere. Somebody here I want you to meet."

Nikki had been unashamedly eavesdropping. She saw Raymond

Cantwell approach, then put down the bag he was carrying. Adelaide opened the screen door and went out, then opened the bag and looked inside. "Oh, my god. Just look at that!"

Marj followed. "What is it?"

"Oh, you didn't hear. Something killed a bunch of rabbits last night. Fred found them this morning. We think it might've been a stray dog."

Marj looked shocked. Einar, who had been left behind, now found the screen door open and slipped out. He stood a moment, blinking in the sunlight, then, unnoticed, strolled toward the edge of the drop-off. Raymond spotted him, ran after him, took him by the arm and steered him back. "Not good to go near the edge. Might fall off."

"That's right, Raymond," Marj said. "Thank you. This is my father. His name is Einar. Dad, this is Raymond."

"Do I know you?"

"You know me. Knock knock. I'm Raymond. *Raymond.*"

"Raymond? Raymond . . . Raymond."

"And you're Einar, Einar, Einar. You want to see some dead rabbits?"

"Oh, don't show him *that*, Raymond." Adelaide said.

"Okay. You want to go to the dump, Einar?"

"Oh, I don't think—" Marj began.

"We can take the rabbits to the dump and watch them sing. Dead rabbits sing white. Death is black but dead is white. White like snow."

"Rabbits?" Einar said. "Can we catch rabbits?"

"I got lots of dead rabbits."

"I don't want dead rabbits. I want live rabbits. Can we feed the live rabbits?"

"Sure. Live rabbits sing—" Raymond stopped and listened. His forehead puckered. He stood looking at rabbits in the park, his face puzzled. "Live rabbits sing yellow and smooth. Live rabbits *always* sing yellow and smooth—but now it's not the same. The rabbits sing . . . they sing pink . . . pink is dangerous. Pink feels sticky. Something's wrong with the rabbits." Raymond, agitated, looked around, spotted Nikki on her deck and moved toward her.

Nikki, embarrassed at being caught listening, started to back away but it was too late. Raymond was right in front of her and she was aware that all eyes were now upon her. Raymond raised his hand and pointed. "There. Something's wrong. It sings home. But now it's rough and dangerous and it sings *red*."

Nikki had no idea what Raymond was talking about, but she realized that he was not pointing at her after all. He was pointing at Boston Charlie.

CHAPTER 14

"I FELT so stupid," Nikki told Marj later. "Of course I shouldn't have been standing there, rubbering."

"Rubbering! I haven't heard that since I left the farm. They used to call it that when you listened on the party line."

"Yeah, short for rubbernecking, I guess. My country aunt used to say that, along with that thing about little pitchers having big ears. 'Better not say any more. I think Annikki is rubbering.' As you see, I have a great and glorious history."

"I don't know what it is with Raymond and your plant. I think I'm right, though, about his being a synesthete. It sounds like nonsense, but when he says something 'sings' and when he talks about colors, he's probably describing what he sees and hears. And if he *is* psychic, he could be picking up on a lot of stuff we're not aware of."

"You believe in that sort of thing?"

"You don't grow up with a Lapp grandmother with second sight without becoming a believer. Mummo was always predicting things and having conversations with the dead. She had a bunch of weird dream symbols that were like a hotline to the future. She'd say, 'I dreamt that Mrs. So-and-so was dancing barefoot, her toes spread wide apart. I'll bet she's pregnant.' And, sure enough, we'd find out that she *was.* Or Mummo would say, 'I dreamed of all my dead friends last night. Just watch, we're going to have a rainstorm.' Even if it was a cloudless day, we all knew enough to go close the upstairs windows!"

"And how many of her strange powers did *you* inherit?"

Nikki had asked the question lightly and was surprised to see it seemed to make Marj uncomfortable. "Uh, well, none that I want—although Mummo was a formidable woman and I learned a lot from her."

"Lucky you! I only have one grandmother living and she's in Florida. I never see her. Maybe yours could have told us what happened to the rabbits. I didn't tell Adelaide, but I found a dead rabbit myself yesterday. I took it to the dump. And last night, during the storm, I swear those animals were acting crazy. They were leaping around, jumping at each other. I meant to ask if you'd seen them too."

"No, I missed that. But Raymond did keep saying there's something wrong with the rabbits, although they look perfectly normal now."

"I wonder what Adelaide thought of it all. She didn't have much to say."

"Adelaide treats Raymond like a pet poodle. Fetch, boy, fetch! She doesn't pay any attention to what he says. But Raymond did seem to hit it off with my father. Dad's asked me a couple of times where Raymond is—and that's unusual because he forgets who *I* am."

"How does anyone cope with something like Alzheimer's?"

"When there's no choice, you just do—but it really makes you live in the present. I mean, watching my father, he's so different now. Sometimes it's as if he's discovering the world for the first time. This morning I found him just staring at my African violet—as if he'd never seen one before. And he loves to watch the rabbits."

"Then he's not having mood swings?"

"Not so far. At least, nothing I haven't been able to handle. I told you what happened when I unpacked his stuff—and that I had to put it away. It's almost like if he doesn't have to *try* to remember, he's okay. It's when he realizes that he *can't* remember, that's when he gets upset. He used to be hard and mean. Didn't care about anything or anyone. My *old* dad would've said, 'You've seen one rabbit, you've seen them all.' Now he wants to go out and catch them! He's like a kid."

"Hey, I have an idea. Maybe he'd like to feed them. I bought a bunch of carrots for Bruno—he's that big white bunny with the black spot. I got him to eat out of my hand the other day. I'll give you some carrots and your dad can try it."

"I think he'd like that. Of course I can't let him out by himself. He might just take off and end up in Moose Jaw." Marj glanced toward her deck where her father appeared to be napping in his chair. "I'd better go get his dinner started. What with you looking after Casimir, and me riding herd on my dad, I miss our meals together."

"Maybe your father would enjoy having Casimir around," Nikki said, a bit too casually. "I mean, he's no trouble to me, of course, but since your dad seems to have taken a liking to small animals. . . ."

"Nice try. But it's not my dad I'm worried about, it's what Casimir might do to *him* if he tries to pat him. I know I'm pushing the envelope of our friendship, but I want to leave him with you a little longer. Has he destroyed anything? I see Charlie looks okay."

"Casimir has a new respect for plants. Casimir is doing fine."

"Are you giving him lukewarm water?"

"Yes, my queen, I have obeyed your instructions to the letter. God forbid His Majesty should experience a cold drop of water on his royal tongue!"

"It's just that if he drinks cold water he'll barf all over your floor."

...

The wind from the lake was becoming chillier, and Nikki took Boston Charlie indoors. *You're a pampered pet too, Charlie. Not used to heavy weather.* Casimir was nowhere in sight. Nikki did, however, notice that the pile of puzzle roughs on her drawing table had been scattered and that each sheet of paper bore a number of tiny puncture marks made by cat teeth. *He's been busy.* She picked up her papers, put them in her office and carefully closed the door.

The phone rang. It was Phil. "And how are things *chez* Nikki?"

"Okay so far. I'm babysitting Marj's cat and she's babysitting her father."

"I'd like your friend to come to my office Monday morning first thing. Do you have her number? Shall I call her directly?"

"I can give her the message and your number so she can call you back. Should she bring her father along?"

"Um—not necessarily as long as she has all his stats. I can take her down to see Willow Acres, and we'll have to work out the arrangements. In these cases it's usually better not to have the person there. It might just upset him needlessly."

"Wouldn't Marj have to prepare him somehow? Explain what's happening?"

"It depends on how advanced his condition is. If he's at the point where he can't remember from one moment to the next, there's no value in upsetting him ahead of time. You friend will have to decide how to handle it."

"It just seems so cold."

"The rules are different with people who don't have yesterdays or tomorrows. Tell your friend I'm at my office for—oh god, I *won't* be in my office. I've—uh—got to see somebody and I'm already late.

Give your friend my home number. If she *can't* make it, have her leave a message on my machine. If I don't hear from her, I'll expect her Monday morning at nine."

Susan. Susan *is the person she has to see and is already late.* Nikki put down the phone, resisted the impulse to slam it. It wouldn't do to keep *Susan* waiting. It had never bothered Phil to keep *Nikki* waiting—and waiting—and waiting. "Sorry about dinner, hon, but the meeting ran late and we got to talking afterwards." *Maybe it wasn't even Susan she had to see. Maybe I'm reading too much into this.*

Nikki was halfway out the door when she remembered the carrots for Bruno. She went back and took three of the slender vegetables out of her crisper drawer, noting how *nice* a newly cleaned refrigerator looks.

Marj was in the kitchen with her father who seemed to be trying to help her prepare dinner. "Dad, this is Nikki. She lives next door."

"Hello, Mr. Kuusisto."

"Do I know you?"

"No, I'm Nikki. I'm your daughter's neighbor."

"Nikki? Nikki . . . Nikki." Einar turned back to what he was doing. He picked up a couple of potatoes Marj had peeled and dropped them into the pot, then gathered a handful of peelings and put them in as well.

"Uh, Dad. Wouldn't you like to watch television? I can turn on the set for you." Marj guided her father to a chair, turned on the TV, then returned to her task.

"Phil just called. Wanted to know if you can be at her office Monday morning at nine. She'll take you to see the place and help you make arrangements. She was just leaving, so I told her I'd give you the message and you'd call back if you *can't* make it. I can come over and stay with your dad while you're gone."

"I don't have to take him with me?"

"Phil says not. Just whatever information is necessary."

Marj looked relieved. "I don't know how I'd manage without you."

Einar Kuusisto wandered back into the kitchen and picked up a carving knife. Marj gently took it from him.

Nikki was still holding her handful of carrots. She held them up. "Would you like me to take your dad out to feed rabbits?"

"Oh, yes. *Yes!*"

"Come on, Mr. Kuusisto, let's see if we can find Bruno."

"Bruno? Do I know him?"

"Not yet. Bruno's a rabbit."

Nikki gently steered the old man outside. Luckily, Bruno happened to be in his favorite spot under Nikki's picnic table. Nikki seated Einar on the bench, then held out a carrot to entice Bruno to come out. By now, Bruno had established a connection between Nikki and carrots. He hopped out, craned his neck toward the proffered vegetable, his nose twitching. Carefully, Nikki placed the carrot into Einar's hand and watched Bruno begin to nibble. "Hold tight, now, or he'll pull it away from you."

Einar, with a delighted smile, held on to the carrot while Bruno did his best to dislodge it. Nikki was smiling too. There was something sweet about the scene. *Mr. Kuusisto, you may have been an S.O.B. but now you're just a kid again.* She thought of her own father. Could the day ever come when that implacable (nifty puzzle word) man would be reduced to childlike vulnerability? Nikki didn't think so. Not *her* dad. If he ended up disabled, in a home, he would be running the place from his wheelchair—plotting, manipulating, issuing orders, and always the center of attention. Her dad had always known just what buttons to push. He would pretend to be on you side until you confided something, then he would twist it around and beat you over the head with it for the rest of time. Her mother had been the target more often than Nikki or her brother. At some time, she must have mentioned an old boyfriend, because it had become a favorite topic at parties: "My son," Nikki's father would expound, "—of course I'm not sure he *is* my son, since my wife was sleeping around before I married her. . . ." Nikki's mother would smile sweetly and say, "And *after* you married me, darling. *After*—so as not to genetically pass on the insanity on my husband's side of the family." It was a game they played. No one, Nikki thought, took it seriously although it made guests squirm. Nor were Nikki and her brother ever shielded from such things. Neither parent seemed to know the meaning of the word "edit." *How they hated each other!* Nikki, pulled up short by the admission, tried to make it better. *Of course my parents didn't really* hate *each other, they just weren't very well matched. Right. Who am I kidding? It was total war.*

Bruno had worked his way along the length of the carrot. "I guess you can drop the last little bit, Mr. Kuusisto. We can give him another one." But Einar didn't want to drop the carrot, he held tightly to the last inch. Bruno gave a tug. Einar laughed out loud. Bruno tugged again. Einar pulled back, teasing. Nikki expected the rabbit to let go and run off. Bruno did let go, but then lunged forward, sinking chisel teeth into Einar's thumb. Einar screamed, then swore, and lunged at the rabbit. Bruno avoided him easily. Nikki, horrified, saw blood dripping from the thumb, took firm hold of Einar's arm and escorted him back to Marj's.

"Marj, I'm so sorry. Bruno bit your dad. I'll take him in the bathroom and wash off his hand."

"It's okay, I'll do it," Marj said, flashing Nikki a look of reproach.

"I'm *sorry.* I just didn't see it coming. Bruno seemed so gentle."

"Doesn't look too bad." Marj had washed off the cut and applied iodine and a Band-Aid. Einar was muttering darkly.

"It's okay, Dad. You'll be just fine. I'll turn the set on again and you can watch TV until supper's ready."

"I feel awful," Nikki told Marj as they walked out together. The two remaining carrots that she had left on the table were gone. "Looks like the bunny brigade struck again, but I don't think your dad will be wanting to feed any more rabbits anyhow."

"Don't be too sure. He may have already forgotten. You couldn't have foreseen it. It wasn't anybody's fault. No real harm done—unless, of course, Bruno gets Alzheimer's."

"I'm glad you can joke about it. I should have been more careful. Anyway, I wonder how you *do* get Alzheimer's. Do they know what actually *causes* it? At one time they blamed aluminum cookware. Phil made me get rid of ours."

"Not really. Bottom line is so far there's no cure."

...

Nikki returned to her house. She was now feeling depressed, and it didn't lighten her mood to find that Casimir had managed to access her bathroom trash and scatter it over the floor—paper towels, lengths of dental floss, an empty shampoo bottle and (*oh god!*) used tampons! Nikki cleaned up the mess, tied up the plastic bag and took it outside to the garbage can. There she saw the orange tomcat. "Still hanging around, I see. Sorry, but I'm under strict orders not to feed you." The cat scurried off.

Nikki went back inside and prepared Casimir's dinner. She knew she should eat something herself, but she wasn't hungry. Day Two of the menstrual period was always the worst, probably for every woman in the world. Nikki remembered the charged atmosphere whenever her Day Two had coincided with Phil's. This day would have been bad enough without cramps. Dead rabbits. Creepy Raymond Cantwell. Marj's dad—and Bruno biting him. And, of course, Nikki had gotten little sleep what with Casimir *rampant*. She lay down on the couch and closed her eyes. At any rate, if there *was* a god, come Monday, Marj's father would be situated and Casimir would go back home—one less mess to clean up, one less egg to fry.

Poor old guy, Marj's dad. She felt bad about the bite, and realized, with a bit of a shock that they probably should have rushed him to a doctor. Bruno seemed healthy enough—and it surely was not rabies that had killed the rabbits, not if they were in the same condition as the one Nikki had found. Still, the rabbits *were* behaving strangely. Maybe they should catch Bruno and have him checked. As she was thinking these thoughts, she felt the jar of cat feet landing on the foot of the couch. Not bothering to open her eyes, she felt Casimir pick his way up alongside her body and then, to her astonishment, crawl on *top* of her and lie down. There he curled up and began to purr. Nikki laughed. It felt good—nice and warm and soft on her crampy abdomen, the purring almost like a soothing vibrator. *I can understand the love-hate relationship people have with their cats. Just when you're ready to kill them, they do something like this!* Nikki dozed off.

She was standing on a wide grassy plain that was filled with people. They all seemed to be waiting and listening. As Nikki watched, every so often one or a number of them would detach themselves from the crowd and begin to walk away toward something in the distance. Nikki could now see that it was a huge musical instrument of some kind, mounted on a hill. It seemed to have strings, and someone—or something—was plucking them to produce notes, not only notes, but chords of amazing sweetness and complexity.

The musical notes seemed intended to selectively summon the listeners, and now Nikki saw that they were not only of all races and colors, but also of others unlike any on earth. Not only that, some of them seemed so insubstantial that when Nikki looked at them directly, they vanished from view, like stars in a night sky that you can see only with peripheral vision. Some were more of a presence than an actuality, while others seemed to be able to occupy the same space, layered, like multiple exposures on film. Nikki tried to see who the musician was, but all she could make out was a haze of colors that flickered and changed shape like footage she had seen of the northern lights.

It was then that Nikki recognized her "own" note being played, realizing in a flash of insight that every entity had—no, *was*, in essence, a musical note, and that when her personal note was struck on the stringed instrument, it reinforced her own tone, strengthened and exalted it, and irresistibly drew her to its source. She could no more have resisted the "siren song" than a falling body could have defied the law of gravity. Nor did she wish to resist, because the note so enthralled her, seduced her, illuminated her, and instilled, in an instant in time, what seemed the wisdom of the cosmic, the realization of her own place and purpose in it, and the soaring desire to fulfill that purpose to its utmost reaches. She also realized a sense of oneness with all the other entities and the exquisite sense of order that bound them all together, each in his exact place, with his exact mission, each striving—striving to *become*, with no limitations or restrictions—all of them joyously in cooperative motion the way atoms are in motion even in the most stationary of objects—all the musical notes forming achingly lovely chords, binding them all together in a common state of blissful purpose in which all were one and yet no individual identity was lost.

In her state of ecstasy, all things negative simply did not exist. All was good. All was benign on this musical harmonious plane. But, as Nikki was drawing closer to the source of the music, like a chill wind, a thought blew into her mind: What would happen if a "wrong" chord were struck? *Was* there such a thing? Could such a thing be? She had not uttered a word, but as soon as these thoughts formed in her head, it was as if she had screamed them out loud. Everything fell silent. All heads turned, all eyes focused on her. Nikki stood, confused and, for the first time, frightened. She felt cold and heard the howl of rising wind. She tried to speak but found she could utter no sound. She tried to say she was sorry, she had not meant to cause a disturbance, but it was as if she were now being isolated from the throng, as if a thick sheet of glass or of ice were forming between them, and that she had somehow been exiled or discarded as unfit—or deemed not ready. And oh, she was so *cold*.

Nikki opened her eyes to darkness. The sun had long set. How long had she been asleep? The only light in the room was the light of the quarter moon spilling in through the window, illuminating the glistening fronds of Boston Charlie. There was no sound at all. It must be late; everyone in the park must be in bed. Nikki didn't move, at first, although she shivered, wished she had a blanket. Casimir was no longer on top of her, and now she saw him in the moonlight, a soft white blur, gazing fixedly at the fern, not moving, but sitting as if hypnotized.

Nikki sat up, noting how lighting can change the atmosphere in a room. Her familiar little living area was transformed by moon shadows into something gothic and alien. Through the window she could see that the night was clear and starry, surprisingly bright with the moon only in its first quarter. But there was something else too. Nikki had to look twice to believe it, and even then rubbed her eyes to make sure she was seeing what she saw. It was the rabbits, of course. Yet again the Eagle Lake rabbits were abroad in the night, but this time, instead of leaping and fighting, they were all standing still, moonbeams caressing every furry body, and they were all looking through the window at Nikki.

The dream! It was like her dream, the memory of which now flooded over her. But why? Why would animals act that way? She looked again, more closely, and saw that the rabbits might not have been actually looking at *her*. They were standing, sitting, fixed in various attitudes, ears up, certainly all focused in her direction, but weren't they doing what Casimir was doing? Weren't they all fixated on Boston Charlie? A fern? A houseplant! Charlie was doing nothing except—and the thought made Nikki smile because of the outrageous-ness of it—spreading its fronds wide as if offering blessings to the multitudes—like the Pope at the Vatican. Nothing was moving, and

Nikki had plenty of time to study the tableau. She noticed something else too. Outside, on her deck, in the same attitude of expectancy, sat the orange tomcat. Then she saw something that made her scalp prickle and sent an icy shock down her spine. On the rabbit-pocked lawn, next to the picnic table, stood a figure. It was a man—a man, just standing there, looking in her window, gazing upward, as were all the animals—there in the moonlight, motionless as a statue, stood Raymond Cantwell.

Nikki threw the wall switch. The room was instantly awash with light, and Nikki experienced a pang of chagrin. *Dumb. If Raymond Cantwell is an ax murderer, he now has a clear view of you.* The light inside made the view outside vanish, which was exactly what Nikki had impulsively wanted—to make it all go away. She hastily closed the drapes, glad, now, that she had installed them. She saw by the wall clock that it was just a little after midnight. When light flooded the room, Casimir blinked twice, then headed for his water bowl. Nikki, now, was by no means sure that she'd actually seen any of it. Had it all been a part of the bizarre dream—series of dreams—she'd been having lately? She turned the light off again, and as soon as her eyes had adjusted to the darkness, pulled back the edge of the curtain and peeked out the window. There was nothing there now except the moonlight shining on water, ground, and picnic table. No rabbits. No orange tomcat. No Raymond Cantwell.

Then, incongruously, Nikki realized that she was hungry. She made herself a cheese and onion sandwich and drank a glass of buttermilk. Then she went to bed where she puzzled over the events of the day until she fell into a dreamless sleep. She didn't even notice Casimir when he leapt onto her bed. She was unaware that the cat sat staring for a long time at her sleeping face before he curled up beside her.

CHAPTER 15

SUNDAY MORNING dawned clear and palely sunny. Nikki awakened a little more refreshed. If, during the night, Casimir had done his impression of a Tasmanian devil, she had managed to sleep through it. Nikki took her shower and went through her morning routine of making coffee, feeding the cat. She pulled open the draw drapes to a reassuringly normal view of Eagle Lake. Rabbits were there as usual— no sign of any dead ones. No sign of anyone at all. It was becoming easy to believe that last night's visitation had been something she had merely dreamt. Mentally, she could hear Phil on the subject. *Stress. Stress causes all kinds of manifestations. What you need, Nikki, is to talk to someone. I'll call my analyst, Dr. Magda Von Buchenwald, and see if she can fit you in.* Phil was a woman foursquare in the system. If you discounted the minor aberration of her being a lesbian, she was the paradigm of conservatism, all the way from her power business suits to her punctual as clockwork annual pap smear and mammogram. If there was conventional wisdom to be bought, she had a standing order. Nikki's blue-jeaned, sneaker-clad world view, that included going to a doctor only when she was really ill, was as jarring to Phil as the rock music Nikki sometimes liked to play.

Nevertheless, Nikki had to admit that her life had gone strange lately. Any one thing, by itself, could, perhaps, be explained—maybe even the rabbits—living *and* dead—but put them all together—the dreams, Boston Charlie, Raymond Cantwell, the earthquake, her paintings, and yes, even the speed with which she was producing her puzzles—and all these things were disturbing. Nikki had a nagging feeling that somehow they were all connected. But how? All she knew was that everything had started with her move to Eagle Lake. More precisely, it had begun when she met Marj.

Marj. It was Marj who had taken her to the nursery where she had bought the fern. If it hadn't been for Marj, Nikki would probably not have gone to Adelaide's coffee and had that embarrassing scene about the cat. And yes, it was Marj who had snitched to Adelaide. She had explained it away, but there you are. It was also Marj who had told Nikki that Raymond Cantwell was a synesthete—when maybe he was only the neighborhood crackpot voyeur. It was Marj who had gotten her to babysit with Casimir—and gotten her involved in helping her with her father, meaning she would then have more contact with Phil. The whole thing played right into Phil's hand, didn't it? If Phil had set the whole thing up it couldn't have worked out better, that is, if Phil wanted to keep a manicured thumb on Nikki's life. Of course it wasn't *all* Marj's fault, Nikki realized *that*—but goddamit, wasn't she getting just a little *too* involved with the woman? And who was she anyway? She pawned herself off as an unemployed, uneducated ex-waitress, but she didn't really seem to be looking for work, did she? As for being uneducated, you couldn't call her that, could you? And how was she using whatever dark powers she may have inherited from her witch of a grandmother?

Nikki stopped short. There was something familiar about all this. What was she doing? She was making a hardass case against her best friend by piling one ugly suspicion on top of another—*like in the dream*. Everything was perfect until she began to think of negative things—and suddenly she found herself cut off. So does that mean that the dream was foretelling the future—or was this an illustrated lecture on what happens when you start entertaining suspicions? They spiral out of control. *Ooh! Deep water. Go back to shore, Nikki, before you drown yourself. Put it down to DTB—Day Three Bitchiness.*

Still, Nikki found herself feeling irritable. Day Three wasn't usually this bad. She vigorously vacuumed up cat hair and even shied the *TV Guide* at Casimir when she spotted him walking along her kitchen countertop. She was curt with a couple of Jehovah's witnesses who came by to warn her about Armageddon. Nikki's old joke, "In that case, Armageddon outta here," had gotten a reproachful look from the older, more experienced campaigner and convulsed the teenaged novice with laughter. The two had walked away in conversation, the younger now looked contrite. Nikki wondered idly where the kid would be in another few years. Still foursquare in the faith, or well away from it?

Nikki's experience with organized religion had been limited to attending the Lutheran church when she was little. It had been somewhat bewildering—the ritual of Communion (which Nikki was too young for) and all those hymns about heavy crosses and being washed in lamb's blood. *(Ugh!)* Her parent's religious devotion had been fugitive. Her mother had been raised a Lutheran, but had not attended church in adulthood until after she married and had a child—who, she then felt, ought to be baptized. Nikki's father also descended from Lutheran stock, but had been raised a Christian Scientist, when his parents converted to the faith after a Reader had brought their son back from the brink of death from rheumatic fever. In the army, when his name had been misspelled as Leinberg, his Bugs Bunny sense of humor had led him to don a yarmulke and attended the Jewish temple. When he married his first wife, he converted to Catholicism, then became a Lutheran again after he married Nikki's mother. He'd taken center stage by being baptized along with his infant son, and had reveled in all the attention he was getting.

The family had attended the Lutheran church until one hot July day. It may have been nothing more than the lack of air conditioning, but her father had suddenly declared that religion was garbage, and, astonishingly, her mother hadn't disagreed! They never went again. Just like that! Nikki had grown up without either the sustaining force or the warping influence of organized religion, whichever way you look at it. Consequently, while she was too young to have developed a philosophy, she'd been left with an open mind. Jehovah's Witnesses, she speculated, must thrive on rejection. Who would actually be willing to discuss something as personal as their spiritual state with a stranger who knocks on their door?

And, speaking of strange, Nikki did *not* want to go to Adelaide's coffee, but, once again, she had promised Marj that she would go, and promises, to Nikki, were sacred. Marj might need help in managing her dad, and, for her sake, it would be politic to kiss Adelaide's ring.

They were a subdued group that evening, walking to Adelaide Moon's—Nikki, Marj and her father. Neither Nikki nor Marj seemed to have much to say. Einar Kuusisto kept pointing out rabbits and taking occasional steps in their direction so that his zigzag progress slowed the pace. It had begun to rain a little—the "Scotch mist" of a West Coast day in late summer—and they were all a bit damp by time they arrived.

Adelaide greeted them with, "C'mon in and find a seat." Raymond Cantwell, behind her, had evidently been given instructions to look after Marj's father. He took Einar by the arm and led him inside. Everyone was there—Paulette and Fred Crushill, Walter and Louise Hatch, Emily and Justin Laderheim (minus their vacation pictures, Nikki hoped), Janet and Bob Lindsay (the newlyweds) and, of course, all the Moons—Hector and Ida, George, Clark and his girlfriend,

Shelley, and even Prince, who was lying under the coffee table in such a position that, if he had suddenly stood up, he would have carried it away with him.

Their entrance—and Nikki realized that it was really Einar Kuusisto's entrance—caused all conversation to stop and all eyes to turn. "I want you to all meet Marj's dad, who'll be staying with her for a few days," Adelaide said. "This is Einar. Let's all make him feel at home." The group interpreted that as meaning they should give him a round of applause, causing Einar to look about in panic until Raymond took his arm and led him to a chair. Marj looked apprehensive and perched on the arm of the couch, while Nikki was left to squeeze past her and step over part of the dog in order to get to the one vacant spot.

Nikki saw that there was coffee and Adelaide's famous upside down cake—and that there was definitely an agenda. Adelaide got right to it. She took a drag on her cigarette, fixed the group with a look. "We all know that somethin' happened to the rabbits this week, but we still don't know what killed them. Now if anyone" (for some reason she glanced at Nikki) "*anyone* here knows of any strange animal in the park, I want them to tell me exactly what it was and when they saw it."

Nobody volunteered, but everyone looked uncomfortable. "You know, it might not have been just a stray dog," Adelaide continued. "We could *all* be in danger. There are *bears* on the island, and wolves, and *cougars*. And maybe it would be a good idea, until we find out what happened, if none of us goes out after dark alone."

Louise Hatch, the English lady, looked visibly alarmed. Her husband, Walter, spoke: "Well, maybe we should organize a patrol. A sort of Neighborhood Death Watch, ha-ha. See what's killin' the little buggers." Louise shot him a glance. "Sorry, m'dear, but how else are we going to find out? Treat 'em like the enemy, I say. Treat 'em like the enemy. Smoke 'em out. *I'm* willin'! Who's with me?"

Justin Laderheim spoke up: "Yes, we certainly *could* do that, *if* necessary. But wasn't it just an isolated incident? As I recall, it was the night of the storm, and we haven't had any more rabbits killed—before or since. We could all end up patrolling till doomsday, losing sleep over something that may never happen again."

Emily Laderheim nodded in agreement with her husband. "It was probably a stray dog," she said, in a slide-lecture voice, "The cougar is known to kill and eat its prey, so does the eagle. Bears are carnivorous, of course, but isn't it more likely that it may have been a canine—perhaps one that was frightened by the storm and broke loose and ran wild?"

"Well, I know that Pierre was *terribly* upset by the storm. Poor little thing wouldn't stop shivering," Paulette Crushill said, and hastily added, "Of course Pierre never left the house that night. He slept with me all night long."

And what about Fred, Nikki thought with black humor. *Did* Fred *sleep with you all night long? Remember now, it was Fred who discovered the dead rabbits. Did you check his teeth for fur?* Nikki could have mentioned finding the dead rabbit the day before, but by now she knew better. She would then have to explain, in front of the group, why she'd disposed of it without telling anyone.

"There's a stray cat that hangs around." Everyone, including her husband, Bob, turned to look at Janet Lindsay. "Well there *is.* I've seen it hanging around the garbage cans. It's a big orange tomcat."

Adelaide sighed audibly. "Has anyone been feeding that cat?"

"Not since you yelled at me about it," Nikki heard herself say.

Adelaide fixed her with a stare. "I wasn't accusing you, Nikki." Then, out of the corner of her eye, she spotted Einar Kuusisto. He had been quietly eating a piece of cake, and had reached for his cup of coffee. When he did, he somehow managed to knock it over, spilling the contents on the table. Marj made a move, but Raymond Cantwell was already blotting up the spill with paper napkins. Adelaide looked annoyed at the interruption. "Raymond, get a sponge from the kitchen—and get Einar a coke with a straw. It'll be easier to handle. Anyway, Nikki, I want you to know that I wasn't accusing you. When I told you not to feed stray cats, you were new here and you couldn't have known. I am certainly not singling you out as the one who's doing it now."

No, Mother. "Well, I *haven't* been feeding any cats—not stray ones anyway," Nikki said defiantly—and rather lamely.

"Oh, I know you've been looking after Casimir for Marj, and I think that's very kind of you, but right now we need to insure that everyone in this park is *safe*. We don't want anyone to feel threatened—residents or visitors. We have people with children who use the park, and we certainly don't want any incident of a child being attacked."

Just how safe would you have felt, Lady, if you'd seen Raymond Cantwell peering in your window at midnight? Nikki didn't say.

"You're saying, then," Emily Laderheim put in, "that you think we have something to fear from a wild animal? A tomcat might certainly attack rabbits, particularly their young, but it seems unlikely that one would kill a number of adult rabbits in a night, doesn't it? You think, then, that we might have a cougar in the area—one that might stalk children?"

"I don't know, Emily, but we can't discount the possibility. All I'm saying is that *somethin'* has been killin' rabbits and until we know what did it, we have to keep our guard up, right?"

"Well, *I* think we're making mountains out of molehills," Justin Laderheim said. "Who really cares about a bunch of dead rabbits? *I* certainly don't. Too many of them around as it is."

"We've got enough rules in this park already." It was Fred Crushill. "I, for one, don't want to end up walking patrol all night just because a few rabbits got chewed up."

"Well, that's all very well for *you* to say, but what if it *is* something that might attack a child—or even an adult?" This from his wife, Paulette. "And for all we know, it might attack Pierre. I know I'd be afraid to take him out at night."

"Why don't we just put out some poisoned bait," Bob Lindsay suggested.

"That's horrible," said his wife.

Hector Moon spoke up: "In all my years I've never known of a wild animal in Eagle Lake Park—except for deer. There's a fence all around this place and bears and cougars can't get in. A deer can jump it, a raccoon can get through it, but a bear or a cougar or a wolf—not bloody likely that they'd even try."

"What about that time, Hector, when the cows from that farm in the valley got loose and knocked down the fence. Are you sure the fence hasn't been damaged?" Ida asked.

"Well, I'm gettin' sick of this whole subject," Walter Hatch said. "If you don't have the stomach for organizing a patrol, then let's just wait and see if anything else happens."

"You mean wait and see what or who gets killed next?" his wife asked.

Justin Laderheim stood up. "Don't we have anything else to bring up at this meeting, because if we don't, I, for one, am ready to go home."

"Why Justin," Adelaide said, "we don't consider these get-togethers *meetings*. It's more like a happy family getting together to talk about what's best for all of us."

"Is that so? Well, how's this? You wanted me to move my camper down by the lake and I did, but somebody threw a rock off the cliff and it fell on my camper roof and knocked a big hole in it—and when it rained the water got in an damaged everything. Are you going to pay to have it repaired?"

"Now, Justin, you know why I asked you to park there. I'm sorry if you've had a bit of trouble, but I couldn't have foreseen it—and *I* don't know who threw the rock. It could have been one of your own grandchildren when they came to visit."

"Right. And you can bet they won't be visiting me here again, because as soon as I can, I'm going to get the hell out of this place. And I'm going home. Are you coming, Emily?"

This is a lot better than home movies, Nikki thought. She looked around and realized something odd. Everyone in the room—*everyone*—seemed to be at some pitch of anger. It's as though all the residents of Eagle Lake Park had decided, today, to be in a bad mood all at the same time. And, to Nikki's secret delight, Adelaide looked to be losing control of her subjects. The group focus had disintegrated to querulous exchanges between individuals and the buzz of voices sounded like a hive of angry bees.

Janet Lindsay, who rarely had anything to say, was complaining to Adelaide about having their parties end at midnight. "It's like being a teenager and having a curfew! I left home because I couldn't stand it."

Then Fred Crushill was saying that if he couldn't keep his wood-working tools where he could get his hands on them, then, by God, what was the use of being retired at Eagle Lake Park? In the background, Bob was scolding his wife for getting them in trouble with Adelaide, and on the other side of the room, Shelley was telling Clark Moon that she never wanted to see him again as long as she lived. Paulette Crushill was saying to Ida Moon that she was sick of getting involved in park projects, like papering Unit One for Clark and his girlfriend. She, Paulette, was getting too old for that kind of slave labor, and all she wanted was to be left alone. Ida was saying that if she had a complaint, she should be talking to Adelaide, not her, and that she, Ida, didn't give a damn—actually using the word "damn." Adelaide had almost vanished in a cloud of cigarette smoke, and the noise level kept rising until:

"Shut up, all of you!" It was George Moon.

It was the first time Nikki had heard George actually say something.

In the silence that followed, the only sound heard was a thin trickle of water. They all turned to look. It was Einar Kuusisto. He was standing as if dazed. In his hand was a can of Coca-Cola, pointed downward, as if forgotten, the contents spilling out through the opening, forming a puddle on the floor. At the same time, another puddle was forming at his feet. Urine stained the crotch of his trousers and was coursing down his leg.

CHAPTER 16

"WHAT A bloody disaster!" Nikki said to Marj as the three of them were making their way back to Marj's mobile home.

"Oh, I don't know, as Adelaide's parties go, I thought it was one of her better ones."

Nikki laughed and Marj joined in. "Do you want me to come in? Do you need any help with you dad?"

"No, I'm beginning to get the hang of it. I think he'll be easier to handle one-on-one. I'll change his clothes, give him a shower and tuck him into bed. Then I'll make myself a soothing pot of English Breakfast and if you'd like to join me on my verandah, I'll be happy to quaff a dish of tea with you. We can test the British theory that a good cuppa is the only answer to anything up to and including the *Luftwaffe*."

"I'd be most genetically altered to accept your invitation, milady."

"In that case, madam, I shall be cryogenically preserved to have the honor of your presence."

Back in her own house, Nikki changed clothes and took a shower as well. In her dive to help clean up the mess on Adelaide's floor, she had managed to set her knee into a puddle of coke or urine, she wasn't sure which. Now, fresh and clean, as she was putting on a comfy jogging suit, Nikki experienced a pang of guilt as she thought of Marj, and how she had been so quick to think the worst of her earlier that day.

Poor Marj. Of course it *had* been a very strange evening. Nikki washed Casimir's dinner bowl, refilled his water, checked her plants and went outside. Skies had cleared and the moon was waxing; there would be a full moon—the harvest moon—in a week or so. She saw no rabbits as she made her way to Marj's. Nikki planned to wait outside until Marj appeared so as not to disturb Mr. Kuusisto who, presumably, would be either in bed or staring at television. Now she saw that Marj was already on the porch. Behind her, the unit was dark, but a cheery candle glowed on the table and Marj called out softly, "Come on in." She, too, had changed clothes and was wearing a pair of knit pants and football jersey. "I think we'll be warm enough out here."

It was pleasant to be on Marj's deck. They were sitting on cushioned plastic chairs in front of a small table. On it, Marj had set the teapot (in a tea cozy, no less) and cups. The candle—one of those candles inside a globular glass chimney—sent forth enough light to see by, but not so much that it interfered with the soft illumination of the moon and all it implied. Nikki loved the night, particularly in Eagle Lake Park. The tall evergreens and view of the water were transformed at night to a mysterious realm evocative—of what? Something primordial. Something prehistoric. Some ancestor of hers would have sat by a fire on such a night, perhaps at the mouth of a cave, perhaps as the edge of a lake, with nothing beyond but forests and animals and unending stretches of wilderness.

Marj poured them each a cup of tea. "Today I almost hated you."

Nikki, startled, looked at her friend.

"And I'm ashamed of myself," Marj said. "I don't know what came over me, but all of a sudden I was thinking all sorts of crazy things—how everything that was wrong in my life was somehow *your* fault."

Nikki opened her mouth to speak but Marj interrupted. "No, hear me out. I don't know what brought it on, but suddenly I found myself thinking how my life was fine until *you* moved into the park. How I miss Casimir—and *you're* the one who has him now. I know, I know! You have to realize that *none* of this makes sense. It's totally unreasonable and unfair, but I was actually convincing myself that even the situation with my father was somehow due to you. If you hadn't been here, maybe things would have been different and he wouldn't be staying with me."

"Odd you should say that, because I went through the same thing. I'd almost convinced myself that all the weirdness in *my* life started when I met *you*. Crazy, isn't it? Are we all under *that* much stress?"

"It's more than that. I thought about it tonight at Adelaide's. Didn't you notice how *wired* everyone was? It was like the ozone in a thunder storm. Like any second there'd be a flash of lightning that would scorch all of us."

"There did seem to be a lot of built-up resentment, that's for sure. I think Adelaide was the focus of most of it."

"It was more than that. You once asked me what powers I'd inherited from my grandmother. I told you none that I wanted, but there is one—a sense of disaster. I can always tell when something godawful is about to happen, and I've had that feeling all day."

"Well, of course! Look what's going on. But if everything works out, by this time, tomorrow, your dad will be in a facility that's able to care for him properly. You'll be able to visit him and give him all the support he needs, and you'll have your life back—and your cat. I know you miss Casimir, and I'm sure he misses you too. Why don't you come over and see him? Your dad's asleep, you'll only be a minute. It'll make you feel better."

"Nikki, I don't know—"

"Go peek in on your dad. If he's dead to the world he'll never know the difference. If you'd rather, I can stay here and listen for him while you go visit with Cas."

Marj got up and went inside, then came out. "He's sound asleep. I think he's getting used to being here—or maybe he's just exhausted. I closed his door. I don't think you have to stay. Let's go."

Nikki turned on her living room light. "Casimir, where are you? You have a visitor."

The light showed Casimir to be curled up on the rug next to Boston Charlie. "Hi, baby, it's mommie," Marj said. Casimir looked her over coolly. "How are you, sweetheart? You're looking beautiful."

"He's allowing me to brush him," Nikki said. "Is that a good sign?"

"Casimir, baby, it's me." Marj advanced.

Casimir looked her over with golden eyes, then backed away. "How's mommie's little man? I've missed you." Casimir kept backing away and disappeared under the couch.

This is not going at all well, Nikki thought. "He's just a bit disoriented. He's had to get used to me and used to being in a new place. I'm sure he'll come around if you just ignore him."

Marj shot Nikki a sharp look. *Who did this woman think she was, telling me that* my *cat will "come around" as though she owned him?*

"Why don't you just have a seat, Marj, and give Casimir a chance to get used to you again? Can I get you anything?"

"No. Nothing. I should be getting back."

"Then I'll come with you," Nikki said. "Don't feel bad about Casimir. I think he's as unsettled right now as the rest of us."

"Oh, I know," Marj said as they crossed the short distance to her home. "Casimir is not above punishing me for abandoning him. He's done it before—gone into a sulk when he felt slighted. Animals do that. You want another cuppa? I think the tea's still warm."

"Speaking of animals, I don't see any rabbits around."

"Wouldn't they all be tucked away in their burrows or wherever it is they go at night?"

"Not the ones around here. I saw them again around midnight last night. They were all standing in the moonlight—and so was Raymond Cantwell."

"*What?*"

"Believe it or not, Ripley. There he was, amongst all the bunnies, staring in my window."

"Ooh, that's *creepy.*"

"*I* thought so."

"Why would poor old Raymond be staring in your window?"

"I've no idea. I don't think he was really staring at me—I mean the lights were out, he couldn't have seen me. I think he was staring at Boston Charlie."

"Oh, for god's sake! Why is that man obsessed with your fern? I mean okay, it's a gorgeous plant but *please!*"

"Charlie hasn't been looking quite as well lately. He's developed a few dry fronds and just doesn't look as robust as he first did."

"You've been watering him?"

"Oh yes, but it's like I said. For me, plants die."

"You've only had him a week. I hope Casimir isn't responsible."

"I don't think so. Casimir leaves Charlie alone—although he does seem fascinated by him. I often catch him just sitting and staring. Good ol' Boston Charlie seems to be a focal point wherever he goes." Nikki sipped her tea. "I don't know what's going on here, but maybe Adelaide was right. Maybe there *is* something dangerous in Eagle Lake Park. I hope it's not Raymond Cantwell."

"Raymond is decidedly odd, but I can't picture him going around killing rabbits. My prime suspect is Prince. Maybe he's learned to jump the fence. We had a Briard once that no fence could contain."

"Nobody mentioned Prince tonight."

"Nobody would dare, but I'll bet a lot of us were thinking it."

Nikki finished her tea. "Right now I'm gonna go home and get some sleep."

"Me too. I'll curl up on the couch and try to get some *zzz*'s in case my dad starts getting restless later. It'll be *great* to be able to get a full night's sleep again."

"I'll be over about eight-thirty to stay with your father while you go see Phil." Nikki let herself out. "And Marj? Keep your doors locked."

Marj secured the screen door. "Yes, and you too."

...

Back in her own living room Nikki confronted Casimir eyeball to eyeball. "Look, you little traitor, was that any way to treat the person who buys your Kitty Gourmet and tends to your hair balls? You should be spelling out an apology in MEOW mix."

Casimir disdainfully tossed his head, turned and presented a fluffy raised tail as if to say, "Fiddle-dee-dee!"

"You scoff, but do the words Humane Society mean anything to you? Marj might just decide life would be easier without kitty litter."

Nikki stopped to contemplate her plants. The herbs outside, in the light from her window seemed okay, although Marj had told her she should repot the rosemary and bring it inside for the winter. The oxalis was a-bloom with a few pink flowers, and Charlie—well, what *was* it about Charlie? The plant didn't appear to be dying. Sure, Nikki had snipped off a couple more dead fronds, but there appeared to be new ones growing. Still, Charlie did not quite have the same presence. She couldn't really put her finger on it, then she laughed. *He looks depressed. If a plant can look hang-dog, then this is it.* Ridiculous or not, that *was* it. The fronds that had arched so expansively looked to be limp, no longer as vital. The green that had been so verdant (nifty puzzle word) was paler, like a suntan two weeks after a Hawaiian vacation. Nikki picked up the pot. It didn't feel as though the plant needed water. Could she be over watering? She didn't think so. Did it need food? Nikki had been using a mild fertilizer solution. "Don't look so discouraged, Charlie. Maybe I should talk to you more."

The phone rang. It was Phil. "Yes, Phil, it's all set for tomorrow. Marj will be at your office at nine. Yes, she knows how to get there. I'll stay with her father."

"That's good but it's not why I called. I need you to do me a favor."

"Well—sure, Phil. If I can."

"It's the IDC fund raiser. We need a banner to stretch across the highway. Actually what we need to do is to update the *old* banner—change the date. Since you painted the old one for us, we were wondering if you'd mind—"

"Well, yes, all right."

"Good. Come by and pick it up next week."

"Yeah, okay." Nikki hung up the phone. A small favor? Or the start of something big?

CHAPTER 17

Nikki woke with a start. Someone was knocking—no, *pounding* on her door. She threw on her robe and went to answer it. It was Marj, wild-eyed and near tears. "Have you seen my father?"

Nikki shook her head. "No, I haven't. Come in, Marj. What's happened?"

"I can't stop, Nikki. I've got to find him. I woke up this morning and he wasn't in his room."

"Okay, just come in a second while I get dressed. I'll help you look." Marj followed Nikki into the bedroom where Nikki quickly pulled on blue jeans, sweat shirt and stepped into her sneakers. "When did he—that is, *how* did he get out?"

"I don't *know.* The doors were locked. He *couldn't* have gone out—but he's not there now." Casimir had come into the room and was now twining familiarly around Marj's ankles. Marj scarcely noticed. "He was in his bare feet and pajamas."

"Then he couldn't have gone far. Maybe he wandered into the park area. I'll call Adelaide. She'll muster the troops. Meanwhile you and I can check with Raymond Cantwell. Your dad may have gone looking for him. If he's not there, we'll start at one end of the park and check every house, every trail. We'll find him. He probably took off after a rabbit."

"He's not anywhere near here. I already looked. Do you suppose he could've gone down to the highway?"

"If he did, someone would surely spot a disoriented old man wearing pajamas. We can call the police station. He might already be there." Nikki picked up the phone and dialed. "Hi, Adelaide, sorry to call so early but we have an emergency. Marj's dad is missing. Yes . . . sometime last night or this morning. . . . Okay, Adelaide. Thanks Adelaide. Yes, we thought of that—and we appreciate it. Marj and I are going to look for him now." Nikki hung up. "Adelaide will call all the residents and get a search party together. She's also going to notify the police."

Einar Kuusisto was nowhere in the mobile home park. He was not at Raymond Cantwell's, nor had Fred Crushill seen him on his morning walk. Everyone expressed concern but nobody knew of his whereabouts. Nikki and Marj checked all the outbuildings, including the communal laundry and showers, and the various storage sheds. As they searched, they were joined, one by one, by concerned neighbors. Nikki, not wanting to alarm Marj, slipped quietly away long enough to scout the area along the embankment. She saw nothing. No sign of a body having fallen off the edge. No sign of a body on the rocks below.

"He must have wandered off into the campground. We'll have to check all the trails," Justin Laderheim was addressing the impromptu search party on Barkell road. "We'll go in twos, that way, if we find him and he's unable to walk, we can either bring him back, or one can stay with him while the other gets help."

"I'll go check the dump area," Walter Hatch said. You, young Bob, you come with me. The women can look along the road to the highway and check the shore of the lake."

The group dispersed. Paulette Crushill and Louise Hatch started down the road toward the highway. Emily Laderheim and Janet Lindsay headed for the campground along with Clark Moon, Fred Crushill and Raymond Cantwell. Nikki and Marj walked down the hill toward the shore of the lake.

The beach was deserted at the off-season early morning hour. Eagle Lake was calm. The sun wasn't up yet but the sky was light, and it looked as though it would be a beautiful day.

"I can't imagine how he could just disappear," Marj said.

"When did you actually see him last?"

"Just before I went to bed, I guess—*no*. The last time I saw him was just before we went to your place to see Casimir. I looked in on him. He was asleep. I shut his door."

"You don't remember checking on him again before you went to bed?"

"No. I remember that I came in, walked down the hall. I was about to look into the bedroom but since I'd closed the door earlier, I was afraid the sound of the door opening would wake him. I went straight to bed myself. I expected to have to get up with him later. Oh, my God! He must have gone out while we were at your place! I remember now. I forgot to lock the screen door! It was open when we came back! He's been out all night! He could be dead of hypothermia. *Why* didn't I look in on him when I came home!"

"You couldn't have known."

"He was fast asleep. He was *snoring*. I was only going to be gone a few minutes—and we weren't gone long, were we? Why didn't we see him? We sat out there on the porch and drank *tea*. Why didn't we spot him?"

"I don't know. And when we find him he probably won't be able to tell us because he won't remember." Nikki was narrowly eyeing the shore, grateful, at least, that no pajama-clad body was floating in the water. "He's not here. Let's go back and see if anyone else has had any luck."

But no one had found Einar Kuusisto. Hours later, when every inch of the campground had been covered, every building checked, every person questioned, it seemed as if Einar had simply vanished. No one had picked him up on the highway. No one had notified the police of having seen him. The search had been thorough to the point of desperation, including even the crawl spaces under each mobile home. Systematically, they had removed panels of skirting and trained flashlights into the areas to make sure nobody could be hiding there. They had looked under Nikki's deck. They had searched every utility shed. They had combed the woods and walked all around the dump area. They had double checked every vehicle including Justin Laderheim's camper which was now parked by the lake next to the embankment, just below the still vacant Unit One—the unit that Clark and Shelley would be occupying once they married. No one had taken refuge in the camper, but inside there was obvious water damage from a leak in the roof.

Nikki had persuaded Marj to come in for a cup of tea and something to eat. She called Phil to tell her what had happened. Phil made a suggestion: "Try to find out if there's any place Marj's father would consider a haven. Sometimes a person with Alzheimer's will try to return to a childhood home or a house they lived in years ago. The memory is a strange thing. They found one old woman in a playground. She was a child again, reliving her school days."

"I'll ask, but I don't think he's lived in this area before. Thanks, Phil. I'll let you know what happens."

Marj had both hands wrapped around her mug of tea, warming her icy fingers. Her sandwich lay untouched. "Oh god, what are we going to do? Where could he *be*? He's been gone for hours!"

"We'll find him, Marj," Nikki said, thinking that she was sounding like a broken record—as all the park residents were sounding, in their attempts to reassure. *I just hope to god we find him alive.* "Phil suggested he may have tried going back to a place he knew. Would there be anything like that here?"

"I don't think so—unless he's made his way down to that farm down the road. He used to be a farmer, you know. He could've gone down that dirt road to the dairy farm—where we think the orange tomcat comes from."

"It's a long shot but worth checking."

"Let's go." Marj left her tea and sandwich.

On their way out, they ran into Adelaide and a few park residents who were, again, standing in the middle of the road, conferring about what to do next. "Marj and I are going to walk down to the dairy farm and see if there's any sign of him there. I was told he might be trying to go home—or someplace that seemed like home. He might have spotted the farm and wandered toward it. He used to be a farmer, you see."

"Oh, that's a good idea. Who thought of that?" Adelaide asked.

"Phil, my—uh—friend. The one who's helping Marj."

"Boyfriend?" Adelaide's antennae were up.

"Girlfriend," Nikki said evenly.

"Oh. Well, we're gonna clear out that area in front of Unit One. All the brush and blackberry brambles. We've looked everywhere else. I'm sure Marj's dad isn't in there, but it's the only place left. In any case, I want to clear it out so Clark and Shelley will have a better view of the lake when they move in. Blackberries only attract kids. It was probably some kid pickin' berries lobbed that rock on Justin's camper. I'm sending George in with the weed whip and chainsaw. The rest of us will go through the woods again just in case we might have missed him somehow." Adelaide looked at Marj's drawn face. "Don't worry, we'll find him."

"Sure, Adelaide. Of course we will."

Nikki and Marj took the route toward the highway, but this time turned right at a dirt road that intersected and sloped down toward a valley where a farm lay in the distance. Nikki had seen the farm many times and thought it would make a picturesque subject for a painting. Now, as they drew closer, the place no longer looked as inviting—a ramshackle barn surrounded by a muddy area pockmarked by the feet of cattle.

"Looks like Farmer Brown's on duty," Nikki muttered to Marj. "Good day, sir. May we talk to you, please."

The heavy-set man in overalls cocked an ear, then, in his rubber boots, squished toward them through the mud. "Yeah?"

"I'm Nikki Leino and this is my friend, Marj Kuusisto. We're looking for an old man who's missing, Miss Kuusisto's father. He disappeared last night, and since he used to be a farmer, we thought he might have come here."

"Hah?"

Oh god, he's deaf as a traffic light.

Marj took over. She leaned forward and shouted, "Have you seen an old man in his pajamas?"

The man seemed to understand. "Oh, you're lookin' for the old guy that disappeared. Yeah, cops been here already. No, I ain't seen him."

"Could we look in your barn?" Marj shouted.

"Go ahead, but he ain't there. You can look till the cows come home."

Nikki couldn't help smiling. "It's not a figure of speech," Marj said. "The cows will be home about five o'clock."

"You two are gonna get your pretty little feet all muddy!" the farmer shouted, cackling with glee.

If it were only mud! Nikki thought as they picked their way through the mire. *I'll have to burn these sneakers.*

Systematically, Nikki and Marj checked the stalls, undeterred by the powerful barn smell that had nearly felled them at first. They climbed the ladder to the upper level where hay was stored—a likely place for Einar to have taken refuge. The only sign of life they found was a number of barn cats, one of whom was the orange tom, curled comfortably on hay bales. "So this is where you belong," Nikki said. "I thought so."

Nikki and Marj backtracked, shouted their thanks to the farmer—who may or may not have heard them—and headed back to Eagle Lake Park.

As they passed Adelaide's house they were stopped at the top of the hill by Adelaide herself. Her expression clearly conveyed that something was wrong. Marj started to push past her, but Adelaide barred the way. "Marj, you don't want to go up there just now."

"What's happened? Did you find him? Is he alive?"

"I'm sorry, Marj. I'm afraid your father is—gone."

The sound of a rescue vehicle entering the park interrupted. Nikki and Marj stood to one side, expecting to see it enter the mobile home area. Instead it continued past them down the hill toward the lake. At the top of the hill, in the newly cleared section in front of Unit One, a group of people stood silently looking over the edge.

It had been George Moon who found Einar. He and Raymond Cantwell had been clearing brush, working their way to the embankment's edge. George, about to take the chainsaw to the last couple of saplings, had looked over the edge to see where they might fall, and spotted Justin Laderheim's camper parked below. George's first thought had been that Justin must have thrown a tarp over the leak in the roof—but then he saw that it wasn't a tarp at all, but the crumpled body of Einar Kuusisto in his blue and white striped pajamas.

Marj made her way to the edge of the embankment. She'd been near hysteria several times that day, but now she was completely calm. Nikki stayed close to her side, and the group silently parted to let them through. Down below, the body had been covered, and was being lifted into the ambulance.

Afterwards, when all the statements had been made, notes taken, condolences offered, Nikki took Marj in hand and led her home.

There, in Nikki's living room, Marj sat on the couch with Casimir in her lap and cup of tea at her elbow. "I knew we wouldn't find him alive," Marj said. "And maybe it's just as well. But, oh my god, how could he have fallen like that?"

"I don't know."

"You saw him, Nikki. They say the fall killed him instantly. They say he had a broken neck. But he was all scratched up, and he looked . . . he looked so *horrified*." Marj shut her eyes. She'd had to identify the body.

"It all fits, Marj. To fall off that embankment last night, your father would've had to get through a thick patch of blackberry brambles, and his facial expression would've been the result of the fall."

"But why would he have done that? I could understand it if he'd been wandering around in the darkness and had toppled off the edge in front of either of *our* units. There's not much to stop anyone from falling there. What was he doing in all those brambles. You saw him. He was cut to pieces."

"Maybe he was trying to catch a rabbit—and it led him right into the briar patch. Maybe he got tangled and tried to fight his way out, but got disoriented and ended up going the wrong way, over the cliff."

"You're probably right. It could've happened that way. Maybe he *was* chasing a rabbit."

Or maybe, Nikki thought to herself, *something out there was chasing* him.

...

Adelaide had been right. There *was* a family feeling to living in Eagle Lake Park—all the way from petty squabbles to solidarity in a crisis. *Yet*, Nikki mused, *I'll bet that when the day comes to move away, I won't be keeping in touch with any of these people—and neither will Marj. For that matter, I wonder if Marj and I will stay in touch. We have a lot in common, but we belong to different worlds.* Nikki remembered her mother saying that nothing brings people together like common endeavor or common disaster, but that it's always a temporary alliance. Of course she'd been referring to her marriage.

And what, Nikki wondered, would a permanent alliance be? Parents die off. Children leave to make their own lives. Friends come and go. Marriage partners? Divorce ends all that. And when you divorce you lose not only your partner but all your partner's friends and family. Siblings? Nikki thought of her own brother. It had been a while since they'd been in touch. A card at Christmas. A phone call—how long ago? She couldn't remember.

Nikki and her brother had never been particularly close, although he'd been supportive when he learned that she was a lesbian. Still, there had not been much contact after that, and Nikki suspected that, to her brother and his wife, she had become the *exotic* member of the family—an object of curiosity, and, possibly, sniggering speculation. Nikki's sister-in-law, a no-nonsense country woman whose family was solidly conservative, treated Nikki with wary cordiality, but there was an undercurrent that made Nikki uncomfortable—a vaguely unsavory way of insinuating herself that betrayed a fascination with lesbian lifestyle. "How do you do it? Which one is the man?" Nikki spoke with her brother on the phone but preferred not to visit.

She looked at Casimir who was, once again, stationed next to Boston Charlie. "I suppose I'll miss *you* when you go back to Marj." What with funeral preparations to be made, Casimir would be with Nikki a little longer.

Nikki had invited Marj to stay with her as well, but Marj had said no, she'd rather sleep in her own bed—now that she had it back. Obviously saddened by her father's death, Marj made no pretense of being grief-stricken. With quiet dignity, she had thanked the people of Eagle Lake Park for their help and kindness, but made it clear that she would rather be by herself—and that seemed to include Nikki as well. Nikki respected that. It was so *Finnish*.

Eddie Kuusisto had been notified and Marj had assured her brother that it was not necessary for him to come all that way to the funeral unless he particularly wanted to. It would be a simple interment in Madrona Memorial Park, attended only by Marj, Nikki, the Moons and a few Eagle Lake residents. Mary, Einar's former companion, probably would not be there. She'd gone away, and Marj didn't know how to get in touch with her, although Marj did leave a message with the woman who had been their nearest neighbor—the one designated as a contact in case of emergency.

Out of courtesy, she had also left a message on Jonah Byrd's service, although she certainly didn't expect her ex to attend. It was more to let him know that she had a lot on her plate right now, so whatever it was that Jonah wanted of her would have to take a number. In the same spirit, Nikki had informed Phil, partly to acknowledge the help Phil had tried to give, and partly so that Phil would understand why Nikki might be too busy this week to worry about the IDC banner. Adelaide was helping with the arrangements, and would serve refreshments at her home after the funeral, which was to be held Thursday, September 14th, at one o'clock.

It was all rather neat and tidy. A person is born, lives a given number of years, dies—sometimes quite suddenly—and life flows in like water to close up the hole. The space he occupied no longer shows any trace of him. What possessions he had become dispersed. Nobody, Nikki thought, ever wants the dead to return, no matter how beloved. Imagine the chaos if only one senior citizen came back and demanded his retirement payments be reinstated—and his bank accounts—and his house. His heirs would probably kill him! *It's just as well that death is a one-way street.*

Einar's death had changed the measure at Eagle Lake Park—slowed the tempo from a scurry to a knell. Nobody really mourned the old man, but death has a way of arresting the living, hushing them, giving them pause. Everything stops for a funeral. *Maybe now things will settle down*, Nikki thought.

But of course it was only the beginning.

CHAPTER 18

MAYBE I should go pick up the IDC banner after all. It was Monday morning and Nikki had time on her hands. She didn't feel like working, even with a deadline looming. Marj was off somewhere with Adelaide, probably picking out a casket. Nikki was at home with Casimir. *I should check my wardrobe. I don't know if I have anything to wear to a funeral. Nothing black—but people don't wear black to funerals anymore, do they? Still, I don't think I can go in a pair of jeans either.* In the end, Nikki did what she usually did when she had idle time. She took out her paints and set up her easel. She looked at her last painting, the one in oils, and wondered if she should try doing something with the sky, then decided it would be more fun to start from scratch with a new canvas. "Who wants to pose for me? Casimir, how about you?" The cat looked startled, then disappeared under the couch. "Guess not. How about you, Charlie? You want your picture painted?"

Nikki did a quick charcoal sketch, then began working with her paints. *I should probably be using watercolors for this, but what the hell, we'll immortalize Boston Charlie in oils.* She soon found that it was not working. Something was wrong. The painting was coming out—Nikki took a step back—*smudgy*. Blurry. Like a double exposure. She looked at Charlie but saw nothing unusual. *Must be my eyes. Maybe I need glasses. Eyestrain from working on computer under a fluorescent light.* Bemused, she looked at the painting again. The plant *did* look out of focus, as if she had painted a moving object—or was it a vanishing object? There was an ethereal quality to the work. Or was it a *disintegrating* object? Some of the fronds looked definitely fragmented. *I suppose it could work as an abstract.* Bored with the project, Nikki put her paints away and cleaned her brushes. It was a pleasant fall day. She would go check the mail.

The air was cool and there was a wind from the lake. Nikki buttoned her denim jacket, as she headed down the road. There seemed to be no one around—except rabbits. She caught a glimpse of Bruno but didn't stop to speak. *Ill-tempered animal!* Maybe it was just her imagination but weren't there *more* rabbits around than usual? Well, perhaps not. Nobody had an actual count of the park rabbits. They were everywhere. You couldn't take a photo without having rabbits in every picture, and park visitors had fun playing count-the-bunnies in their vacation snapshots. Even with something killing them, the rabbit population did not seem to have suffered.

Nikki turned right at the "T" and walked past the Moon's. She was strolling along, deep in thought, when a sudden noise almost caused her to lose her balance. Prince, the Moon canine, loose in the yard, had run up to the chain link fence and, seeing Nikki, began leaping up, throwing his body against the metal and barking as if crazed.

"Prince, you idiot, it's *me*. You scared hell out me!" Prince kept on barking, jumping against the fence as if trying to claw his way through it. "*Down, Prince!* Fool dog. Don't you remember me or have you got Alzheimer's too?" The dog seemed not to hear her. He was barking incessantly, foaming—no, maybe just slobbering—at the mouth, trying now to leap the fence but each time just falling short. Nikki backed away. *Must be that the Moons aren't home and this is Prince's guard dog mode.* She hurried on past. *He probably can't clear the fence, but I don't think I'd bet my life on it. If he got excited enough, like the night of the storm, he might just be able sail right over that thing.*

There was nothing in Nikki's box but junk mail—advertising flyers, a couple of catalogs Nikki had no interest in, and a "free gift" of gummed address labels from some charity that wanted a donation. The gummed labels had her address wrong. *Why don't they just put a garbage can next to the mailboxes?* She started back, then paused. Instead of having to walk past the demented Prince again, why not cut through the woods, direct-deposit her mail at the garbage dump, then circle back through the hiking trails and the campground? It would give her a bit of exercise.

There was a little footpath that led from the road into the forest. Nikki followed it, noticing the vegetation—low-growing Oregon grape with its stickery, holly-like leaves, and salal, a leafy plant that was annually picked and sold to the florist industry by whoever had the ambition to go into the woods to gather it. The island vegetation had a rainforest lushness, always green, but autumn still brought color. Nikki loved the change of seasons. The blazing foliage in the eastern part of the country had been gorgeous, but when the West Coast poplars and broadleaf maples turned yellow, the sight could take her breath away. That first year she and Phil had spent on the island there had been a spectacular autumn. The weather had been mild with no windstorms and little rain. As result the leaves had remained on the trees till nearly Christmas. Nikki had gone around snapping photos that never did do justice to the landscape.

The woods Nikki walked through were mostly cedar and fir with a few poplars, maples, alders, and arbutus trees. It was too early yet for fall color, but there would be plenty in another month or so. The path, as Nikki had guessed, led to the clearing where the dump moldered—a dismal mountain of burnt-over trash. Without breaking stride, Nikki tossed her mail on it and continued on to re-enter the woods on the other side. She was now in the area of numbered campsites. The place was deserted. Huge trees surrounded her like buttresses of a cathedral. Some were covered with a thick green moss that glowed a brilliant emerald when illuminated by a stray shaft of sunlight. Nikki wished she had her paints with her. She left the trail and climbed over a fallen log—a big "nurse" log—a giant that had been allowed to lie and now grew, on its decaying back, vegetation of all kinds, including young evergreens. Nikki had seen huge trees that stood on two "feet" with an opening underneath big enough for an animal or a child to crawl through—trees that had sprouted on just such a log and continued to grow there, straddling it, while the log decayed away, leaving the characteristic hole.

Nikki walked a bit farther to examine a huge stump. It looked like an idol from some lost civilization, with two black eyes staring at her. Nikki knew that the "eyes" were the result of the old logging method of cutting holes in the trunk of a tree and inserting wooden springboards for the "fallers" to stand on. The men worked in pairs, using a two-man saw to make the under-cut, then chopped out a wedge to determine the direction of the tree's fall. They would then saw from the other side of the tree, and it must have taken split-second timing to scramble off the springboards when the tree began to topple. There were several such stumps in the woods, their "eyes" hollow and dead. Nonetheless, the sense of being watched was very real to Nikki—by what? A cluster of gnomes? A vanish of Sasquatch?

Here there seemed to be no rabbits, or if there were, they would be the wild brown ones that were on the increase on the island. The Eagle Lake Park rabbits were a breed apart. It was interesting that one could virtually be wading in rabbits one minute, then quickly leave them behind on entering the trails. Nikki was musing on their absence as she returned to the needle-covered path. Animals seemed to have their own agenda, their own rituals, their own taboos, their own relationships—friendships, hatreds, pecking orders. Would we ever even come close to understanding them? She thought of Casimir, and of Bruno, and of Prince. *No, I think not.*

Nikki knew that if she continued on down the trail she would soon come to the edge of the wood, then into the open part of the campground where barbecue pits and rabbits abounded, but she was reluctant to leave the quiet sanctity of the forest. It was the first time Nikki had hiked the trail, at least all the way. Until now it had always been full of campers and hikers, and Nikki had avoided it. Now, off season, Nikki vowed to make this a regular part of her fitness routine, and, on impulse, decided to prolong her walk by exploring a little side trail that disappeared behind a clump of cedar trees.

The trail underfoot was a little rougher. Nikki had to step across tree roots and pick her way down over rocks as the path dipped sharply downward. *I'll have to get a walking stick!* The path continued on down, doubling back on itself in a hairpin turn. *I seem to be going down a sharp slope—which means I'll also have to climb it when I come back. Are my leg muscles in shape for this?* The path wound behind a large boulder and then leveled out. Nikki stopped to examine the rock, or, more accurately, the moss that covered it. There seemed to be several varieties of moss and lichen clinging to stone, and Nikki, once again, mentally mixed paints to reproduce their color.

Seen from the side, the stone seemed to have a profile—Nikki fancied it as an Indian chief with his bottom lip sticking out. From the front, the lip looked like a table—or an altar with moss as the altar cloth. *And if I back up a bit, the whole thing looks like*—Nikki took another step backwards, then gasped. She had felt something brush against her ankle, then encircle it, as if grasping it. By reflex action, she kicked out and pulled her foot free, then looked to see what she had stepped into. She would have screamed, then, if her voice hadn't failed her. It was a human hand!

Her heart pounding, Nikki looked to see that the hand belonged to a body stretched out on the ground, almost hidden by vegetation. Nikki's first impulse was to flee—run for her life—but something stopped her. What *was* this? Was it a drunk? Was he ill or injured? She realized that the sane thing to do would be to leave quickly and go for help, but Nikki also had the instincts of a writer, a recognition of the bizarre experience, and the curiosity that goes with it. Gently, she nudged the hand with her toe. It didn't move. "Sir? Do you need help?" *Dumb question but I have to say something.* The body was lying face down and did not appear to be moving *or breathing.* "Oh god, he's dead. I've found a dead body. *I've found a dead body!*"

Nikki leaned over and took hold of the hand. It was cold and Nikki could detect no pulse. She knelt down and pushed back fronds of fern. *I guess I should try CPR—if I can just remember how to do it.* But it was obviously too late. She saw that the man was beyond resuscitation, and, to her horror, she recognized him. It was Raymond Cantwell.

CHAPTER 19

STUNNED AND disbelieving, Nikki knelt by the body of Raymond Cantwell. There seemed to be no hurry now about getting help; poor Raymond was beyond it. It was all so surreal—like a dream with none of the rational reference points of normalcy. Raymond Cantwell! How had he died? Had he fallen, slipped on the steep trail? Had he tumbled off the rock? If so, wouldn't he have been at the foot of it instead of a few yards away?

Raymond was wearing tan trousers, a long-sleeved flannel shirt and leather hiking boots. His body was lying prone, his head turned to the right, eyes open, staring glassily, with his mouth open and drawn back, much as Einar Kuusisto's had been. His clothing was stained by bodily fluids and fecal matter—the purging of a body after death. Had he had a heart attack? Was his face frozen in a grimace of pain or in the final scream of a man falling to his death? What had he been doing here? Had Adelaide sent him on an errand—perhaps to take something to the dump—and had he been taking the long way back? Or had Raymond Cantwell been wandering around at night again, on some mission or his own? And why was he almost hidden under ferns and shrubbery? Had he crawled? If so, he must have been crawling toward the trail, not away from it. One hand was extended—the one Nikki had stepped into—as if he had been reaching. *I don't know what killed you, knock-knock Raymond. Accident? Two accidents in two days? If it wasn't an accident, then something or someone did this.* Nikki glanced around and a shiver went through her body. *And maybe I'd best get my ass out of here. There may be more things watching me than the stump idols.*

Nikki emerged from the forest, shaken. She knew she would have to report what she had found, then most likely be questioned by authorities and forced to give a statement. Well, might as well get it over with. She went to Adelaide's but Adelaide was still not at home. Prince was still patrolling the yard. What should she do? Should she call the police herself? Yes, she supposed so, although she instinctively knew that Adelaide would resent that, as if by reporting the death directly, Nikki would be going over Adelaide's territorial head. Perhaps she should go to the senior Moons—Hector and Ida. Let *them* call 911. *To do that, I'd have to go all the way back to the lake. I know! I'll tell the Crushills. Paulette and Fred. Fred was the dead-rabbit-picker-upper and Paulette is Adelaide's number two dogsbody—number one, now that Raymond is gone.*

As she passed her own unit, Nikki was tempted to go straight home, make a soothing cup of tea, and let someone else find the body on the forest floor. She hated the thought of being questioned by police and maybe even ending up on the six o'clock news. Marj had once said that she had trouble with authority; Nikki did too. Whether interrogated by her sharp-tongued fifth grade teacher, a customs agent at a border crossing, or even quizzed by a popular opinion poll, Nikki, who never had anything to hide, always feared she would say something stupid or incriminating that would get her into trouble. *If I just go home and pretend nothing's happened, they'll surely find my sneaker prints in a bit of mud at the scene, and then I'll get accused of doing in poor old Raymond. Why did I have to pick this day to go exploring in the woods?*

At least someone was home at the Crushills. Pierre, the poodle, sounded the alarm as Nikki approached. Paulette opened the door. "Oh, hello, Nikki. Come on in. Never mind Pierre—*quiet, Pierre!*—don't worry, he won't bite. Come in and sit down. I just put on a pot of coffee." Paulette looked at Nikki sharply. "Is something wrong?"

"Yes, Mrs. Crushill. There is. Is your husband home? I'd like to talk to both of you. I need your advice."

"Fred's not here right now. He went to get his band saw from the shed. He should be back in a few minutes, though, unless he's found someone to chat with. We're all so upset about poor Mr. Kuusisto. You'll be going to the funeral, won't you?"

"Yes. Yes I suppose so, but I'm afraid I have some more bad news." Nikki went on to tell Paulette about Raymond Cantwell.

Paulette, mouth agape, headed for the door, opened it and yelled, "Fred! Fred Crushill!" She got no reply and Nikki watched her pick up an object from the top of the refrigerator. It was a large cowbell. She opened the door again and vigorously shook the bell up and down. The noise was deafening. "That'll bring him home!"

From Ethiopia, Nikki thought.

"You poor little thing! What a terrible experience for you." Paulette poured Nikki a cup of coffee. "Here, drink this."

The door opened. "Goddamit, Paulette, I'm gonna throw that perishin' bell into Eagle Lake. I've told you never to ring it unless you're in trouble." Fred Crushill noticed Nikki. "Oh."

"Stop your fussing, Fred. There's *big* trouble."

Sitting in Fred and Paulette's tiny living room with its overstuffed, antimacassared furniture, Nikki, sipping hot coffee, felt relieved. She felt like a kid again with the Crushills *in loco parentis*—wise adults who would know what to do in a crisis.

"You say you found him in the camp area, off the main trail?"

"Yes, it was near campsite number three," Nikki said, surprised, herself, that she remembered that. "There's a little path that goes down the hill and around a big rock. I stopped to look at the rock, and when I backed up to get a better view I nearly stepped on Mr. Cantwell. I wouldn't have seen him otherwise. He was hidden under a lot of ferns and stuff. I guess we should call the police." Nobody had ever referred to Raymond as Mr. Cantwell, but it seemed, to Nikki, more respectful of the dead.

"Yes, of course. But first we should let the Moons know. It's their park."

"I was going to tell Mrs. Moon—Adelaide—but nobody was home. Just Prince."

"I think I should go take a look—and maybe Adelaide will be back by now. Maybe we should all go."

"Not me, Fred. My old knees won't go down *that* trail anymore."

"Very well, Paulette. Nikki and I will go. You can show me the exact spot—that is if you feel up to it. I know you must be upset, so if you don't want to come, I'm sure I can find it myself. Sounds like altar rock."

"That's okay, I don't mind." *The way things are going around here, it might be safer to use the buddy system.*

Nikki and Fred could see, as they went by, that nobody was home at the Moon house. The dog was still in the yard and the vehicles were missing. "Do you think we should go over and notify Hector and Ida?" Nikki asked.

"Let's not upset the old folks. I want to see this for myself. If Adelaide's not home by time we get back, I'll call the authorities."

This is good, Nikki thought. Fred's presence diffused responsibility and diluted the enormity. *This way I won't be the only one to have seen the body.*

"I didn't see any of these rabbits in the woods although they're all over the place out here." Nikki remarked, just to have something to say. Their silent trek reminded her uncomfortably of times in her childhood when she had led a disgruntled parent to the site of some minor disaster, like the time her bike had rolled into the river and she had to get her father to pull it out.

"Damn fool critters. Dig everything up. Nearly broke my ankle steppin' in one of their holes yesterday. Oughta barbecue the lot of 'em." Fred, it seemed, was not a rabbit lover.

"Where did they come from?"

"Don't know for sure, but there's a story about this bein' an old rabbit farm. Guess a few of 'em got loose. That's all it takes! They've been here longer than I have—longer than the Moons even."

"I thought I'd see a lot of them in the woods, but I didn't."

"These rabbits are tame. Least they started out bein' tame. They hang around the campground because that's where everyone feeds 'em."

"I don't know much about rabbits, but these seem to be kind of weird. They sure were acting wild the night of the storm—jumping, fighting, chasing each other."

"Wild hares do that in their spring mating season. Saw 'em once, in a field in England. Not this time of year, though. Anyhow, they're a different animal."

"Hares and rabbits? How are they different? They look pretty much the same, don't they?"

"Hares have longer back legs. Their coats change color in the winter. They don't live in burrows, like rabbits. The leverets—" he glanced at Nikki, "baby hares are called leverets, are born with fur and can take care of themselves right away. Rabbit kittens are born naked and helpless in burrows."

"I haven't seen any burrows, but there are plenty of places where they've scooped up holes in the ground. And I've never seen any baby rabbits."

"Hm. Neither have I, come to think of it, but they must be breeding. I think they make burrows along the edge of the bluff or just inside the woods. Lots of eagles around, so the kits would have to be kept out of sight. I you look carefully, you'll see that some of the rabbits are smaller. They'd be the young ones."

"I wonder what's been killing them."

"Dog, I'd say."

"Prince?"

"Wouldn't put it past him."

"Do you think he can jump over that fence? He scared me when I went for the mail. That's why I cut back through the woods. He was acting crazy."

"Lot of that goin' around lately."

"But if Prince jumped the fence and killed the rabbits, he'd have been stuck *outside* the fence, wouldn't he? They'd have found him out on the grounds, wouldn't they? They'd have known it was Prince that killed them."

Fred considered this a moment, then shook his head. "Not necessarily. Prince could've slipped into George's shop when George took the truck out early in the morning. Adelaide would've thought that either Clark or George put him in there for the night."

They'd left the rabbits behind and were approaching Campsite Three. Nikki didn't need to point out the trail, Fred seemed to know exactly where to turn off. With surprising agility for a man his age, he descended the slope and followed the path to the curve around the rock, and, in fact, walked right to Raymond Cantwell's body.

It was lying just as Nikki had left it. Fred bent down to examine it. "Been dead awhile. Looks like *rigor mortis* has come and gone." He turned Raymond Cantwell on his side, noted discoloration of the left side of the face. "Lividity. Blood drains down and puddles under the skin."

"He looks like he might have been crawling toward the path." Nikki said.

Fred straightened up. "Yeah. Or maybe something or somebody

dragged him *away* from the path. Dragged him by the feet. Concealed him in the underbrush."

Nikki hadn't thought of that. "But—but who would *do* such a thing? And *why?*"

"I don't know. Don't know what killed him. Probably nobody. Could be he just had an accident—or a heart attack. He could've fallen into the underbrush and been trying to crawl onto the trail. Medical examiner will probably do an autopsy. Nothing more we can do here. We'll go back and report it."

Nikki had been staring at Raymond Cantwell, remembering that the last time she had seen him was when they were all searching for Einar Kuusisto. *Poor old knock-knock Raymond. Psychic? Synesthete? Oddball. What nightly ritual brought you into the light of the moon? Did you die in the night—and, if so, how?* It was then Nikki noticed something she hadn't seen before. Raymond had been lying with his left arm extended and the other screened by vegetation. Now that Fred had partially turned him over, the right arm and hand were visible, and Nikki noticed that the right hand was missing the index finger—not the entire finger, but the first two phalanges. *Creepy! I never noticed Raymond had a missing finger. Or maybe it happened after he died. Did something come along and take a bite out of him?* It didn't look like a raw wound; the finger just seemed not to be there. *Wonder what the medical examiner will make of it.* For some reason, Nikki didn't mention it to Fred; all she wanted to do was get out of there.

CHAPTER 20

WHEN NIKKI and Fred came out of the woods to Barkell road, they saw that Adelaide Moon had still not returned. Fred went home and called the police. Adelaide arrived later, accompanied by her son, Clark, and by Marj, to find, yet again, emergency vehicles and police cars in Eagle Lake Park. Nikki was questioned, but, to her relief, not thrust in a starring role. Fred Crushill offered his measured opinion as to time of death, explaining, when asked whether he had a background in medicine, that he had been in Korea. If anyone ended up on the six o'clock news it would be Adelaide. Her performance of shock and grief and outrage would have won her an Oscar.

Nikki and Marj had edged away as soon as they could, to talk the matter over privately in Nikki's living room. It was mid-afternoon— too late for lunch (which Nikki had skipped), too early for dinner. "I think we could use a cup of tea." Nikki said.

Marj nodded wordlessly and Nikki went on to also arrange a little tray of cheeses with crackers and salmon paté. "You probably haven't eaten anything at all. Better have a nibble."

Marj was sitting on the couch with Casimir who, now the devoted pet, lay with his head on her knee. She took a sip of tea, looked at Nikki and said, "I think we should all be running for our lives."

"I guess we all feel that way. When you said something godawful was going to happen, you weren't kidding!"

"It's not over yet."

Nikki started to say something reassuring, then changed her mind. "What do you know that I don't?"

"I don't *know* anything. It's a feeling. Have you ever seen a tornado?"

"No."

"It's not like a regular storm. The atmosphere turns thick and yellow and you feel the terror in your gut, and you know that if that thing comes at you, you might as well lean over and kiss your ass good-bye. That's the feeling. Something is stalking Eagle Lake Park. So far it's swallowed two people, but it's still hungry. We're all terrified, and I think it's starting to drive us all out of our minds. We're starting to have weird thoughts and impulses to do desperate things—alien things. Things we'd never think of on our own. You know what I thought today? *Anybody here could've killed Raymond Cantwell, and you know why?*"

Chilled, Nikki said no.

"Because you don't need a reason if you're crazy. And it's like all of Eagle Lake is on its way to becoming psychotic. People are reacting—I should say overreacting—like Adelaide this afternoon. Like everyone did at Adelaide's coffee. It's like we're all headed for a nervous breakdown—even the animals. Did you see Prince today? It's only the beginning, and if we stay here we'll all go bonkers."

"God, Marj. I'm sorry I asked! Okay, I've noticed the weirdness too, but we don't know that anybody *was* killed. I'll bet the autopsy shows Raymond Cantwell either had an MI or fell off the rock."

"Or committed suicide. What was he doing in the park in the middle of the night? And what sent my father over the edge? What are the chances of two people dying like that? And who'll be next? You know who it's going be? "

"No, do *you?*"

"The next person who starts showing unusual behavior! It could be me. It could be you. I notice you did a painting of Boston Charlie. Look at it! Is that your usual style? It doesn't look like Boston Charlie either. It looks like his evil twin—and it looks like you painted him when he was moving."

"Yeah, well I guess it's not a very good still life."

They both laughed, then, and the tension lifted. Marj sipped her tea. "I seem to be doing a wonderful impression of my grandma Kuusisto, peace be on her. Talk about the voice of doom! She was a Finnish Lapp, you know. Tiny little thing. Less than five feet tall. Lapps are like gnomes—and they're magic. They can see things. My grandmother would put on a pot of coffee and say, so-and-so is coming over for a visit, and sure enough, by time the coffee was brewed, that person would show up. I asked her how she knew, and she said she could see his *etiäinen*—his forerunner. She said if you *think* of a place, or you're *going* to a place, you send out a mental picture of yourself that precedes you. Most people can't see them but Lapps can."

"That's *so cool!* Have *you* ever seen one? I mean, you're part Lapp."

"No. At least not yet. I asked my grandmother why I couldn't see them and she said I was too young. She said I'd need to grow in age and wisdom and I'd have to have—oh dear, what was that word—*valaistus?* I gather it meant some sort of epiphany or illumination."

"I envy you your relationship with your grandmother. Mine lives in Lantana, Florida. I've only seen her once when the family took a guilt trip to visit her. We didn't hit it off. I was fourteen. To her I was an obnoxious teenager who didn't speak Finnish, and, to me, she was a crotchety old lady who lived in a stiflingly hot house, spoke broken English, and disapproved of everything. I always think of her when I see stale bread. She had a waste not, want not ethic. She'd buy fresh bread but we always had to finish the *old* bread before we could eat the fresh. As result, the fresh bread became stale before we were allowed to touch it. We spent a month eating stale bread."

"Bit of a culture gap."

"Yes, but I still have the uncomfortable feeling that the loss is mine."

"Maybe you should try contacting her while you can still do it without an Ouija board."

"Yeah."

Marj got up to go. "Your parole is up. I can take Casimir off your hands." The cat had awakened and was stretching his legs.

"It's your call—and your cat—but he seems comfortable here, if you'd like to leave him until after the funeral. We can haul back all of his stuff then and you won't have to worry about him destroying your plants while you're out."

"Well, okay, thanks. I'm surprised he seems to be leaving *your* plants alone."

"He took a couple of swipes at Charlie when he first got here—and got whacked in the nose by a flying frond. Maybe that's all it takes. You want to come over for dinner later?"

"I'd *love* to but I can't. Adelaide invited me and I couldn't very well refuse. I'll be dining with the Moons. I only hope they lock up that crazy dog. He threatened to tear me to pieces today."

"Yes, me too." Nikki saw Marj out. *And if it hadn't been for Prince, I'd never have walked through the woods, and Raymond Cantwell would probably still be lying there until somebody noticed him missing. I wonder if anyone noticed the missing finger. Einar Kuusisto got his thumb bitten and ended up dead. Raymond Cantwell ended up dead with a missing finger.* Nikki looked at Casimir. "Tell me, my dear Watson, what does that suggest to you? Not a thing? Me neither."

...

Nikki prepared for a quiet evening at home—her last with Casimir. She served him a dish of Moist & Tasty beef dinner with a side order of Crunchy Bits and a bowl of tepid water, then prepared a salad and a glass of milk for herself. Nikki was beginning to realize that she was going to miss Casimir. She gave him a pat and cupped his chin with her hand: "I guess I've grown accustomed to your face."

Casimir pulled loose. The cat seemed restless. He ate only part of his dinner, and afterwards, when Nikki tried to brush him, he sprang off the couch as if to say, no time for that now, and took up his favorite position facing Boston Charlie. Then, moments later, he got to his feet and began pacing again.

"What's the matter, Cas?" Nikki checked his litter box. "Pristine, Your Highness. Ready for your use if that's your problem. Or are you just having yourself a jitter?"

Nikki felt a little jittery herself. She closed the curtains against the gathering darkness, and turned on the TV. She'd missed the six o'clock news, went on to watch part of *Wheel of Fortune*, then *Jeopardy*. She couldn't get interested in the fact-based TV movie, and found she had already seen the episode of *Home Improvement*, so she opted for a *Nature* documentary on the Arctic, but soon turned off the set. She wondered what sort of evening Marj was having with the Moons, and wondered who else would be there—Paulette and Fred, probably, and Clark and Shelley. Bob and Janet weren't at home but Nikki knew they'd gone into town to spend the evening with Janet's folks. Hector and Ida would be at Adelaide's, maybe even the Hatches and the Laderheims. It would be a "happy family" gathering.

Nikki had not been invited. Nikki had committed a *faux pas* by discovering Raymond Cantwell's body. Nikki knew it that afternoon when Adelaide had looked at her with such hostility that it could only be described as hatred—a hatred that had no reason and knew none. Nikki had seen that look before. All gays have seen it—the mindless, fanatical surge of odium reserved strictly for those whose sexual orientation is not straight and narrow. Rapists, child-molesters, serial killers may be viewed with fear, disapproval, sometimes even compassion. But gays, in some members of our society, trigger a hatred that can only have been forged in Hell. Too often it occurs in their own families. *I wonder if she's found out I'm a lesbian. Maybe Marj let something slip. Or maybe she just hates me because she knows Marj and I are friends. Maybe she thinks I'm a bad influence on her little girl, what with wandering through woods and tripping over bodies. She looked at me as if I'd killed Raymond, and as if Raymond's death was a direct attack on her. Well, I guess she felt she owned him. Yep, Adelaide, we're just one big happy family here in Eagle Lake Park.*

It was then she heard the shots. The sound, though some distance away, made Nikki jump, and startled Casimir so that he dove under the couch where he turned himself into a trembling ball of fur. *What the hell?* Nikki opened the curtains and switched off the light. She could see nothing. She went outside and stood on the deck where she could hear men's voices in the distance. *Ah, I'll bet there's a patrol to protect us all—but who will protect us from trigger-happy nitwits firing guns in the dark! What were they shooting at? Some poor animal, most likely.* Nikki hoped that the orange tomcat was safe in his barn. She went back inside. *Not a good night to be out. Not when the good people of Eagle Lake Park are having a* Lord of the Flies *moment.*

Nikki coaxed Casimir out from under the couch with a handful of Kitty Treats and an onion skin. She'd discovered that Casimir loved chewing on the dry outer skins of onions—the crackly sensation of his cat teeth puncturing parchment. When Nikki had hit on the idea of giving him onion skins, Casimir had stopped perforating her puzzle roughs. Tonight, though, Casimir seemed preoccupied.

He barely nibbled the Kitty Treat, ignored the onion skin, and when Nikki reached over to give him a reassuring pat, the cat responded by uttering a sharp *grreow* and took a swipe at her hand with his claw.

"Hey! Watch it, Cas. What *is* the matter with you tonight?"

Casimir gave Nikki a baleful look and backed away. Nikki watched him go stand next to Boston Charlie, as if listening. It reminded Nikki of Raymond Cantwell—Raymond Cantwell who claimed he could hear the plant "sing home" and "sing death." Could Casimir hear it too? The cat certainly looked as if he were hearing something. Somewhere Nikki had read that cats can hear sounds that humans cannot—the way dogs hear a dog whistle. What was Casimir picking up on whenever he stationed himself in front of the fern? And that night, the night she'd seen Raymond Cantwell in the moonlight, was Raymond hearing it then? Had the rabbits heard it too? Had the orange tom heard it? Had Prince? How far did it carry? Nikki tried, straining, to hear something—anything—but no, she couldn't.

She looked hard at Casimir. Whatever the cat was hearing was having an effect on him. Normally Casimir was content to sit and stare at the plant, but tonight the cat was reacting differently. He seemed to crouch as if to spring—or was he poised to flee? It was almost as though he wanted to escape, but was, by something, held fast. The hair on his back rose slowly to a ridge and his ears flattened. His eyes were open, pupils full and black and staring. Whatever Casimir was hearing was frightening him. Then as if with an effort, the cat sprang free and bounded down the hall into Nikki's bedroom. *Well, I wonder what that was all about.*

Nikki saw that Marj's lights were on. She picked up the phone and dialed. "What's with the shooting? It's too late for Fourth of July and too early for Halloween."

"Oh, that was probably Clark Moon and Walter Hatch. Somebody found more dead rabbits at the other end of the campground, and with this business of Raymond Cantwell, Adelaide wants the park patrolled all night. The guys are pairing up and taking turns."

"Not the women?"

"No, and I wasn't about to start pushing equal rights."

"Hey, I *enjoy* being a girl! What were they shooting at?"

"I don't know but I wouldn't want to be out there tonight."

"So how was the evening? Did everyone except muggins here turn up?"

"It was just the Moons and me—at first. Then, after dinner, Fred and Paulette showed up and Justin Laderheim and Walter Hatch. Adelaide had arranged it. She ran the show, as usual, but the woman seemed near hysterical. Kept bursting into tears. I wondered if she'd been drinking. Guess she was really upset about Raymond. *Strange* vibes all evening."

"Was the dog still on a rampage or had he calmed down?"

"Prince? Oh god, that animal's vicious! I don't know what's wrong with him. He actually tried to attack *Clark*. George had to drag him out and lock him up in his shop."

"Sounds like the social event of the season."

"In a week full of funerals it was right up there."

CHAPTER 21

THE DAY of Einar Kuusisto's funeral dawned gray and rainy. Nikki, who had slept badly, awakened feeling stiff and out of sorts. She fed Casimir, who'd had a restless night as well, alternately prowling and galloping through the house. Nikki assumed it to be a house cat's way of getting exercise, but why did he have to do it at three in the morning?

Nikki had never been to a funeral, didn't know what she should wear. The weather decided it: gray skirt and sweater, matching boots, gray trench coat and Irish tweed hat. Her outfit would be understated and practical, considering the drizzle. Marj was being chauffeured by the Moons so Nikki had to go alone. She drove to Madrona Memorial Park and, at a quarter to one, parked her truck in the lot.

It was to be a simple graveside service, and Nikki was one of the first to arrive. Madrona Memorial Park was a wide expanse of lawn studded with massive junipers and the arbutus trees that had given the park its name. No headstones impeded the work of mowing the lawn, and most graves were clustered in family groupings, each designated by a flat metal marker and a small vase recessed into the ground into which flowers might be placed. Within these groupings the sizes of the plots varied depending on whether the interment had been a casket or an urn of ashes. Unused to cemeteries, Nikki, wandering among them, idly and naively wondered if they were the graves of children or midgets.

Einar's last resting place, freshly dug, stood empty. Beside it was a mound of earth covered by a sheet of green Astroturf. Cars began arriving. A few people straggled into the park, greeted each other, exchanged comments about the weather, then walked around, visiting familiar and unfamiliar graves, reading inscriptions, remembering, explaining. "Oh yes, he was Julianna Morgan's son. Died when he was only sixteen," Paulette Crushill was telling Louise Hatch. "You remember Julianna. She used to be a nurse at the hospital." Then, in a whisper, "The boy was retarded, you know, and sickly. One operation after another. His death was a mercy." Finally the hearse pulled up and everyone gathered. The coffin, a cheap cloth-covered gray casket, was carried out by the pallbearers—George Moon and his son, Clark, Justin Laderheim, Walter Hatch, Fred Crushill and Hector Moon—and positioned over the grave on straps.

A minister delivered a short religious message, than offered a few remarks about Einar Kuusisto's life—remarks obviously gleaned from scanty sources and delivered by one who had never met the deceased. Somewhere in the distance, a bagpiper played *Amazing Grace*, and Nikki found that cliché strangely affecting. With a handful of sand, the minister traced a tiny cross at the head of the coffin. There was no symbolic partial lowering of the casket. Mourners formed a line and filed by, each touching the coffin in passing in a gesture of farewell, some leaving a single flower, a sprig of evergreen or a leaf upon the lid. It made Nikki think of a documentary she had seen about African elephants who made a ritual of touching the bones of a dead comrade, sometimes picking them up and carrying them some distance before dropping them.

Then it was over. Nikki regarded the raggle-taggle group. She need not have worried about what to wear; there seemed to be no dress code. Paulette had on a floral print dress under a thick Cowichan sweater; Clark Moon, with his hair in a pony tail, wore blue jeans and sneakers. Louise Hatch stood thin and straight in a red wool coat, and Ida Moon was clad in a house dress and loafers over which she had thrown a plastic rain cape. Marj had on a raincoat buttoned to her chin. It had not rained during the service, but a cool mist made the air dank and chilly.

Then, with more than a slight chill, Nikki recognized one other figure on the edge of the group—a woman so smartly dressed in black that she looked totally out of place—Phillida Lowry! *Oh, my god. Phil. What's* she *doing here!* Nikki had the urge to turn and run—get into her Mazda and peel out of there. Too late. Of *course* Phil had seen her. How long had she been there, watching her? Phil was heading toward her now, her face a Kabuki mask of sympathy. At the same time Nikki felt a hand touch her arm. It was Marj. "Can I ride back with you?"

Before Nikki had a chance to say yes, Phil was upon them. "You must be Marj. Nikki has told me so much about you. I'm so very sorry about your father." Phil extended her hand, and pulled the slightly surprised Marj into what, for Phil, served as a hug—a symbolic gesture of embrace she somehow managed with a minimum of physical contact. She then turned to Nikki. "Such a sad occasion." She did the hug thing again, and in so doing, whispered in Nikki's ear. "I have the IDC banner in the trunk of my car. You can put it in your truck or I'll follow you home and drop it off."

The absurdity of it almost made Nikki laugh out loud. This was *so Phil.* Nikki gave Phil's shoulder a pat as she disengaged, only to find herself looking into the penetrating eyes of Adelaide Moon. "Nikki, Marj, I don't believe I've met your friend."

Nikki glanced at Marj but read nothing in her expression. *What* was I expecting to see? *"I told her you were a lesbian" flashing on and off on her forehead like the time and temperature sign on the bank building?* "Oh, Adelaide, I'd like you to meet Phillida Lowry. Phillida is head of the Institute for the Developmentally Challenged, and was helping Marj get her father situated before all this happened. Phillida, this is Adelaide Moon, the owner of Eagle Lake Park."

"So happy to meet you," Phil said and extended a gloved hand.

Somehow conveying surly suspicion in her broad smile, Adelaide touched hands briefly. "Likewise." Adelaide's eyes took in Phillida's expensive pantsuit and accessories. "You're not from around here, are you?"

"A transplanted easterner," Phil smiled. She, in turn, took measure of Adelaide's brown slacks and wool plaid jacket, nicotine stained teeth and lank hair, with the imperturbable politeness of a mission-ary meeting a naked savage. "I understand Eagle Lake Park is lovely. Nikki was fortunate to find such a beautiful spot after—"

"*Yes!*" Nikki leapt in. "And you'll be seeing it very soon. Marj and I will be heading back *right now*, and you can follow us."

"Oh, is Marj riding back with you?" Adelaide asked. "Well, all right then, we can all meet at my place for coffee and sandwiches. Of course you'll come too, Miss Lowry."

"Oh, I'm not sure—ah, well, perhaps for just a moment." Phil was being ushered away bodily by Nikki.

...

"So *that* was Phil," Marj said as they drove back to Eagle Lake Park. "Stylish! But isn't she quite a bit older than you?"

"And a lot richer." Nikki could see Phil's new gleaming silver Volvo in her rearview mirror.

"Good-looking woman. Self-assured. Accustomed to command."

"*Born* to it. That was part of the problem."

"Yeah, I can see how it would be. Not too different from Jonah and me. He didn't show up for the funeral—but he did leave a deeply caring message on my machine: 'Marj. Sorry about your dad, but you know how I am about funerals. The only one I'll go to is my own. Call you later.'"

Nikki drove past the Moons to her own place and parked the truck. Phil pulled in behind her into the small parking area. "We'll unload the banner first." Nikki said to Marj. "It'll give Phil a chance to exit gracefully before we go to the Moons."

But Phil seemed in no hurry to leave, and Nikki was beginning to wonder if the banner hadn't been an excuse to come check out Nikki's new domain. "Well, since you're here, come on in and see my new digs."

Casimir greeted them at the door. Phil gave the animal a look of genteel horror. "Oh, of course, that's your cat, isn't it, Marj? Still here, I see. I haven't been near one in years. I'm allergic to animals." Casimir gave her an appraising look, then retired under the couch.

"Shall we all sit down for a moment," Nikki said, a bit awkwardly. The old Nikki would have scurried to catch Casimir and lock him up in a bedroom. Early in their relationship, Nikki had discovered that any animal Phil was not allergic *to*, she had a phobia *of*. It had been Nikki's province to try to rid the yard of snakes, frogs and spiders, warn all visitors not to bring their pets, and always stand ready to position her own body between Phil and any approaching stray dog. Now Phil's allergy might work in Nikki's favor. If she started sneezing, she would surely go home. If that didn't work, Nikki had an ace up her sleeve.

"You have a very nice view here," Phil was saying as if trying to find something to compliment. "And look at all the bunny rabbits. It's really quite charming for a mobile home park." She glanced around the room. "I love what you've done to the place." Phil was using her insincere voice.

Her mouth is on automatic pilot and her brain is taking photos. I wonder what her agenda is. "We're all expected at Adelaide Moon's," Nikki said, pausing to give Phil a chance to make her excuses.

"I suppose I really *ought* to be getting back," Phil said slowly, glancing at her watch, "but maybe—"

"Oh, I'm *sure* you'd enjoy meeting the Moon family—of course I should warn you that Adelaide has a large dog—a Great Dane. His name is Prince, and when he jumps up on you, all you have to do is tell him to get down. Adelaide says he never bites."

"—ah, maybe—maybe another time." Phil got up to go. As if having waited for just the right moment, Casimir emerged from under the couch, walked up to Phil and rubbed up against her leg, leaving a skim of white hair on her black slacks. Phil left.

Everyone had arrived at Adelaide's by time Nikki and Marj got there. Bob and Janet were missing. They hadn't been at the funeral; they had not returned the night before. Nikki guessed they were staying in town with Janet's family—a lucky escape for Bob, as he would miss taking part in the all-night patrol. The group was subdued as they drank coffee and helped themselves to a lunch of deviled eggs, ham sandwiches and chocolate layer cake prepared by Paulette Crushill and Ida Moon. It had been Einar Kuusisto's funeral, but it was the ghost of Raymond Cantwell that cast a pall over the gathering.

"Did they ever determine the cause of death?" Nikki asked Paulette.

"They say it was a brain tumor. Nobody knew he had one. Killed him instantly," Paulette told her.

"Natural causes, then." Nikki felt a small sense of relief. At least no one had done him in. "I guess we'll be going to another funeral."

"Adelaide says not. He'll be cremated and there won't be a service. Raymond had no family."

With the ashes buried in unhallowed ground, as a witch's familiar? Nikki thought. *Or maybe it's too much of an expense—or too much of an anticlimax.*

"Your *friend* didn't come after all?" Adelaide had joined them and was addressing Nikki.

"Phil asked me to convey her thanks for the invitation, but she had to get back to the Institute. She said to tell you she enjoyed meeting you and looks forward to seeing you again soon." *Snapping to grid again. How often had Nikki smoothed over, made excuses, bought the gift, sent the card, acted as diplomat?*

"Interesting woman," Adelaide said. "*Close* friend of yours?"

"Yes." Nikki could feel herself beginning to bristle. This was like being questioned by a suspicious parent.

"I understand the two of you used to live together."

How would she know that? "I don't remember mentioning that."

"No, I don't suppose you would." Adelaide's eyes were leaden and her mouth an ugly line.

Paulette had been standing next to them, glancing from one to the other. Now she grabbed Nikki by the arm and steered her away from Adelaide. "Better not talk to her when she gets like this."

"I don't understand. The woman seems to hate me. And what business is it of hers how I live my life?"

"Adelaide is—Adelaide. Her park, her rules. She's upset because she thinks you and Phil Lowry are gay."

"You mean lesbians. And how would she know that?"

"She doesn't *know* anything. She only suspects. When you moved to Eagle Lake Park she did some checking, got your old address and learned you'd shared it with a Phil Lowry. Naturally she thought you'd been living with a man. *That* she could forgive."

"And where does that old woman get off *forgiving* me? She's not my mother and she's not the boss of me." *When was the last time I used that expression? When I was twelve?*

"All I'm saying, Nikki, is that if you're wondering why Adelaide is acting like she is, that's the reason. I've known Adelaide Moon for a long time. She's not an easy person to like, but she's not as bad as she seems. It's just that lately—well," Paulette's voice dropped to a whisper, "don't tell her I told you, but she's going through menopause—mood swings—and now, of course, she's upset about Raymond. Give her some time."

Nikki was still seething when she and Marj walked back together. "That miserable witch! What the hell does that sanctimonious old mother—uh—obscenity—"

"*Surrogate* mother-obscenity," Marj said. "You know, that's why she drives us crazy. Some part of her really reminds us of our mothers!"

"*I'm* getting the hell out of this park as soon as I find another place. I wonder how much it costs to move a mobile home."

"Might be better just to sell it. It's pretty old. Could fall apart."

"And have to have Adelaide's approval of the sale? I'd sooner set fire to it."

Marj changed the subject. "I guess you heard the latest on Raymond Cantwell."

"Natural causes and no funeral. Paulette told me."

"Did you hear about Prince?"

"No. Where *was* he anyway?"

"Prince, as they say, is no longer with us."

"What happened?"

"You remember those shots we heard last night?"

"Somebody accidentally shot the *dog?*"

"It was no accident. The dog went mad. Yesterday he would've attacked me if there hadn't been a fence between us, and last night he would've bitten Clark if George hadn't pulled him away. George had to shoot him."

"Just like you said. You did say that the next one to go would be the one who shows unusual behavior. I didn't think of Prince, but he sure scared me when I went by yesterday. Speaking of animals acting funny, Casimir was in a weird mood last night. He kept pacing around, and when I tried to pat him, he took a swipe at me."

"Oh, that's not unusual. I could show you scars. Cas has a long list of things he hates—going to the vet, getting his nails trimmed, being left alone, *not* being left alone, being picked up, *not* being picked up, being brushed, *not* being brushed, loud noises like thunder and gunshots. The shots probably spooked him."

"I suppose that was it." Nikki decided not to mention Boston Charlie.

"Anyway, it's time for little boo-boo to come home to mama."

Casimir showed nothing but indifference to being moved back to Marj's. "You know, I'll miss the little critter," Nikki said, as she carried the litter box. It took the two of them to transport Casimir's life support system—bowls, cat toys, kitty litter, grooming tools and food—all things that had migrated to Nikki's during Casimir's visit. Marj carried the cat in her arms and set him gently on the floor. Casimir glanced around briefly as if to say, I see nothing's changed, then began a leisurely stroll through the house.

"He didn't even say good-bye," Nikki said.

"Humbling, isn't it? If you want rejection, get a cat."

The phone rang. Marj picked it up, rolled her eyes and gestured to Nikki that she should stay. "Yes, it was a lovely funeral. You'd have enjoyed it Jonah, specially the part where we all kissed the corpse on the lips. No, I am *not* grief-stricken and yes, I *am* being unseemly. This is the new me. Or should I say, this is the *old* me—the one who doesn't give a crap about *what* you think."

Nikki listened, a bit wistfully. How long before she'd be able to talk to Phil that way?

"What, exactly, is it you want of me, Jonah? I keep getting these little cryptic messages. Is there some irregularity in one of our old tax returns? Can't you find your monogrammed cufflinks? *Trust* me, Jonah, *whatever* it is, you *can* tell me on the phone, goddamit. Whatever your little game is, I don't have the time or inclination to play."

Nikki had quietly taken a seat in Marj's living room. Casimir, finished with his tour of inspection, joined her, jumped onto the couch and climbed into Nikki's lap where he rubbed his whiskers against Nikki's caressing hand and purred his sputtering purr. Nikki became aware that Marj had gone silent on the phone. She looked up. Marj's expression was unreadable as she slowly hung up the receiver.

"Is something wrong, Marj?"

"Yes. And I don't know how to handle it."

"Jonah wants to get back together again."

"Not that simple." Marj's eyes filled with tears.

"Oh my god, Marj. What *is* it?" Nikki always felt ill-at-ease with raw emotions. She envied people with the instinctive ability to comfort others. Nikki felt that she did not *hug* well, and tended to stammer banalities that left her squirming with embarrassment, later, when she remembered what it was she *had* said. It was worse than *esprit de l'escalier*—when you think of all those brilliant *bon mots* as you're leaving via the staircase.

Marj waved a hand as if to say, just give me a minute. Nikki did the practical thing and fetched her a box of tissues from the bathroom, then put the kettle on for tea. Marj dried her eyes and blew her nose. "I didn't expect to react that way." Nikki said nothing, just waited. "That, of course, was Jonah. He's been saying he wants us to talk. He didn't want to tell me over the phone, but I goaded him into it. He's ill. He's going to die."

"*What?*"

"AIDS."

"Good god, does that mean—uh, how long has he had it?"

"HIV? I don't know. Neither does he."

"Is it full blown AIDS or just HIV?"

"I'm not sure. He says he's been in the hospital. That may be why I didn't hear from him. He says he's not working. I don't know whether that means he quit, lost his job or can't work."

"And he needs your help."

"Yes."

"And he'll get it?"

"Yes."

"He should have told you as soon as he found out. The bastard should have *told* you."

"Yes."

"It doesn't mean you have it, Marj. Get tested as soon as you can. Put your mind at ease. What are you going to do?"

"Right now, nothing. But I have to make decisions. I need more information. I'll have to go see him. I'm going over there tonight."

The kettle blew its whistle. Nikki got up and made tea, then brought the cups over to the table. "You know, of course, that if there's *anything* I can do—get information on AIDS, look after the cat, run errands—"

"Thank you, Nikki. We may be doing all that. You probably know more about AIDS than I do."

"Because I'm a lesbian? Lesbians very rarely get it, by the way. Straight people get it all the time these days. Blood transfusions. Needles. Plain old heterosexual sex. I take it Jonah is not a drug user."

"Not to my knowledge, although I know he's smoked pot—I mean who hasn't? He may have snorted cocaine at a party or something like that. No, it was probably the classic unprotected sexual encounter. Jonah liked his sex the way he liked his coffee—fresh, hot, and plenty of it."

"I thought you were going to say 'instant.'"

Marj giggled. "Sweet, white and mountain-grown!"

"Black and freeze-dried!" Nikki and Marj were both laughing now. "I'm glad you can still see the humor, Marj."

"Yeah, well. I'll think about it later."

"Tomorrow is another day, Scarlett."

CHAPTER 22

"Well Charlie and Company, I guess it's just you and me," Nikki said to her plants as she checked to see if they needed water. The house seemed empty now without Casimir in it; the big cat had filled the room, not only in size but in presence. She wouldn't have Marj as a dinner companion either; Marj was off to see Jonah, to whatever end. Nikki opened a can of salmon and made herself a sandwich, thumbed through the *TV Guide*, then tossed it aside. *I should've rented a couple of movies. Maybe I'll find something to read instead—but first I'll make myself a cup of hot chocolate.*

Hot chocolate had been a childhood comfort drink, her favorite to sip after playing outdoors in winter, or while watching, yet again, *The Wizard of Oz* on TV. On those days when family tensions were thick enough to skate on, hot chocolate was the drink Nikki quietly took to her room. Now she mixed cocoa, sugar, a few grains of salt and a bit of water in a cup, put it in the microwave long enough to bubble, added milk and nuked it again until it just started to foam. A dash of vanilla, a handful of mini-marshmallows and a sprinkle of cinnamon—no, chili powder. Ah! She carried it out on deck.

Eagle Lake Park was quiet. There were no rabbits in sight. A breeze was blowing from the lake, and Nikki wondered if she should put on a sweater. It would be dark soon; a light cloud cover blotted out emerging stars. She sipped her hot chocolate and wondered whether Adelaide was still having the park patrolled. As if in answer, she saw Fred Crushill and Walter Hatch approaching through the gloom, walking along the edge of the drop-off. Walter was carrying a hunting rifle. *The walrus and the carpenter.*

"Hi there! On patrol, I see. How long does Adelaide plan to keep this up?"

Fred Crushill started a bit at Nikki's voice, then approached followed by Walter. "Oh, it's you Nikki," Fred said. "My night vision isn't what it used to be."

"*Day* vision isn't what it used to be either, ha-ha," Walter said. "Still, job's got to be done, I say. Job's got to be done."

"Are you two going to be walking around all night?"

"No, thank God," Fred said. "George and Clark will be taking over in an hour or so."

"I though maybe it wouldn't be necessary now. I mean, Raymond died of natural causes, didn't he?"

"According to Adelaide, we could all be murdered in our beds," Fred said. "Damn nonsense if you ask me. I don't know what she expects us to find."

"Reminds me a bit of the old days. France, it was, 1942. We were holed up in a stone barn outside a little town called Sérifontaine. It was nighttime and we didn't know how many jerries were in that town so we had to—"

"Yes, yes, Walter. I'm sure it was all *very* exciting, but we'd better keep moving. Standing still in this cool night air is not helpin' my rheumatism. Besides, Nikki doesn't want to hear your old war stories."

Walter sighed. "No rest for the wicked, eh? Ha-ha! Young lady, I advise you to go inside and keep your doors locked. If there's a dangerous animal on the loose, we'll be the ones to deal with it." Walter patted his rifle. They started off, cutting across Bob and Janet's place and on toward the end of the park. Nikki could hear their bickering voices fading in the distance.

"I don't know why you bothered to bring that thing. You can't see worth a damn. *You* walk ahead of *me*. I don't want you shooting me in the back if that thing goes off when you step in a rabbit hole."

"It's gettin' too dark. Where's the flashlight. Did you bring the flashlight? *You* should be out in front if you've got the flashlight."

"Yes, of course I brought the flashlight, but I'm *not* going to walk in front of *you*."

Nikki grinned. She picked up her cup and headed back inside, then stopped, surprised. There, in front of her door sat an animal—a cat. The orange tomcat!

"Well, hello," Nikki said. "You'd better high-tail it back home before somebody takes a shot at *you*." The cat didn't move. Nikki realized that if the cat *did* head homeward, there was an excellent chance he would run right into Fred and Walter. But if he hung around longer, he might run up against George Moon who had much better eyesight and no mercy.

"So what am I going to do with you?" Nikki reached across and opened the door. To her surprise, the cat slipped quietly inside. "I hope you're house trained."

Nikki locked her doors and shut the curtains to bar the Eagle Lake Park monster. Once again, she had the company of a cat. The orange tom took a few minutes to check out his surroundings, as cats do, sniffing, satisfying his curiosity. Nikki didn't know what to expect. Outdoor cats can panic if they find themselves indoors. Nikki remembered a time when one of their yard cats became trapped between the kitchen door and the screen. When the inner door was opened, the cat shot into the room and went on a rampage scattering bric-a-brac, smashing china, until it finally wedged itself between appliances on the kitchen counter. There, they'd managed to throw a blanket over it and wrestle it back outdoors.

To Nikki's relief, the orange tom, seemed much more laid-back. Having taken measure of the room he strolled casually to Nikki's plant shelf and stationed himself in front of the fern. Nikki sat down on the couch and shook her head. "You too, huh? What *is* it that you cats can hear that I can't?"

The orange tom stood up, stretched, as cats do, in a sort of yoga sun-salutation, extending front legs, toes spread, claws gripping carpet, while he lowered his chest to the floor with tail raised and rump high in the air. Then, rising slowly, he transferred his weight to his front feet, and alternately stretched each hind leg backwards, spreading toes, extending claws, then ended the exercise with a bit of a shake, as if removing water from his coat. He then walked directly over to Nikki, looked into her eyes and said, "Hello, Luv. I'm Boston Charlie."

CHAPTER 23

Nikki sat still as stone but inside her mind was racing like a computer on speed. *I didn't hear that. I'm dreaming. I'm imagining things. I should pinch myself. I'm crazy. That's it. Marj was right. I'm the next to go. They'll find me dead. Nononono. I can't die. I don't have a cut finger. Idiot. What does that have to do with anything? I'm having a nervous breakdown. Cats don't talk. Plants don't sing. I'm hallucinating. Oh god, I'm losing it!*

The orange cat with tabby markings sat and looked long at Nikki, as if giving her time to digest. He got up and rubbed against her shin, turned, sat down, looked up at her again, then *whispered*, "I really *am* Boston Charlie. Can we get past that?"

Dream. Gotta be. Alice in Wonderland talking to a caterpillar. "I don't understand. You can't be real."

"That's not important. I'd like to have a word."

"Am I dreaming?"

"Yes, of course you are. People in your plane of existence dream continuously, the same way that your stars shine continuously, although you don't see them in the daytime."

"Who *are* you and what do you want?"

"For now, just continue to call me Boston Charlie. I find I can speak through this little creature. You don't really hear my voice—or his. I do not use his vocal cords—although I find that I *can* use his eyes, and can now see *you* for the first time. I use this little creature's mind and brain to send messages into *your* mind. Your mind uses *your* brain the way that you use your computer."

Nikki was staring, fascinated, and now saw that the cat was not actually speaking. Its mouth didn't move. For a moment Nikki suspected some sort of crazy ventriloquist's trick. But who? How? Was she expected to believe that this really *was* her Boston fern? "What are you? An alien from someplace? How come you speak my language?" Indeed, in a bizarre twist, the cat seemed to have a British accent.

"We're not using language at all. Your brain translates my thoughts and makes them intelligible to your ego. As to my British accent, that's because your mind links me with Bert, the man at the nursery."

And now he just answered a question I never asked out loud. "Then I'm the only one who can hear you?"

"If there were others in the room, they probably wouldn't hear me, although some might. It's a matter of neurological patterns being the same. First of all, try not to be afraid. Your fear is setting up barriers and making communication difficult. If you can control your fear, we can go on."

Nikki was now able to draw a near normal breath. "Go on to what? Who *are* you?"

"I am a voyager from another place. A refugee, don't you know? Sometimes there is an intrusion from one plane of existence to another."

"You're a *plant.*"

"Imagine my surprise when I found that plants are, in your world, a primitive life form! In mine, we are highly developed and the dominant species."

"You mean in your world plants are intelligent?" Nikki's mind flashed back to her teacher plants dreams.

"Yes, we are. And yes, I did have some success in communicating with you in what you call a dream state. Unfortunately I found that, in your system, there is too great a gulf between what you call the conscious and the subconscious. Your egos are still too territorial and protective, and your present level of development makes it difficult—perhaps impossible—for you to grasp the fundamentals of our sciences."

"The shaking? That first night when you began to shake?"

"In my world we move freely. I didn't realize at first that, in yours, plant movement is slow and limited."

"The earthquake. Was that you?"

"That was a failed experiment on my part. I tried manipulating matter. I hoped it would result in communication. It only gave you a fright.

"Your life forms, to me, appear only as electrical impulses. As a stranger, I didn't know which ones were dominant. I reached out to what you call plant life, but soon found yours to be of a low order. They responded to me the way pets respond to loving care."

"The rabbits?"

"I sent out probes to contact other forms of life. The creatures you call rabbits appear to have an unstable group consciousness that made them unsuitable. So did the animal you call Prince. Their reactions were deranged and violent. Then there was the man named Kuusisto and the man named Cantwell. I was able to communicate with them, assimilate knowledge of your system, but the results were equally chaotic. I concluded they were both inferior or defective. It was frustrating to find that I could not form a link with intelligence. Your other cat proved too fearful. As I said, fear sets up barriers. This little creature here has elongated brain waves and an uncluttered consciousness. He needs a name. We can call him Charlie too; he'll be here long after I've gone."

"Charlie Two."

"Even better."

"Are you from another planet?"

"Not planet. My plane of existence occupies the same space, so-called, as yours, but normally we're not aware of each other. We use building blocks of matter that are less dense than yours, so you can't see our world, nor can we see yours. Our scientists had been conducting certain experiments. One of them went wrong and here I am!

"At first I was in what you might call shock. I could not function in your alien world. My normal senses did not operate here. I had to *reconstruct* myself by using *your* building blocks—the basic units of matter in your system. You think of them as atoms and molecules but there are much finer units than your scientists have yet been able to detect. I had to operate according to the physical laws of your system as best I could."

"And you ended up as a Boston fern?"

"*You* see me as a Boston fern. To myself, I look different. You only see the part of me that lies within your range of vision, just as I could only see you as an electrical field. Your cat can hear sounds that a human can't. In the same way, your eyes are not equipped to see more than the narrow band that intrudes into your three-dimensional world."

"Like the tip of an iceberg?"

"A multidimensional iceberg."

"But why don't you just go back to your own world?"

"It's not that simple. I will, of course, *try*. Maintaining this form is difficult. It's ironic, that although I come from a realm in which time does not exist, in *your* world, I seem to be running out of time."

"Then what do you want from me?"

"It won't be as easy as I'd hoped, but I am cautiously optimistic, as *your* people might say, that if you are willing to help me, we may be able to avert disaster."

"Disaster? What kind of disaster? And how can I be of help to a—uh—you?"

"We'll take it one step at a time, and hope my time will suffice. Communicating this way puts a strain on my resources. You might say I need time to recharge my cosmic batteries. But even more important, we need to give this little animal time to reaffirm the sovereignty of his own existence. We mustn't compromise the integrity of his psyche. I suggest you keep him as your own cat. He won't be missed at the farm. Treat him well. He is our only link."

"What—what happens next?"

"Try to keep your composure. Tonight, just before you go to sleep, give yourself the suggestion that when you awaken you will remember your dreams. I shall be contacting you in your dream state. Tomorrow, depending on the results, we will resume. I think Charlie Two would like some dinner."

And with that, it was over. Nikki stared at the fern, then at the cat. Boston Charlie looked like a Boston fern. Charlie Two sat blinking, as if newly awakened, then began walking around the kitchen. Almost mechanically, Nikki got up, opened the refrigerator and took out the leftover salmon. She set it down beside Charlie Two and gave him a bowl of water. The cat wolfed down the fish, purring as he did, producing orgasmic grunts of pure pleasure.

While Charlie Two finished licking his bowl, Nikki tried to size up the situation. She needed kitty litter! She might also need a psychiatrist, but right now she needed kitty litter. Marj! Marj would have some. Was Marj home yet? If so, how would she, Nikki, explain all this? Of course she *couldn't* explain. Marj would think she had lost her mind—and she might be right. No, this was *not* something Nikki could just willy-nilly blurt out even to Marj. She would have to be very, very careful.

"Kitty litter? Yes, but what—"

"I'll explain later. Come over."

Marj arrived in minutes, carrying a bag of Kittyfresh. "You'll need a box."

"I have one here. The one we used for the herbs. That will do for now."

"When I said you should get a cat, I didn't expect you to conjure one up so fast."

"Me neither. Meet Charlie Two." The cat was lying on the rug like a Roman at a feast, licking his paws, sprawled in such a way as to expose the white underbelly of his marmalade coat. "He showed up at my door and since the storm troopers are apt to shoot anything that moves, I thought he'd be safer in here." It was a true explanation, as far as it went, and although Nikki had tried to sound casual, she wondered if Marj would notice her nervousness. She rubbed her clammy palms against her blue jeans. *Take a deep breath, calm down. Try to get into a holding pattern over the airport of sanity.*

Marj, however, seemed to be abstracted as well. "Charlie Two? Doesn't that show a lack imagination—I mean for a writer?"

"I never thought of that. Well, too late now. He seems to like it."

"Charlie Two it is. Nikki, I really could use some of your hot tea therapy."

Grateful for the diversion, Nikki busied herself with kettle, teapot and cups. She noticed her hands were trembling and clasped them briefly to steady them before she picked up the tea tray and carried it to the table. "And, how did it go with Jonah?"

"That *bastard.*"

"Ah—did I miss something? Is this the same Jonah who's dying of AIDS?"

"Jonah will not die of AIDS. Jonah will die when I kill him."

"You mean he found out he doesn't have AIDS after all?"

"He's not sick. He only said that."

"But why would he lie about a thing like that? What could he possibly gain?"

Marj sighed. "Oh, you'd have to know Jonah. I was demonstrating too much independence. He had to shoot me down."

"He *said* that?"

"No, what he did was apologize all over the place. I'd upset him. He was reaching out to me and I was treating him lightly. He had to know if I still had any feelings for him so, on impulse, he told me he was dying. He knew it was a cruel and horrible thing to do, but I'd hurt him, you see. In a way, though, it turned out to be a *good* thing because it made him realize that I still *care* about him. Jonah knew he'd have to see me face to face, and Jonah always gets what he wants—and doesn't care how he does it."

"He wants to get back together? Is that what all this is about?"

"Wait, it gets even better. By showing up, I demonstrated that he could *count* on me—as he'd *always known* he could. And he does need my help, desperately, but it has to do with his finances, not his health. It seems that my ex has gotten himself in a complicated mess. Bottom line is he wants me to get involved in something shady. He wants to transfer assets into my name to keep his creditors from attaching them. All I have to do is sign a few papers and do everything he tells me."

"Oh, is *that* all? Golly, what gal wouldn't do *that* for her man?"

"Indeed!" Marj sipped her tea. "Jonah was always into a lot of stuff I suspected was illegal. I know that when we got divorced he only declared a fraction of his assets. My lawyer told me I could've come out with a lot more if I'd hired detectives to ferret out his holdings, but I didn't care. I just wanted out."

"If you play your cards right, you might end up owning all of them."

"Yeah, and I could also end up in jail—which, I think, is exactly what Jonah needs—a patsy."

"You mean he would coldly set you up?"

"I think he would if he could."

"I take it you said no."

Marj slowly stirred sugar into her second cup of tea. "I said I'd *think* about it."

Nikki looked startled. "Really? I'd have hit him with a lamp!"

"If I hadn't said I'll think about it, I'd still be there, wouldn't I? To Jonah, the word 'no' means 'pressure me some more.' I just kept my poker face like I always do."

"What are you going to do?"

"Maybe I can come up with a sting operation. Throw him a lifeline that's really a bungee cord. Something that will slingshot him straight into the Pit of Peril."

"Monty Python would be proud of you."

"And now I'll go home and leave you to your quiet evening with your cat. He's a *relaxed* beast, isn't he? Are you sure he's not stuffed? At least he won't discombobulate your life like Casimir. If you plan to keep him, you'll need cat food. I've got tons and I'll be glad to bring some over in the morning. Least I can do when you took such good care of Cas for me."

...

After Marj had gone, Nikki washed teacups and wondered how life always managed to return to normal. Someone dies. You go to a funeral. You come home and start doing the laundry. You discover that your Boston fern is an alien entity that talks to you through a cat, and the next thing you're having tea with a friend who is telling you about her troubles with her ex—and then you do the dishes. Life, she concluded, zigzags between the good stuff and the bad stuff, but always returns to the middle which is filled with *small* stuff. *Mm. I must send that in to* Guideposts.

Keep your composure, the fern had said. Nikki took a long, soothing hot shower—but not until she'd emptied the bag of Kittyfresh into the cardboard box and placed it conspicuously in the middle of the kitchen floor. "I don't know if you grok kitty litter, Charlie Two, being an outdoor cat, but I do *not* plan to demonstrate it for you."

Give yourself the suggestion to remember your dreams, the fern had said. Considering the strange dreams Nikki had already been having, she wasn't worried about not being able to remember. *I just don't know if I'll be able to get to sleep at all.* But she did, very quickly, and slept so soundly she didn't even stir when Charlie Two climbed into bed with her, as if he were her cat—as if he had *always* been her cat.

CHAPTER 24

Nikki found herself walking along a footpath in a woods or a garden. Her companion—her guide—might have been a man or woman. It was hard to tell because the entity seemed to be shifting, vibrating, moving in such a way as to always be a little out of focus, and dressed either in a white robe or surrounded by a white mist. Nikki was being shown something very important and knew it to be vital that she understand it. At the same time, the strangeness of her surroundings was so distracting that she found it hard to concentrate. The place looked somewhat familiar to her, and then she realized why. It was the landscape of her paintings. There were the trees, the shrubs, the flowers and stream that she had done, first in watercolor, then in oils. Only now that they surrounded her, they all appeared to be infinitely more colorful and vivid.

There was also something about the place that seemed to energize, vitalize, and infuse Nikki with a feeling of well-being. She took a deep breath. *Like breathing oxygen!* Everything around her, she realized, was surging with vitality. Plants, birds, fish, stones—and people. Yes, there were people too—adults and children—as well as animals and insects. A huge blue butterfly floated gently to settle on a big yellow flower. A small animal darted behind a bush. People walked about leisurely. Children played. A vine twined up a tree. A fish swam slowly in the stream, its filmy fins graceful in the water. A bird swooped by in a *whoosh* of wings.

"This is the experiment," Nikki's guide was saying. "Here everything is composed of the basic components of life—units of awareness, infinitely tiny, but each coded to contain within it the blueprint of a universe. Awareness—consciousness—combines and recombines to take on form. Everything is made of the same material." He pointed to the ground.

"When that blade of grass on the bank of the stream has fulfilled its destiny to the fullest as a blade of grass, it will then seek to become a flower, perhaps like the one that grows next to it. And once it has reached its ultimate peak as a flower, its consciousness will fly apart and perhaps choose to blend with a more complicated gestalt of consciousness to form a tree, or an animal or someone like yourself.

"*Any* object, no matter how small or mundane is made of the same material, tiny bits of consciousness, units of aware energy, taking on form."

As Nikki stood and watched, her guide brought his hands together then opened them to reveal an indistinct shape. Nikki saw the shape solidify and, to her amazement, become—of all things—a hot dog! Not just a wiener, but a ball park red hot—a frankfurter inside a bun! He handed it to Nikki.

"You have before you what is to you, a very familiar object—an illustration of how thought forms matter. Everything here has recombined, is recombining and *will continue* to recombine to form everything else. The process is governed by the power of *intent*.

"Notice that little water plant that floats in the stream. Its roots have become separated from the soil. If it has fulfilled itself, its components will disintegrate—ah, but no. I see it is re-rooting itself in the stream bed. That means it has not yet completed its cycle as a water plant."

Nikki looked sharply at her guide. "Are you a human or a plant?"

The reply was not exactly a laugh, more of an impact of good-natured humor. "In your honor, Nikki, I'm approximating a form that will be somewhat familiar to you. But the people you see about you, are much like yourself, though of a different density. This is a laboratory, you see. A biosphere enclosed in a dome. We are doing an experiment in creation. Everything here is changing constantly. Everything is *becoming*. Everything is infused with the—you might call it joy of living, the creative thrust, the passionate desire to strive and develop. We have nature rapturously and rambunctiously rampant." (Again the wave of humor that swept like warm wind.)

"Creativity, Nikki, knows no good or evil. It's just creates. Creativity, in our system, however, is mostly benign. We have no wars or crime or illness. Your system is still very much concerned with these things, and therefore your creativity must be of a more cautious nature, with built-in safeguards like time and distance and death. Our experiment here is to introduce, under controlled conditions, elements of different systems to see what the effect of such combinations would be on the creative principle."

"Why? If you have no wars or crime or illness, why would you want to introduce them?"

"Not the wars, crime of illness, although since it is a possibility that that sort of contamination could occur, we set up a small, self-contained experiment. No, our aim is different. You see, we are creators of worlds—environments for education and development. To provide all possible climates, it is our purpose to combine elements to produce new fields of endeavor. As you know from yours, worlds are not designed to be free of conflict and challenge, but a spectrum of various environments that afford maximum opportunity for experience and learning. In this experiment, there was some disagreement among our scientists. This biosphere is a compromise between different schools of thought."

"You create *worlds*?"

"Yes, and you do too, although at your level of development you're not aware of it."

"Where are these worlds?"

"The concept of space is meaningless in realities that are beyond your own three-dimensional system. Each system is separate and quite different, yet all systems are like open doors that no one notices. Consciousness roams freely. You are here. I am there—although in my case, as you will soon see, it was not pre-planned. Instead of just projecting my consciousness, I became an anomaly in your reality."

"Uh—okay. If you're there, how come you're also here? Or is it just something that happens in dreams?"

"In our plane of existence, not bounded by time, it's possible to be in more than one place at once. It's true in yours too but you perceive it from *within* the context of time. Some of you think of it as reincarnation. No need to go into that now."

"What am *I* doing here? "

"Right now, you're here to experience this place and witness what happens."

Nikki was still holding the hot dog—the so-familiar object in an alien world. She spread the roll a bit, and, as she did, the wiener split in two, revealing, inside it, as if just forming, a tiny *folded paper napkin*. The wrapper! Nikki stared, dumbfounded. Her host looked at it too. "Well, I *did* say it was experimental!"

Nikki looked up to see that her guide had disappeared—and so, she saw, had the hot dog. Now that Nikki was alone, she found her surroundings entrancing—the heady fragrance of flowers, sweet warm air, soft grass beneath her feet. She listened to the sound of a bird and mentally tried to describe its call, but could only come up with "liquid diamonds." The longer she remained, the more peaceful and joyous Nikki felt. If only she could stay here forever! She was experiencing a limitless sense of freedom. She could do *anything* here. She could *be* anything. Her spirit could soar to heights of fulfillment undreamt of in her own world.

Nikki did notice that the other people in the biosphere appeared not to see her. What was it her guide had said? They were made of a different density of matter. She was tempted to go over and touch one of them to see if her hand would meet solid flesh. Everything else seemed substantial enough—at least her senses were reacting in a way that seemed to be normal. She wasn't floating in the air or walking through matter like a ghost. She found she could touch a flower, at least gain the sense of the flower. She wondered if she could pick one, but that, here, would be unthinkable! Here one had to be very careful. The consequences of the smallest act could be infinite. Suddenly she found herself concerned that her feet were trampling grass. She looked down and saw that as she walked, the grass seemed to *welcome* her footsteps. It was, indeed, reaching up to caress her, as if exploring her bare feet. It was as if the grass was as curious about her as she of it, and was touching her feet the way a blind person might run his fingers over someone's features, gently, almost lovingly. It was very sensual, and Nikki wondered if she was really feeling the grass or whether her brain was picking up the sensation in some other way.

On impulse, Nikki sat down on the bank of the stream, then lay back and looked up. For the first time she noticed the "sky." It wasn't readily apparent that it was a dome, but as she studied it, she could see that it did, indeed, enclose everything within it—and her paintings of it had been accurate. It did lend a sense of being contained—perhaps even of being oppressed. There *was* something foreboding in the way it seemed to imprison everything beneath it.

Nikki sat up. Something was different. What was it? What was happening? Nikki noticed, then, that everything had gone absolutely still. In the three-dimensional world there is always a sense of motion even when nothing is moving—motion as compared with the frozen stillness of a photograph. Nikki was aware now that there *was* no motion. *It's like a freeze frame in a movie!* It only lasted a moment and then motion flowed back again. Nikki experienced a momentary feeling of disorientation, almost dizziness. She had the sense that something was about to happen and knew that she was there to observe.

It began when a small boy ran out of the woods followed by another. The taller child seemed to be chasing the smaller one. A game of tag? No, it was a *fight!* Nikki watched the bigger boy tackle the smaller one and begin to beat him with his fists. "Hey, you two. Stop that!" Nikki ran to the children. By then the smaller boy had sunk his teeth into the older one's arm and the two were locked in a fierce and ugly struggle. Nikki tried to pull the boys apart, but found then that while she had a sense of their being there, she was unable to grasp them and that they did not seem to hear or see her. It was like trying to stop a fight in a movie. She looked around to see if one of the inhabitants would interfere, but saw now that it was the beginning of something else entirely.

As Nikki watched, her horror grew. The inhabitants who had seemed serene and happy were now behaving erratically. As if some control switch had been thrown, their movements were becoming, at first graceless and uncoordinated, then eccentric, then frantic and violent. Like inmates in an asylum, some were fighting, some weeping, while some wandered aimlessly. Some howled like animals or did injury to themselves as well as each other. Nothing, at this point, was as it had been a few moments ago. The plants and trees were taking on gnarled and twisted shapes. The animals were becoming grotesquely deformed. *My god, it's like a Frankenstein theme park!* It was exactly as if everything—plants, animals, people had simply gone mad and then begun to deform—and then—and here Nikki had to rub her eyes to be sure she was seeing correctly—to *disintegrate*. Nikki saw a man run wildly past her—a man with no arms. A woman was carrying a legless child, clutching it with fingerless hands. *Are they falling apart or are they turning invisible?* Nikki caught glimpses of things so strange they would be indelibly etched in her memory: a vine actively strangling a small animal as the animal writhed and changed shape; what looked like a dog covered with grass instead of hair; a tree trunk with a man growing out of it like a centaur, who thrashed his body about and screamed as he tore at his own flesh which came off like slabs of bark.

Then the earth began to shake. Huge cracks began to appear. Nikki felt herself being knocked off balance. By reflex, she reached out to clutch a tree branch for support but was unable to grasp it. She realized then that she could remain upright and unaffected as long as she didn't look at the ground. The sight of the heaving earth was giving her vertigo. There was a deafening sound like thunder from overhead and Nikki knew that the biosphere dome was cracking. The light darkened and a cold wind blew—stronger, ever stronger, like a hurricane, destroying everything. Nikki tried to run but was caught by the arm. She saw that it was her guide who held her fast. "This is what happened in my world. We must see that it does not happen in yours!"

CHAPTER 25

N‌IKKI CAME awake, wide-eyed, grasping her pillow. Her goose down duvet was twisted into a rope. The fitted sheet had pulled away from the corners of the mattress and lay, crumpled and lumpy, under her body. *What a nightmare!* Nikki was still breathing hard and her body was covered with sweat. She got up and took a shower, then combed her wet hair in front of her bathroom mirror. Except for puffy eyes, she looked normal enough. The morning itself *seemed* normal enough. The thing yesterday—the thing with Boston Charlie and the orange tomcat—had it really happened at all? "Is it possible," Nikki asked her reflection, "that *you* are having a nervous breakdown?" Nikki was thinking how nice it would be to discover that there *was* no Boston fern, no orange tomcat, no paintings, no weirdness, when she felt something soft brush against her ankle. Nikki sighed. "Good morning, Charlie Two. What have you got to say for yourself?"

"Meow."

Nikki put on clothing, then coffee. She gave Charlie Two a saucer of milk. "Later I'll get you something more substantial from the grocery store."

She was pouring herself a cup of coffee when Marj arrived bearing cat food. She unloaded tins and foil packets on the table. "I hope this will be okay. Charlie Two is a barn cat, probably used to eating mice, so he shouldn't have a delicate stomach. It took me three or four different brands before I found one that Casimir wouldn't hurl. I find that the more expensive it is, the less likely it'll be that Cas barfs it up. All I can advise is try these, see if they agree with Charlie Two. I see, at least, he's litter trained."

Nikki hadn't even noticed, but Marj's eagle eye had spotted the little mound in the litter box where Charlie Two had done a neat job of covering whatever he had deposited. Nikki yawned and poured Marj a cup of coffee.

"You look as though you haven't slept. Charlie Two keep you awake?"

"I slept. Just kept having nightmares."

"Maybe you should go back to bed. I'm going into town to see my lawyer."

"The Jonah thing?"

"Sort of. I want to find out to what my legal position is in case my ex tries blackmailing me."

"How could he do that?"

"Easy. If he's in deep, he can threaten to lie and say I was in on whatever it was. I don't trust the man."

"Can you trust the lawyer?"

"I shall, as they say, proceed with caution. Get some sleep. You look awful."

When Marj had gone, Nikki opened a tin of sliced chicken and liver Kitty Gourmet for Charlie Two. Whatever the cat may have been, he was not a finicky eater. He wolfed down the gravy soaked meat then licked the bowl clean. Nikki watered her plants, then addressed Boston Charlie. "Well, what now? Do we hold a séance or what?"

The plant made no comment and Charlie Two showed no signs of uncatlike activity as he purred and licked his paws. "I guess I'll just have to wait for orders, eh guys?" *Listen to me, I'm awaiting orders from a cat and a houseplant. I guess I should at least try to get some work done.*

There was a knock at her door. Marj must have forgotten something. Nikki opened it. It was *(oh god!)* Adelaide Moon.

"Good morning, Nikki. May I come in?" If Nikki looked puffy-eyed from lack of sleep, Adelaide looked terrible. It was if she had aged rapidly in the past few days and Nikki tried to remember if her hair had always been so gray.

"Uh, sure, Adelaide. Come on in." *Damn.*

Adelaide stepped inside and glanced around the room. "I see you took down the wallpaper Paulette and I put up. Guess by now it was gettin' old and faded. We papered the place five years ago for the Hennessys when they moved in."

"Yes, it was stained with cigarette smoke, and since I don't smoke myself I—" Nikki's voice trailed off as she saw Adelaide stuff her pack of cigarettes back in her pocket. "If you'd like a cigarette, we can go out on deck. How about a cup of coffee?" Charlie Two seemed to have disappeared but there was the telltale litter box in the middle of the kitchen floor.

"I hear you have a cat."

Who squealed? Marj again? "I guess you could say that. He's a stray. I was afraid someone would shoot him so I took him in."

"I can't have cats roaming the park. If you're going to keep him, you can't let him out."

"Fair enough. I'll keep him inside."

Adelaide was behaving a little like a cat herself, prowling about the room, looking at Nikki's work table, her plants, her paintings. "You're quite the artist, I hear."

You hear a hell of a lot, lady. "I like to paint." Nikki felt that some sort of confrontation was coming and feared she would have to meet it head-on. Was it about the cat? Or was it about Nikki being a lesbian? Was Adelaide going to tell her to get out of Eagle Lake Park? Nikki hated conflict, wasn't good at it, and did her best of avoid it—one of the traits that had gotten her into trouble with Phil. She suspected that if she had been less of a wimp and more of a bitch Phil would have had more respect for her. Now she was mentally preparing to tell Adelaide to butt out of her affairs—if she could only carry it off without stuttering or bursting into tears of anger and frustration.

Adelaide had stopped in front of Nikki's paintings, and all at once Nikki found herself feeling sorry for the woman. She looked so *old*. Her hair hung in oily locks. She was, if possible, even more thin and gaunt, her cheeks sunken and with black hollows under her eyes—as if something were sucking the life right out of her. *She's ill. She's very ill.* "Adelaide, can I offer you something? Coffee? Tea? Hot chocolate?"

Adelaide didn't appear to hear her. She walked over to Boston Charlie. "That's what killed him."

"I'm sorry, *what?*"

Adelaide turned to look at Nikki. "Raymond. That's what killed him. Your plant. It got into his brain and it killed him. It made him do things." Her eyes looked feverish.

"Adelaide? Are you all right? Please sit down." The woman was babbling. Had she lost her mind?

Adelaide smiled faintly, sat down at Nikki's table. She fumbled for her cigarettes, remembered, pushed them back. "It's okay if you want to smoke, Adelaide," Nikki heard herself say.

"No. I'll live by your rules, Nikki. Rules are important."

"Then let's go sit outside."

"No. I won't stay. I just want you to know that I know what's going on. You think I don't know things but I do."

Nikki groped for a straw of common sense. "Adelaide, of course you know things. You're an intelligent woman. But nobody killed Raymond. He died of a brain tumor, didn't he? I don't know why he was in the woods but I know he liked to wander around at night. I saw him outside my window at midnight a week ago."

"Raymond knew things too. He heard things. He saw things. He warned me. He warned me about your power. *The woman with the plant that sings death.* Terrible things will come when *everything* sings death."

"Adelaide, Raymond Cantwell was, I believe, something called a synesthete. That means that his senses weren't like yours and mine. He could *hear* a color as well as see it. He could *feel* a sound or see it visually. It's uncommon but there are others like him."

"I know that. I also know that there's something here that affected his mind—something here is affecting all our minds. Prince went mad you know." Adelaide smiled as she said it, displaying irregular yellow teeth. There was something ghastly about the smile and the way she said it, as if she'd said, "I just bought a new hat."

"I was sorry to hear it."

"I want you out of my park."

"Adelaide, surely you don't think that I—"

"*I want you out of my park.* I want you and your devil plant and your cat and your hellish paintings out of my park—before you kill us all."

"Adelaide, *Adelaide. Listen to me.* I am not going to kill anyone. I never have. I never will. Look at me. I'm just a woman. I'm not a witch or a devil. I bought the plant from *your friend* Bert, remember? The paintings are just a watercolor and an oil of a garden scene."

Charlie Two, as if wondering what the shouting was about, came down the hall and sat next to Nikki. "And this is just a cat. He's the orange tomcat from the farm down the road. I don't plan to stay in Eagle Lake Park any longer than I have to. I don't like people with guns patrolling the place. I don't like living this close to neighbors, and, frankly, I'm not terribly crazy about you, Adelaide, but I don't wish you or anyone else any harm."

"Beware the woman with the plant that sings death. That's what Raymond said."

"Adelaide, I know you and Raymond Cantwell were friends, but we both know that Raymond had the mind of a child."

"Raymond Cantwell was my brother."

There was a moment of silence. "I'm sorry. I didn't know."

"Not many people did. Half-brother, really. Old family scandal." Adelaide sat looking at Nikki for what seemed a long time. "You probably mean well. Maybe you don't even know what's going on. But it's best that you leave here as soon as possible. Do you understand me?"

Nikki met her gaze. "Perfectly."

"Good." Adelaide got up to go and reached for her cigarettes. She would light one just as soon as she was outdoors. Nikki noticed that her hand was shaking, and then she saw something she *hadn't* noticed before. While they'd been talking, Adelaide had kept her left hand in her coat pocket. Now she withdrew it and Nikki saw that her hand was missing two fingers.

CHAPTER 26

TOO ASTONISHED for words, Nikki had said nothing. Her mind was racing. Raymond Cantwell had been missing a finger. Adelaide was his half-sister. Was it something genetic? Had the fingers been missing all along and Nikki just hadn't noticed? No one else had commented on Raymond's missing digit. *How could I have failed to see something like that?*

She tried to remember an earlier Adelaide—Adelaide serving her upside-down cake, Adelaide at the barbecue, Adelaide blowing clouds of smoke as she interviewed Nikki when Nikki bought the trailer. It was a little thing, but somehow more monstrous and horrifying than if Adelaide had suddenly begun shedding her skin. Leprosy? Leprosy caused people to lose fingers and toes. But leprosy was not a disease anyone worried about anymore—at least not in North America. Besides, there would be other symptoms as well, Nikki was sure of that. Not just a cut—well, it wasn't even a *cut*; there was no bandage, no sign of stitches. The fingers, just like Raymond Cantwell's, were just missing. The little finger and the ring finger of Adelaide's left hand were simply *not there.*

It was like the dream. Nikki had avoided thinking about it, but now, in her mind, she clearly saw all those people who seemed to be disintegrating and distorting, losing body parts. What had her dream guide said? "This is what happened in my world. We must make sure it doesn't happen in yours?" Was something like that happening in Eagle Lake Park? The rabbits? Had they attacked each other? Had they attacked Einar Kuusisto? Raymond Cantwell?

Maybe this is what madness is. Some tiny little thing in your life becomes skewed. You barely notice at first. Then you begin to explore it, toy with it playfully perhaps, brood on it, give it validity. Bit by bit you venture farther and farther into a world in which the real and the unreal are so intertwined that you can't separate them anymore. You end up as if you were lost in the woods, unable to find your way back. Eventually you become a prisoner, then a citizen of your own alien country, to the point that you no longer even speak the language of your old world. Is that what's happening to me? Have I gone too far? Should I be seeking help? And from whom? A shrink? From Phil? Phil would send her to a psychoanalyst. Nikki had no faith in analysts. Phil had been going to one for years and there seemed to be no detectable relaxation of any of *her* neuroses. *But if I am out of my mind, I'm not alone.*

Adelaide Moon! It seemed bizarre that, of all people, Adelaide was the only other person who seemed to have an inkling of what might be going on in Eagle Lake Park. What would she have said if Nikki had told her about Boston Charlie and Charlie Two? Nikki hadn't, of course. The woman was so clearly on the edge that Nikki had done her best to reassure her that everything was normal. Normal? Adelaide had called her a witch and a murderer. *She'd have me FedExed to the nearest psycho ward—or maybe she'd just have me burned at the stake along with my Charlie collection.*

Still, it would have been a relief to have someone to talk to. But when things got this far—this bad—this strange, whom *could* you tell?

"You're not out of your mind, you know."

Nikki looked down. Charlie Two was sitting at her feet. *Oh god, it's beginning again.*

"Just try to trust us, then, Luv. It'll be over soon—and then you can choose to remember it or not." Once again, Charlie Two was gazing at Nikki intently and *talking* to her in that rather ludicrous British accent.

"You remember your dream?"

"God, yes. I'll never forget it!"."

"You understand that it was more allegorical than real—a shorthand version. It was easier to show you than to describe it to you. If I had said that an experiment in the natural propensity of consciousness to fulfill every aspect of possible development had resulted in an accelerated transformation from one probable pathway into another, causing so sudden a shift that the integrity had become compromised—all due to an imbalance in the sustaining framework, would you have understood me?"

"No."

"I could have also compared it to a child smashing his modeling clay city so he could build a new one out of the same Plasticine."

"*That* I would've understood. A sort of 'back to the old drawing board.'"

"Right."

"So your world was destroyed and you ended up in mine."

"Temporarily. Nothing is ever destroyed. Remember the modeling clay. The important thing is not *that* it was destroyed, but *that which destroyed it.* Remember what I said about the unforeseen imbalance in the sustaining framework? It's the imbalance we have to worry about, and it's why I'm still here."

"Are you telling me that this imbalance of yours is now in Eagle Lake Park?"

"I regret to say that when I was caught in the multidimensional point of entry—I *do* wish we had more time. Multidimensional entry points are such an interesting subject, and I wish I could explain them more fully. Perhaps later.

"At any rate, I fear that I've introduced what, to you, would be a negative principle in the form of basic universal vitality, which means it will become assimilated into your system—a little like one of your computer viruses—although that's an oversimplification. If I hadn't been so disoriented—it happens when you try to travel between systems in corporeal form—not unlike your jet lag—I wouldn't have probed your life forms. I realized what had happened when they reacted as they did. I tried to correct the situation, but it appears I only made it worse."

As she listened, Nikki had a mental picture of the rabbits' frenzied behavior on the night of the storm, and another of their rapt attention the night she had seen Raymond Cantwell. "Does *any* of this have *anything* to do with Adelaide Moon's missing fingers?"

"It's beginning, you see. I'm going to tell you this although it may be so foreign a concept that you won't believe it: You form your bodies and all earthly three-dimensional objects continuously. Nothing in your world is solid. Matter is formed by aware energy, not the other way around. It springs from an inner pattern and is created constantly anew. When the pattern changes the object changes. What you perceive as aging, for instance, is a weakening of the pattern, the blueprint that creates the form. Things don't age or wear out. They're just created with signals of increasing and decreasing intensity as cosmic vitality enters your system, passes through it, then leaves. The process is so seamless that you're unaware of it."

To Nikki, oddly, this was sounding somehow familiar. She remembered her teacher plant dreams and how, in them, everything made such exquisite sense. Something in what she was hearing was striking a chord, and she felt that she *almost* understood, *almost* remembered. Yes, there was something evocative and familiar about all this, on beyond the teacher plant dreams, as if all this was knowledge that she had somehow once known but forgotten.

"You're telling me that everything in Eagle Lake Park could just begin to disintegrate—because somehow the invisible blueprint got screwed up? Then why stop at Eagle Lake Park? Wouldn't that mean that your virus will go on to wipe out everything on this planet?"

"It *can*. In our system the deterioration was almost instantaneous because time, as you think of it, was not a factor. In your system, it will be more gradual. The less stable life forms will be affected first, as well as those that are under stress. Their patterns are already somewhat compromised, you see. As the sustaining blueprint begins to break down, the result will be what you would term madness, followed by an actual disintegration of matter. In our system there was severe distortion when life forms flew apart and recombined instantly in what seemed chaotic ways. That would not happen here because of your time factor—at least not quite that way. In your system, time permitting, it could appear in future generations as a series of mutations—similar to those caused by radiation."

Nikki remembered the monstrous plant-animal combinations in her dream. She envisioned a world in which everyone had gone mad, then proceeded to breed monstrosities. "You mean if there *are* future generations. Wouldn't it be the end of the world?"

"Yes. But remember, it's only the end of *one* of your worlds. The principle has been introduced; unchecked, it will go on to its natural conclusion. But, like everything else, your world is multidimensional. There are and have been many worlds. One of your worlds was destroyed in an atomic war. Another was rendered uninhabitable by industrial pollution. Your version of the world was not one of those, at least not yet."

"Is there any way to stop it?"

"We can try."

"What can *I* do?"

"There are two possibilities. In the natural order of things, you create your own circumstances. By that I mean you physically move into the future you visualize. You and others on your planet did *not* get blown up in a war because you chose to move into a future in which it didn't happen. You do that all the time, each time you make a choice. You leave one reality and move into another. Usually you do it without any awareness of having done it—and you are totally unaware that your old reality continues on to a different end. There *will* be a world in which these events *don't* happen."

"What's the other possibility?"

"The other option would be to try to confine the contamination to Eagle Lake Park. Keep it as a 'hot zone' as your scientists might say, and try to line it up with a major—remember I mentioned this?—*a major multidimensional entry point.* A multidimensional entry point is also, of course, a multidimensional *exit* point."

"Let me see if I understand. One, we can, perhaps, ourselves, move into a world in which nothing has gone wrong—but if I understand what you're saying, there'll still be an earth someplace where people are going crazy and falling apart. If we want to avoid *that*, we can do what? Blow up Eagle Lake Park—or whisk it away into space someplace?"

"It shouldn't be quite that dramatic. There are complicated factors at work. We would be reversing the process that brought me here and that does carry certain risks. What we would hope to do is *reverse* the flow of the negative principle, remove it from your world."

"What are the risks?"

"There's always the risk of the unexpected, as happened in my case. Then there's another risk in isolating and manipulating any part of universal vitality. There's always a chance that it may not be precisely possible."

"You mean it might not work? Or are you afraid you might remove something that shouldn't be removed—remove too much or not enough?"

"Something like that."

"Okay. We can change to another future and let the old one go to hell, or we can try to confine the problem to Eagle Lake Park in which case we, in it, might *all* go to hell. What's my place in all this?"

"In your world you are not so much doers as *deciders*. Creation is a matter of intent rather than action. Therefore *you must make the decision*. I have no authority to do that. You, as your friend Raymond Cantwell said, are the woman with power. You are the woman with the plant that sings death. You are the delegate, the representative of your world, in office by virtue of being a link between our systems. Had I been able to connect with someone else, you would have been spared the responsibility. There is no time to confer with your authorities, no time for any kind of referendum. It's all up to you and me. Now you must have a little time to think it over. Give Charlie Two a drink of water and let him take a cat nap. And tonight, instead of the packaged cat food, give him a tin of your excellent salmon. He also tells me he doesn't fancy the litter box. He'd rather go outdoors, but will tolerate it for now. Your friend Marj will soon be knocking on your door. I will contact you later. Ta-raa!"

...

Nikki drew a long breath. She didn't have much time to pull herself together before Marj arrived, carrying a bag of Kittyfresh.

"While I was at the store I picked this up for you since Charlie Two is now a house cat."

"Let me pay you for that." Nikki said, a bit abstractedly. "I can't expect you to subsidize Charlie Two's regularity."

"Not this time. I think I still owe you for fostering Casimir, but after this you're on your own. How are you feeling? Did you get any sleep?"

"No, I've just been sitting around talking to my houseplant and my cat about the end of the world."

"Knowing you, that sounds normal enough."

"And I had a visit from Adelaide."

"*Did* you? What did Her Nibs want?"

"Not much. She wants me out of Eagle Lake Park before I kill everyone here, like I killed Raymond Cantwell."

"*What?*"

"She thinks I'm a witch. She also told me Raymond Cantwell was her half-brother."

Marj sat down slowly. "Well, that would certainly explain a lot about him—why she kept him in the park like a household pet, why she was so upset when he died. It may also explain Adelaide. The woman's obviously operating on reduced wattage. Half-brother! I never thought of that. I think I would have believed a perverted sexual relationship between them, but *family*? Raymond and Adelaide. Now I'm wondering if Raymond, himself, knew."

"He must have known—or could it be possible he didn't? Ida and Hector would surely know—and George."

"I suppose so. I wonder where he came from and how they got together. Ooh, that's so convoluted. I love a mystery."

"We'll probably never find out. None of our business anyway. Did you see your lawyer?"

"Yeah. I don't think I'm in any serious trouble. Technically I'm liable for any tax evasion during the years we filed joint returns. In a court of law I think any jury would believe that I knew nothing—if it comes to that. I'd take my chances before I'd let Jonah drag me into something illegal. I'd love to kill him a few times, but bein' the lady what I am I'll probably do a Nancy Reagan and just say no—and hope that'll be the end of it."

"It probably will be. I have a hunch that your Jonah is bluffing. He sounds like my dad in that he was always selling, always trying to bend everyone to his will. As long as he thought he could do that, he'd keep it up, but once he realized that it wasn't going to work, he lost interest and went on to something else."

"I gotta go. Casimir will be wondering where I am. I still think you should take a nap."

"Maybe I will."

When Marj had gone, Nikki stretched out on the bed though she doubted that she could sleep. Odd, she thought, how easily and quickly the unthinkable can become the norm. Is that how people survive in places like Bosnia? Here she'd been having an impossible conversation with a plant that was telling her that she, Nikki, would somehow have to decide on how to save the world. (Nikki couldn't help laughing at that.) And the next minute she'd been casually chatting with Marj. *I didn't tremble or blubber or even dither.*

Well, I've been told I have to make a decision. What are my options? I can tell someone about my experiences and end up in a long-sleeved jacket. Am I ready for that? No. I can ignore it all and toss the fern into the lake—but then if more weirdness happens, like Adelaide's fingers, am I ready for that? And I wonder why I didn't mention Adelaide's fingers to Marj? Marj could have told me whether Adelaide has always been minus her left ring finger and pinky. It wasn't that Nikki had forgotten; something had stopped her.

This was her decision and hers alone. Could she go back to what she hoped she might find of her normal life? Could she pretend that none of this had happened? Or could she, as Boston Charlie had intimated, move into a future in which there would *be* no disaster—but still leave behind a world in which people would go berserk, decompose, be destroyed—not suddenly and mercifully, oh no, but over a period of time, since we live in a world that *has* such a thing as time. The virus would spread from Eagle Lake Park to the rest of the country, the continent, the world. How long would it take? Would it be a matter of a few months, a few years? Or would there be generations of chaos—generations of mutants doomed to inhabit a world gone mad? Is this what Boston Charlie had meant when he said we all create worlds? Nikki realized, with a bit of shock, that she would not even be plagued by guilt because she *simply wouldn't remember* any of this. This was her only point of power to make a decision. That decision might have been easier if Boston Charlie had explained exactly *how* he planned to extract the negative principle. Nikki should have asked him. But would she have understood even if he had given her the details? Anyway, she had to make a decision. What would it be? It might not work. There were no guarantees. It might be that no matter what they did, the virus would still do its worst, and that a chaotic, horrible version would be added to whatever cosmic inventory of worlds, according to Boston Charlie, already existed. What should she do? Nikki already knew the answer. She would have to try.

CHAPTER 27

IT WAS seven o'clock in the evening. Nikki had given Charlie Two a tin of salmon and made do, herself, with a cup of yogurt. She drew the curtains, closed the blinds, locked the doors. She had called Marj earlier to tell her that since she couldn't keep her eyes open, all she planned to do was to take a hot shower and go straight to bed. If she'd had that "Do Not Disturb" sign, Nikki would have hung it on the doorknob. Lacking that, she turned out all the lights except for one small battery lamp on the end table. She was just about to take the phone off the hook when it rang under her hand, sending a shock wave through her body.

"Hello, Nikki, it's me."

"Oh—hi, Phil."

"Are you all right? You sound funny."

"I'm okay. The phone startled me."

"Is there someone there with you?"

"Just a cat and a couple of houseplants."

"Are you *still* taking care of Marj's cat?"

"No. I have one of my own now."

"Since yesterday?"

"Yeah. Cat's are like shark's teeth. One goes, another pops up. What do you want, Phil?"

"Well, I didn't think I had to *want* anything in order to call you. I'm just checking to see how you are."

"Since yesterday?"

"I don't suppose you've had a chance to work on the IDC banner?"

"Well, no, I haven't. There no rush, is there?"

"I *was* rather hoping I could have it up by Monday. It's not as though it's a big project. All you have to do is change the date. I *was* planning to come by and pick it up tomorrow evening so Susan can hang it on Sunday. But if you have a cat in the house, maybe it would be better if *you* brought it by."

"I'll try. If Eagle Lake Park is still here and we haven't been zapped into another dimension by then, I'll drop it off Sunday morning. It's the best I can promise."

There was an audible sigh. "Well, I suppose that will have to do. I never could understand your black sense of humor."

Well, that's the first mention Phil has made of Susan. Susan will hang the banner. Susan is now the dogsbody. Nikki sat down on the couch and reached down to pat Charlie Two on the head. "Except for you she'd be here tomorrow night. Thank you, Charlie Two."

"You're welcome, I'm sure."

Nikki felt the same ice-water-in-the-veins sensation she always experienced when Charlie started talking, and wondered if she could ever get used to it. As if in answer, Charlie went on. "This will be the last time we'll be able to communicate this way. You've come to a decision?"

"I don't think *I* should be the one making the decision, but if the choice is whether we let a whole world to go crazy—even if we're not in it—or try to get rid of the virus, even though it's risky, I guess I'll have to go with getting rid of the virus. I wouldn't want that world on my conscience—even subconsciously."

"Then here's what you must do."

"*I?*"

"I'll be needing your help."

"Somehow that doesn't surprise me."

"Good. Tomorrow evening between your eleven o'clock and midnight the—how would your people put it?—the 'window of opportunity' will be open. It will be my last chance to return to my own dimension, and, if all goes well, I'll take the virus with me."

"And what do you want *me* to do?"

"I have made the mathematical and cosmic computations. I shall have to be situated in an exit point. Remember I mentioned multidimensional entry and exit points. It's a field in which all dimensions overlap, you see, so that travel between them is facilitated. By the way, this is something your scientists will discover one day and then you'll have true space travel."

"Do you know where to find one?"

"They exist everywhere. There are several inside your home here, but they are minor entry points. You may have noticed that you prefer to do your creative work in front of your window rather than in your office. You've sensed the presence of an entry point and you tap into the energy it emits. All energy in your system enters through such points. The universe isn't running down like a clock, nor was it created with a Big Bang. New energy is always being fed into the system, or perhaps 'recycled' is a better term—although, that, too, is more complicated. One of your scientists once said that ideas come from space. Indeed they do. For my purposes I'll need a much larger field of energy, and there is one in Eagle Lake Park that I hope will be powerful enough."

"Good. I was afraid I'd have to take you back to Bert's. Where is it?"

"It's right along the edge of the drop-off to the lake. You recall the spot where the old man fell. He sensed the presence of the energy field and was pulled toward it. That's where I must be placed tomorrow night."

"You mean you want me to carry you out there and leave you in the spot where the brambles were cut down?"

"Yes, but there's more. I may need your further help, but I'm not sure just how much I should tell you."

"I think you'd better tell me everything."

"Very well. I'll have to trust your discretion. Fortunately, the residents of Eagle Lake Park will be asleep, but there's always the chance of someone being about."

"Adelaide Moon's night patrol."

"When the process begins, no one, *no one*, is to approach the area I'm in. It could be very dangerous. This is why you'll have to keep watch. Under no circumstances let anyone come within a radius of ten of your yards—or is it your meters? I can never remember."

"Neither can anyone else in this country. Never mind. I get the idea. You want me to stand outside and keep an eye out for anyone who might be approaching and try to keep them from it." Nikki was wondering how she would be able to do that.

"You'll have to think of a way," Charlie replied to her unvoiced thought.

"It'll be dark. Nobody should be able to see you or anything else."

"I'm afraid, at least for some, there will be a great deal to see, once the process begins. Timing is vital and the conditions must be met. I will need—how should I say—a jump start. For that, I must have a fusion of all four of your earthly elements. Air is present everywhere. There is earth on my roots, and if you pour water over them, that will serve. I'll need fire. A simple candle should do. Place it next to my container, then move away, and remember that no matter *what* you see, *do not approach*. You'll know when it's over and safe to return to your home."

"Hey, wait a minute. What do you mean 'no matter what you see'? What's going to be happening?"

"In your case, you may be able to witness the entire event. Not everyone could. It's a matter of neurological pathways. In our dream association, and when you were doing your plant paintings, you've awakened certain areas of the brain that open up abilities that are latent in your species. It was necessary so that we could communicate. Some people have developed these pathways on their own, or in other dimensions—other incarnations. Some have the ability but need something to trigger it, like your friend, Marj. You might compare it to the fact that some people see ghosts while others do not."

"I'm going to see *ghosts?*"

"You may see forms. You see, in retrieving the contaminant, I will have to recall a replica of everything that might contain it. I will have to contact the individual consciousness units of all matter, and gain the cooperation of all of them in the emission of a replica that will then act as a carrier for the virus. With your heightened sensitivity, you may see these replicas as people or you may just see them as lights—or as a luminous mist. The replica of grass and trees might appear to you as a fog, for instance. Creatures with group consciousness, like birds, insects, fish in the lake, your rabbits, may appear as just bands of color."

"So what will be happening? You're going to suck up replicas of everything and everybody like some sort of a Noah with a Hoover? What will happen to the people?"

"When your replica leaves you and you see it go, you won't feel any different. You send out such replicas naturally all the time."

"*My* replica?" Nikki felt a shiver. The process Charlie described was one thing, but the idea that a part of herself would be included was something else again.

"Of course. Any life form that has had a mind link with me will have to be cleansed of the invading element, even those you might think of as being dead—if any strand of their consciousness still lingers in Eagle Lake Park. In addition, any life form that has had mind contact with *you* or others in Eagle Lake Park will have to be included as well. It would astound you to know the numbers involved in this. I will contact them all and request their compliance. Of course they won't be consciously aware of any of it, although those who remember their dreams may find them intriguing."

"And the only danger will be in getting too close?"

"Too close could mean being transported bodily and that is disastrous. It could also be disastrous to the process itself, causing a cosmic short circuit. There is also one other danger. Because your species is so varied in its development, there is always the possibility of a personality becoming splintered. The more integrated a personality is, the more easily it can withstand a—what should I call it?—a virusectomy? A personality that is entertaining a number of negative principles already could, conceivably, lose more than one—which could, then, alter your world. If someone had performed this operation on your Hitler, for instance, World War II might not have happened in that particular reality."

"That wouldn't have been a bad thing."

"No, but another might have taken his place—another who might have been successful in world domination."

"I see what you mean. But if you guys have that kind of power, why not just rid the world of all evil?"

"We *don't* have that kind of power or authority. I've already overstepped and am taking desperate measures to undo. Only *you* as a species can remake your worlds, and that is the great lesson of living in your plane: Learning to create your own reality in a responsible manner. My only concern now is to try to correct the situation by transporting the harmful influence back to my own plane, where I hope to be able to dispose of it."

"Like nuclear waste?"

"Not a bad analogy."

"I hate to say this, but are you sure your world will still *be* there? I mean, it was destroyed, wasn't it?"

"The biosphere certainly was. As to the extent of the damage, I'm hoping our scientists will have been able to contain it. In any case, there will be much work to do, and I will be needed. Wait until late evening, tomorrow, to move me to the spot. Oh yes, and according to my mathematical computations, it would be best to raise me up to a level of three or four feet above the ground. Perhaps you can hang my container by the hook to a tree.

"Good-bye, Nikki. We *will* meet again, but in a different way. And remember: *No matter what you hear or see, do not allow anyone to come near me.*"

"But what if—" Nikki saw that it was no use. It was over. Charlie Two blinked twice, turned and headed for his water bowl. Nikki felt the settling of a huge weight of responsibility. Boston Charlie had stopped talking. Boston Charlie was not going to help her now or tell her what to do. From here on it would all be up to her. Could she do it? *Would* she do it? Could she *not* do it? It was like being given a post-hypnotic suggestion, except that she was aware of it. If a person had been given a post-hypnotic suggestion to climb into a toilet bowl and sing show tunes, would he do it if he knew the suggestion was there? He'd feel stupid if anyone saw him. Could he just dismiss it? Nikki didn't belabor the point. A promise was a promise even when made to a plant.

It was too late in the evening—too dark out—for Nikki to go check the area Charlie had described. She would do that in the morning. She realized that she was tired. *I think I'll go to bed early.* "Good night, Charlie Two. I guess your job is done, and I suppose I could turn you loose if you'd rather go. What do you think?" Charlie Two yawned, stretched, then settled himself into an orange doughnut on the rug. "Wise choice. There are always the night patrols."

CHAPTER 28

Nikki awakened early. To her disappointment, she remembered no dreams of any kind. She had been hoping that Boston Charlie might still be in contact. Mechanically, she went through her morning routine—fed the cat, watered plants, even Charlie, as if he'd been any other Boston fern. *Are we really going to go on with this?* Part of her mind was resisting, urging her to not be an idiot, urging her to deny everything that had happened, urging her virtually to reconstruct her past.

You can change the past and you can change the future but you can't alter the present because that is your point of power. The words seemed to just appear in Nikki's mind and hang there, as if written on a blackboard. "Okay, Boston Charlie, I get the message."

Nikki went out and, carrying her cup of coffee, walked past Marj's mobile, past the Laderheims, past Raymond Cantwell's empty home, past the Hatches to the spot where Unit One awaited Clark Moon and his bride. *This would've been a lot easier if Charlie's cosmic entry point had been in front of my place.* She checked the area that had been a tangle of briars and brush but now had been leveled so that not a sapling remained. There was nowhere to hang Charlie's basket. She could bring a lawn chair, she supposed, and stack something on it to get Charlie to the right height. She would also have to do it in the dark tonight, or think up a really good story for anyone who came along and asked what she thought she was doing.

The picnic table! The picnic table in front of Unit One would work. All she would have to do is move it about twenty feet to the edge of the embankment. If any of the residents noticed, they might think the Moons had moved it for reasons of their own. A rough plank table with built-in benches, the structure was heavy. While a score of rabbits watched blankly, Nikki tried lifting one end. No way! To move it, she would need help. There was only one person she could possibly ask. *Marj* would help her move the table and maybe Marj would even help her stand watch that night. Nikki didn't relish the idea of cowering alone in the darkness. There was one sizable hurdle. She would have to tell Marj what was going on, at least some of it, and risk having her call the men in white coats.

Marj was on her porch. "Hi there! Early to bed, early to rise?"

"Sort of."

"Come on in. You want that coffee warmed?" She took Nikki's cup, then looked at her sharply. "What have you been up to?"

"Well, right now I was wondering if you'd help me move the Unit One picnic table to the edge of the embankment."

Marj put down the cup. "Of course. Do you want to do it now?"

"Now's good. Nobody seems to be around."

Marj nodded and the two of them, with no further discussion, headed for Unit One.

"If I take one end and you take the other, we may be able to lift it. If not, we'll have to 'walk' it one end at a time."

"Where, exactly, do you want this thing?" Marj asked as they muscled the wooden hulk closer to the edge.

"Right where the brambles have been cut. The spot where your father fell."

It took a combination of lifting, pulling and shoving to get the table situated where Nikki wanted it. It stood, tilted, on the rough ground. Marj gave it a final push that wedged it in place and sent one of the legs partly over the edge, thus leveling the top. "Is that okay? It's not entirely steady. I take it you don't plan to serve food on it."

"Perfect. I hope nobody saw us."

"Now we'll go back and finish our coffee."

"Aren't you going to ask me why we moved the table?"

"No. I'm rather enjoying the speculation. I can think of a whole list of reasons. Yours might be an anticlimax."

"I don't think it would be."

On Marj's screened porch, with Casimir sleeping in a patch of sunlight, Nikki told Marj everything—well, almost everything. She made every effort to sound sane and reasonable as she explained about Boston Charlie and Charlie Two, very much aware, here in the bright light of day, how all of it must have sounded. Marj, wearing her poker face, listened without comment. Nikki's voice began to falter along with her self-confidence. "I don't *think* I'm crazy. Would you please *say* something!"

"You're right. It's *not* an anticlimax." Marj shifted her gaze out into the sunlit morning. "Nikki, I don't know *what* to say. I can't just say I believe you because I *don't*—although I'm not saying you're lying. You sound like *you* really believe all of this—unless you're just trying out a plot line on me."

Nikki sighed. "I know. I should be seeing assorted shrinks. And if I end up sitting up all night with a sick fern and nothing happens, I may do just that."

Marj looked uncomfortable. "You're asking me to believe that this plant—this fern—is an alien from another system. And that somehow this alien has contaminated Eagle Lake Park, and that's why everything has been so weird lately. Now he's going back to his own world but he has to take the virus with him. Is that right?"

Nikki closed her eyes, nodded, but said nothing.

"And if we don't do this, our world will be destroyed?"

Nikki had not gone into detail about the manner of destruction. She had tried to keep the explanation as simple as possible. Now she just nodded again.

Marj sat silent for a long time.

"No matter how crazy it sounds, I have to do this." Nikki told her. "If you don't want any part of it, I understand."

"Who says? Hey, how often do I get to take part in a full blown delusion? Look, Nikki, my gut feeling is that while I have no idea what this is all about, you're *not* out of your mind. It's also intriguing as hell. Maybe if we go through the motions, we'll be able to reason it out. My thinking is, if we do this thing, you'll come to realize how preposterous it is. Once, when I was a kid, I actually believed I could fly. I told my grandmother about it and instead of telling me I couldn't, she took me to a rock in the woods and asked me to show her. Well, you can guess what happened. I jumped off the rock and landed on my ass on a bunch of moss. Object lesson. If it hadn't been for her, I might have jumped off something bigger and hurt myself. Okay, you're not a kid, but something's got you convinced that Eagle Lake Park will self-destruct."

"Convinced? There's a big part of *me* that thinks this is some brain disorder caused by gulping down pond water when I was swimming as a kid—or that any minute I'll wake up in my jammies with the sheets in a twist."

"Hey, with all the strange things that have been happening here lately, *I'd* be willing to believe a lot of things—although, I admit, not this."

"I don't think I expect anyone to believe it. I'm just glad you're not dialing 911."

"And just so nobody else does either, we're going to have to make it look reasonable. We can station ourselves at *my* picnic table and hope the night patrol will be able to tell we're not a couple of bull's-eyes."

"I have a spotting scope. We can say we're looking at craters on the moon."

"That's *good*. It looks like it might be a clear night. We can move my table a bit closer so we'll have a better view. What is it we're going to have a view of?"

"We have to make sure no one goes near Boston Charlie."

"Okay, and what else?"

"I don't know what we'll see," Nikki said a bit reluctantly. "Charlie said we might see lights and things."

"Like the northern lights?"

"Maybe. And maybe—uh—ghostly forms. Charlie called them replicas of people."

Marj gave her a long look. "Replicas? Like the ones my grandmother said she could see?" Nikki saw that Marj's attitude had, at that moment, changed. This was no longer just a game to humor Nikki; this was something else.

...

With the mind of a crossword puzzle constructor, Nikki planned and cross-planned strategy. She set up the tripod and mounted the spotting scope. The scope was a relic from her past that Nikki had bought to observe planets in the solar system, even though it wasn't an astronomical telescope. Phil had never had any interest in the heavens, and Nikki hadn't used the scope in years. Tonight it could serve as a cover story if it turned out that they needed one, and a way of viewing, from a distance, whatever Boston Charlie was doing. She put the telescope on the deck for the time being and rounded up other things she might need—a flashlight, binoculars, a thermos (for hot chocolate), an additional sweater and jacket, two pairs of gloves—and stuffed them in her survival bag. The night might turn cool if there was a wind from the lake, and Nikki had a feeling it might not be possible to run home for warmer clothing.

She and Marj moved Marj's picnic table to the edge of the Laderheim property line. There was no sign of the Laderheims or of the Hatches, nor had any of the Moons happened by. It had been unusually quiet all day. Nikki learned why, later, from Paulette Crushill, who came over to tell her that Emily Laderheim had suffered a stroke and been taken to Nanaimo General Hospital during the night. Paulette and Fred were going to the hospital to see how she was doing and did Nikki want to come? The Moons were there already, along with the Hatches who were good friends of the Laderheims. Nikki lied and said she and Marj would go later if it turned out that Mrs. Laderheim could have visitors.

Nikki was sorry to hear about Emily Laderheim and wondered, darkly, if it had really been a stroke at all or the next step in the disintegration of the human race.

CHAPTER 29

THE EVENING routine became almost ceremonial. Nikki fed Charlie Two a can of tuna. Marj came over and the two women ate a Spartan meal of soup, bread and cheese. Both too keyed-up to be hungry, they nibbled rather than relished the meal that seemed more symbolic than sustaining. To Nikki, a former Lutheran, the repast made her think of the Last Supper, ritualistic, momentous, and ominous—nifty puzzle words! Nikki made a pot of tea and served it on the deck.

Eagle Lake Park had been deserted that day, but now people were returning to their homes. They heard the sound of Fred Crushill's old Chevrolet and Paulette's voice as she greeted Pierre, their poodle. The Laderheim unit was dark; presumably Justin was remaining at the hospital to be near Emily. The Hatches were at home; at least there was a light in their living room. Janet and Bob's trailer stood dark and empty. The evening was calm and mild enough to be comfortable. A few ragged clouds cast a bit of cover.

"We might as well set up our telescope. If the clouds don't get any thicker, we'll be able to get a good look at the harvest moon."

Nikki said.

"I don't think we'll have to worry about anyone patrolling the park tonight," Marj remarked, as they carried out the spotting scope and tried to find a level spot among the rabbit holes for the feet of the tripod.

"You think?"

"I think the excitement is dying down, what with Emily's stroke or whatever she had. The Hatches and Justin won't be concerned with anything else—Justin, if he comes home at all, will want to be near the phone. That leaves Fred Crushill and the Moons to do any patrolling. If anyone at all is out tonight it'll have to be George and Clark, and my guess is they only do it to humor Adelaide. And if Adelaide's been at the hospital all day, chances are she'll be so preoccupied with Emily that there'll be no night marchers."

"From your mouth to God's ear, as my mother used to say. I feel foolish enough already without having to explain to anyone."

"*You* feel foolish! What's in this bag of yours?"

"Oh, just a couple of sweaters and jackets, a flashlight in case we need one, a thermos—survival stuff. Everything looks quiet. I guess I could take Boston Charlie out and put him on the picnic table." Mindful of Charlie's instructions, she gave the plant a good watering while Marj looked on quizzically.

"Charlie said he'd need the four elements: earth, air, fire and water. I don't know what for, but we're covered on three of them—but I'm going to need a candle."

"Take the one off my porch table. It sits in a glass so it won't blow out—and take the flashlight so you won't step in a hole and break a leg. I'll wait here and try to come up with a logical explanation if anyone comes by and wants to know what we're up to."

No one saw Nikki carry the plant to the far picnic table and place it on top, like a centerpiece. Charlie looked rather nice there, a bit ghostly in the moonlight, with his fronds spread out in all directions;

Nikki wondered whether she'd be sheepishly retrieving him in the morning. "Charlie, if this is your idea of a cosmic joke!" She backtracked to Marj's mobile and picked up the candle and a book of matches, then returned to Boston Charlie, placed the candle next to the plant, then lit the wick, almost expecting to create some sort of explosion. Nothing happened. *I forgot to ask, but there's probably some kind of split-second timing involved in all this, assuming, of course, that I'm not the world's biggest idiot.*

As Nikki was returning, a light went on in the Laderheims' unit. Justin must have come home after all. Nikki scurried past, avoiding, as best she could, rabbit holes. She hadn't turned on the flashlight for fear it would make her conspicuous.

Back at Marj's picnic table, Marj was rummaging through Nikki's survival bag. "It's getting a bit chilly out here. If you don't mind I'll borrow one of your sweaters."

"That's why I brought them. You know, you're really being a *very* good sport. With all you've been through lately, you didn't need this." Nikki looked at Marj. She appeared pale and beautiful in the moonlight, but she also looked gaunt and thin, as if she'd lost weight, and the shadows under her eyes seemed more than a trick of the lighting. "When all this is over, you could use a good rest Take a vacation. Get away from Eagle Lake Park and Jonah and his problems—and friends who get you involved in crazy stuff. Right now there's a part of me that's saying, what the hell are we doing out here anyway?"

"I'll have to admit, *all* of me is saying that."

"Right now I'm hoping that *nothing* happens here tonight." In the distance they could see the pale flicker of the candle flame.

"So am I."

"Even if it means I must have a severe psychological problem."

"I think we could deal with that easier than with a universal disaster."

Nikki noticed that Marj was still shivering. "You want cocoa?"

"Sure."

Nikki poured two cups of hot chocolate and handed one to Marj. As Marj reached for hers, Nikki saw, by the light of the moon, that Marj's hand was missing two fingers.

Nikki stifled a gasp, then looked at her own hands. They seemed, at least so far, normal. Marj had picked up her cup and was sipping chocolate, seemingly unaware that there was anything unusual about her right hand. Nikki looked again. Was it a trick of the moonlight? No. Clearly, Marj's hand was missing the ring finger and pinky, much as Adelaide's had been. Adelaide hadn't appeared to notice it either, although Nikki remembered that she had kept her hand in her pocket. *It's real. It's really happening. It's not a nightmare and it's not my imagination. We're in danger, all of us. I mustn't panic. And I mustn't panic Marj. Maybe that's the way it works—you don't notice at first that it's happening.* Nikki recalled the fleeing people in her dream. They were being dismembered, disintegrating before her eyes, but they didn't seem to be aware of it themselves. She remembered the woman with no hands holding the child with no legs. The woman seemed only intent on fleeing the earthquake. *God, Charlie, I hope whatever you're going to do works!*

"*Great* hot chocolate, Nikki. What did you put in it?"

"A shot of Curaçao." It *was* getting colder, or was it just that Nikki felt chilled from within. "There seems to be a wind coming up from the lake."

"Yes, and the clouds are getting thicker."

Nikki put on a windbreaker and wordlessly handed one to Marj who put in on over her sweater. Marj looked at the heavens. "I'm afraid it's going to rain on our parade."

"What time is it?"

Marj looked at her watch. "Nearly midnight. Maybe it might be a good idea to go inside. We could still watch from my porch." The minute the words were out of here mouth, there was a flash of lightning that transfigured everything in livid flare.

"You go ahead, Marj. I'll stay here."

Another flash of lightning seemed to transform them both into white marble statues. "I'll stay with you."

"No, go ahead. It's starting to rain."

"Not if you're not coming with me." The wind was stronger now and drops of rain were beginning to splatter.

"Oh *shit!*" Nikki was peering into the darkness. "I don't see the candle flame." She moved to the spotting scope, trained it toward the picnic table. "I can't see anything. The rain must have put it out. I have to go back and light it!"

"Forget it, Nikki. You'll never be able to get it lit now, and you're not supposed to go near—" but Nikki had already grabbed her survival bag and was racing through the darkness.

Somehow she managed not to trip on a rabbit hole, although her progress was hazardous on the uneven ground. As she approached, she saw that yes, indeed, the candle had gone out, and that the book of matches she'd left next to it was now wet as well. *Dammit! Well, this is where we get to try out our survival kit.* She unzipped the bag, rummaged inside and took out her Swedish FireSteel. *Am I not the goddess of fire? Okay, amalgam of nineteen metals, do your stuff!* But of course she'd need something to light! She couldn't expect to send a spark flying into the candle holder and have a wet wick flame up, could she? She went through the stuff in the bag. Socks? Underwear? No! Something even better. She pulled out a tampon, removed it from its dispenser and fluffed up the cotton, positioned the FireSteel over it. She pulled the striker across the rod and watched as sparks flew— but didn't ignite. Raindrops continued to fall and now the tampon was wet as well. Frustrated, Nikki kept striking, sparks kept flying, and then, it seemed as if a very large spark flashed from the striker with such brilliance that Nikki dropped it and fell over backwards. Light was everywhere now, and she frantically pushed with her feet, backing away from the table, then got up and ran back to where Marj was standing transfixed and calling her name.

"I'm here! I don't know what just happened but—" Nikki didn't have a chance to finish. Another flash of lightning, then a growl of thunder, was followed by a flash of light that seemed to rise up out of the ground. Both women stood astounded as the light appeared out of everywhere and nowhere, then began to dance and swirl around them. It was no ordinary lightning, this, but a pale glow that seemed, somehow, alive, and composed of many colors—colors that kept shifting and changing so rapidly that the effect was almost subliminal. The light whirled around them, like water draining from a tub. Then it vanished.

"What the hell was that?" Marj said. "I've never seen lightning like that before!"

"I think it's starting," Nikki said. "Charlie said there'd be lights."

"Oh God!"

Rain was coming down harder now, and it was clear they were in the middle of a thunderstorm. "Go inside, Marj," Nikki shouted. "Casimir will be frightened." At that, both Nikki and Marj were astounded to see Casimir himself. Somehow the cat had gotten out. They could see him in the flashes of light, streaking away, heading toward Boston Charlie. "Oh my god," Marj shrieked. She started to follow the cat but Nikki held on to her arm. "It's not Casimir, Marj. It's his apparition. Can't you see? He's transparent. You can see right through him."

Marj gave her a wild look and tried to pull free. "It's like your grandmother said, it's just his forerunner," Nikki yelled. "Charlie said we might see them. Look, there's Charlie Two. Marj, Boston Charlie is pulling in replicas of everything that has the virus. We'll probably see ourselves but we mustn't try to follow."

Marj's eyes were huge and dark, her expression shocked. "Just hold on, Marj," Nikki shouted above the noise of the storm. She gripped Marj's arm while the thunder and rain crashed around them, and strained to see what would be the most bizarre spectacle of her life:

There were forms, now, hundreds of them, in ghostly motion, all moving toward Boston Charlie. Nikki couldn't make out who they all were, but she did recognize a number of them—inhabitants of Eagle Lake Park, moving in a deliberate manner, like sleepwalkers. She saw the Crushills, the Laderheims, the Hatches, the elderly Moons. She thought she recognized Janet and Bob, and even Bert from the nursery. Boston Charlie wasn't taking any chances! It was a lot like Nikki's dream of people being called when their musical notes were sounded—and it was then she *did* hear her own note and saw her own form leave her body and walk away. At that moment, Nikki panicked. It was one thing to watch the shades of other people, but when her own detached itself and moved forward, Nikki impulsively tried to follow, but stopped when she heard Marj scream.

Marj was grasping her by the arm. "Look, she said, it's my father!"

Nikki, near hysteria herself, peered through the rain. Indeed it was Einar Kuusisto. He was wearing the blue striped pajamas he'd worn the night of his death and was moving, zombie-like, in the ghostly parade. "Why?" Marj sobbed. "Why is he here? He's *dead!*"

"I don't know." Nikki was holding Marj now, preventing her from following her father. "Maybe—maybe that's what a ghost is—the part that doesn't die."

Marj covered her face with her hands and sobbed. Nikki put an arm around her while the rain fell and the wind blew and the specters kept coming. Part of Nikki wanted to run inside and hide under the blankets, but another part of her was so fascinated by the spectacle that she feared if she blinked she would miss something. Now Nikki could see Marj's shape in the group, then, to her mystification, she thought she could make out Phillida Lowry. Phil? Why Phil?—except that Phil had visited Eagle Lake Park. And wasn't that Susan? Nikki couldn't be sure. There were many she didn't recognize at all—hundreds, it seemed. Thousands? Then she laughed, although the laugh was on the edge of hysteria, as she spotted the two Jehovah's Witnesses who had come to her door. Was Boston Charlie calling in everyone? At that moment Marj looked up and grabbed Nikki's arm so hard it hurt. "Look, there's Jonah."

"Where?" Nikki had never met the man.

"There, right in front of—oh my god, it's Raymond Cantwell!"

They peered through the rain, and yes, indeed it *was* Raymond Cantwell, at least the phantom of Raymond Cantwell, moving purposefully forward along with the rest, and beside him stalked the ghostly replica of a dog—Prince. It was then they saw that the form of Raymond Cantwell was being followed by Adelaide Moon.

"Look, there's Adelaide," Marj said.

Nikki looked, then gasped. "That's not the ghost of Adelaide," she said. "That's really *Adelaide!*"

Adelaide Moon did look different from the rest of the throng. Unlike the other forms, she was obviously fighting the storm. Her wet hair was blowing in the wind, and she was leaning against its force, lurching as she made her way over the rough ground. She seemed to be following Raymond Cantwell and calling out to him, her words swallowed up by the tempest.

"Oh, god, we've got to stop her," Nikki said, and pulled herself free of Marj's grip. She started to run, then slipped and nearly fell on the wet grass, regained her footing and managed to catch up with Adelaide just as she was nearing the picnic table where Boston Charlie stood. Only it was no longer a picnic table. Nikki could see that it was a globe of light. She momentarily was transfixed by the sight of the huge field of white light into which forms of people were disappearing, as if into an immense ball of lightning. Adelaide was almost upon it when Nikki threw herself forward and tackled the woman, bringing them both down onto the grass and mud.

"Adelaide," Nikki screamed. "Stop!" She tried to pin Adelaide down but the woman fought her with the strength of the demented.

"Let go of me!" she yelled. "*Let go of me!*"

"No!" Nikki shouted. "It's not Raymond. It's his ghost. Don't try to follow him."

With an animal-like snarl, Adelaide threw Nikki to one side and sprang to her feet like a cat. "Get out of my way you filthy bitch!" Her eyes were wild and her face contorted. She screamed, then, and lunged at Nikki, knocking her off balance. To Nikki the woman looked totally insane. Nikki struggled to regain her footing, then rushed at Adelaide grasped her around the waist. "Adelaide, stop!" she yelled over the sound of the storm. "You'll be killed!" Adelaide screamed in fury, and as she twisted herself free, hit Nikki a stunning blow on the head with her elbow. Nikki saw her run toward the light into which Raymond Cantwell had already vanished. She swayed, stumbled toward Adelaide, tried to tackle her again, but her arms closed over air, and the last thing she saw was Adelaide Moon throwing herself into the dazzling whiteness.

Then everything went dark. The storm raged on, but the light and the phantoms had vanished. Blinded by the sudden darkness, Nikki groped her way toward the spot and found it empty. She realized that Adelaide must have pushed the picnic table over the edge of the embankment, and fallen with it. Her foot caught on wet stubble and Nikki felt herself falling as well. Wildly she grabbed for support, but her footing was unstable in the cut briars, and in a final effort to keep from going over the embankment, Nikki threw her body backwards as she fell down and into unconsciousness.

CHAPTER 30

Nikki woke to find Marj either shaking her by the shoulders or just holding on to her. She looked around wildly, to see she was in her own bed, and awakening, she thought, from the mother of all nightmares. But what was Marj doing here? Everything was blurry. Was it morning? It looked like morning, and there was a cup of coffee on her bed stand.

Marj had let go and was now looking at her intently. "Are you awake now? Are you okay?"

Nikki took a deep breath. Her throat felt dry, as if she'd been running and breathing through her mouth—and she had a headache, but otherwise she seemed to be . . . normal. Sort of. She was feeling panicky, as if she were in danger, but obviously there was nothing threatening her now. "What happened?"

"Don't you remember?"

"Uh . . . I don't know. Was it a dream?"

"Just lie back for minute and try to relax. See if you remember anything."

Nikki leaned back, then suddenly sat up again. "Oh my god, Adelaide! I tried to stop her but she fell over the edge. Is she all right? Did somebody find her? Did that really happen or did I dream it?"

Marj silently handed her the cup. "Take a sip of this." Nikki too a big gulp of coffee that had cooled enough to make that possible. It felt good going down her throat and made it easier for her to talk. "I . . . I keep remembering all kinds of crazy stuff. It must have been a dream, and you were in it. And so were *you!* Nikki was looking at Charlie Two who had leapt up on the bed. My god, I sound like Dorothy."

Marj smiled thinly. "We have the Tin Man, and the Cowardly Lion, but I'm afraid we lost the Scarecrow. No, it wasn't a dream, at least not entirely."

"Adelaide! The part about Adelaide. Did that happen?"

Marj spoke carefully: "So far, nobody knows *what* happened to Adelaide."

"What do you mean? I saw her go into—there was a bright light. She jumped into it. I tried to stop her, but she fought me and I fell. And then the light went out and I saw the picnic table had gone over the edge so she must have fallen with it. I . . . I don't remember what happened next."

"You blacked out. I found you. You were lucky you didn't go over the bank yourself."

"But Adelaide must still be down there. Did she fall on the roof of the camper like your dad? Has anyone looked? We have to tell somebody!"

"She's not there. She's nowhere."

"How is that possible?"

"The picnic table fell on Justin Laderheim's camper and pretty much totaled it, but there was no sign of Adelaide."

"Charlie! Boston Charlie! What happened to Boston Charlie!"

"Gone."

Nikki had the feeling that she'd missed something. "What time is it? How long have I been asleep?"

"It's noon."

"Why didn't you wake me up? I have to tell everyone what happened. We have to find Adelaide!"

"There's a search going on for Adelaide, and she'll probably be found. But she's not where you think she is, and, trust me, if you go telling a story about Boston Charlie and Charlie Two and Adelaide jumping into the light, do you think anyone will believe you? What I want you to do now is get up, see if you're steady enough on your feet to go take a shower. Meanwhile I'll make us some lunch. We can talk this over calmly afterwards."

Nikki looked at her own disbelieving face in the bathroom mirror and slowly pieced together events that seemed impossible, but, somehow, must have happened. Showered and dressed, she saw that Marj had put together a light meal from ingredients in Nikki's kitchen: a bowl of Lipton's chicken noodle soup and a cucumber sandwich. Suddenly hungry, Nikki wolfed it down with another cup of coffee.

"Now," Marj said, as if she were delivering a rehearsed speech, "Nobody knows anything about last night. All they know is that Adelaide must have gone out into the storm and didn't come back. Everyone assumes she'll be found eventually, but nobody knows you were the last to see her. It would be best to keep it that way! Neither you nor I know what happened to Adelaide. Maybe she did go over the edge. Maybe she managed to survive the fall and just wandered away. We know she was unstable, and she could have gone anywhere. There is no need for either of us to become involved in this. If she turns up, she'll have her own wild story to tell, and nobody will believe her anymore than they'd believe us. We'd all just come off sounded totally crazy."

"But we can't just do nothing, can we? It's all my fault, isn't it? I feel responsible. I should do *something*."

"And what would that be?"

"Go look for her?"

"Where?"

"Oh, I don't know. I keep thinking of what Boston Charlie said about being transported bodily, and that it would be disastrous. Is that what happened? Did Adelaide end up in Boston Charlie's world?"

"If she did, you'll never find her. If she didn't, then someone will. I think we should just close the book on this. Don't discuss it with anyone. No one would believe you."

"They *might*. You saw it all. You could back me up."

"We'd come off sounding like a couple of loonies, or a couple of pranksters. But if anyone took it seriously, it could be worse. We would then become prime suspects in the disappearance of Adelaide Moon. Picture the police interrogation! It would be best if we just forgot it ever happened. Call it a dream. Who's to know? Maybe it *was*. After a while, after a spell of normal living, it *will* seem like a dream. Just let it go."

"I don't know if I can do that."

Marj got up to pour more coffee when the telephone rang. She picked it up. "Hello?" She held out the receiver and mouthed, "It's Phil." Nikki looked annoyed and shook her head, then changed her mind and reached for it.

"Hi, Phil. No, I'm sorry but I don't have the banner done. In fact, I won't have time to do it at all. I'll have to drop it off at your office, maybe tomorrow. If you give Susan a paint brush. I'm sure she can change the date for you." Nikki rolled her eyes at Marj. "I know I promised, but that's not important now. The important thing is, you and I won't be involved in each other's lives in the future. We had some good times, but now we need to move on." There was a pause. "Really?" Nikki looked puzzled. "Generous of you to say that, and of course I wish you and Susan the best too . . . 'bye. . . ." She slowly put down phone and stared at it thoughtfully.

"Are you okay?"

"What I am is *gobsmacked!* She said she totally understood, apologized for having imposed, and that it was perfectly all right about the banner. She wished me well. What the hell just happened?"

Marj shrugged. "Some kind of trick? Or maybe Susan is having a good influence on her. Want any more of this coffee? We can go out and see how Eagle Lake Park looks now."

"No coffee, but I do want to take a look around."

Eagle Lake Park was looking battered. The storm had littered the area with branches, fir cones, leaves, and bits of greenery. The deck was trashy with maple wings and brown sprigs of cedar. Nikki stopped to pick dried cedar debris out of her planter, liberating the herbs. Someone's garbage can had tipped over and rolled across the grass to come to rest against a picnic table. The wind was no longer blowing, but the skies and lake were both gray. Nikki's spotting scope was propped against the deck railing. No one seemed to be about except for a few rabbits as Nikki and Marj walked past the Laderheims and the Hatches to where Charlie Two's picnic table had stood.

Nikki approached the edge of the bluff, stepping carefully into a bristle of stems left behind from George's weedwhipping. She looked down to see Justin Laderheim's camper with the picnic table crushing its roof. Certainly no sign of Adelaide—or Boston Charlie—except for an empty plastic pot with hanging wires lying on the ground as if thrown.

"Seems awfully quiet. I wonder where everyone is."

"There was plenty of excitement earlier this morning. Everyone was looking for Adelaide. They're probably all reconnoitering at the Moons'. Maybe they stopped for lunch."

"Did anyone wonder about the picnic table?"

"I think they decided there must have been a tornado spawned by the storm. It seemed to be the only possible explanation. You were still sleeping and I didn't want to leave you alone so I didn't stick around. I found your survival bag and brought it back, and your spotting scope had fallen over, so I brought that back too. Nobody asked me anything."

"Did you stay with me all night?"

"I slept on your couch. I left you sleeping while I went and fed Casimir."

"I don't remember anything past Adelaide diving in, and then the light going out." Nikki backed away from the edge. "It's almost unbelievable now. Everything looks . . . ordinary. Like there's just been a big windstorm that blew things around, and that's all."

"And that *is* all, *isn't it?*"

Nikki had spotted something on the grass and picked it up. "Look at this. It's my FireSteel. I was trying to save the world with a FireSteel and a tampon!"

"Must have worked. We're all still here."

"I wanted to light the candle, and the FireSteel is supposed to work when it's wet, but I needed something dry to light—so I took out a tampon to use as tinder, but of course the rain just soaked it and it didn't work. The steel *did* work in the rain, just like it said in the instructions. I kept trying and I was getting sparks, then everything just flared up. Might not even have been me; might have been the lightning that did it. Anyway, I knew I wasn't supposed to get too close, so I got out of there. Now I'm wondering what happened to Boston Charlie. Did it work? Or did Adelaide screw things up? As soon as she went into the light, everything stopped. It might have been too soon for Charlie to finish what he was doing. God, I hope they find her. I'd hate to think that I—"

"—sent her into the Pit of Peril? Not likely. She'll probably turn up of her own accord. She may have been dazed by the fall, wandered off, may not remember who she is. If so, somebody's bound to find her, or, when she regains her memory, she'll come home. If she was able to walk away, she couldn't have been that badly hurt."

"You don't sound too worried about her."

"No, I don't, do I? The Adelaides of the world always seem to land on their feet, and wherever she is, she'll be a force to be reckoned with."

"Do you think it's possible that she *could* have been transported, along with Boston Charlie, into another dimension?"

Marj yawned. "Be the trip of a lifetime! Talk about an adventure! She'd certainly be a challenge for Boston Charlie! Excuse me, I didn't get much sleep last night. That futon couch isn't all that comfortable."

"Marj?"

"Yeah?"

"I'm getting out of here."

"I'm hoping we both will, eventually."

"I mean *now*. I can't stay here. I *won't* stay here. All this has been just too weird for me. I'm going to pack up my stuff and my cat, and grab the first vacancy I can afford. I don't want to be here whether they find Adelaide or not. You're right, if I told anybody what happened, I'd end up in a rubber room, but I don't want to be here with these people, knowing what I know, and having to pretend that I *don't*."

"I'll miss you, old thing, but I have a feeling I'll be out of here quite soon myself. I'm getting one of those major life change vaticinations."

"Ooh, nifty puzzle word! I've never heard it!"

"I've been waiting to spring it on you."

"I take it that it means prophecy, but where did you find it?"

"I think it was the *Reader's Digest*. One of those word power quizzes."

CHAPTER 31

Nikki Leino shut off her computer. Enough for one day. Chapter ten had come in well. Her creative processes operated in predictable stages these days. Whenever she was about half way through a book, she would "get" the raw material for the next one. By time she was ready to start writing it, the story would have worked itself into shape in her mind—or her subconscious—so that when she began to type it up, it flowed almost as if she were taking dictation. She never used an outline, just put it down as it came, then polished the prose later. She'd been working in her favorite spot, a counter next to her office window upon which she'd situated her latest Macintosh computer— the fourth in a series of computer upgrades through the years. The spot by the window was what Boston Charlie would probably have called a multidimensional entry point, because there Nikki always felt energized and did her best work.

Charlie Two, who had been curled up, asleep, at Nikki's elbow, woke and stretched his legs. Nikki picked him up and gently deposited him on the floor. Charlie Two was showing his age, not that Nikki knew how old a cat he was, but he *was* slowing down and Nikki suspected that his eyesight was not all that sharp anymore. She'd had him now, for what?—thirteen years!

"What's up, Charlie? You want out?" Nikki stretched too. She followed the cat down the hall to the kitchen door, opened it and let him out into the fenced back yard. "Try not to get fleas." She looked at the clock. Time to shower and change. Nikki was meeting an old friend for dinner at the Mahle House, which was fortunately only a five minute drive from her own little house near the sea. It had been over ten years since they'd last met, and there had been little contact between them since Marj left the island.

As Nikki drove her green Jeep Cherokee to the restaurant, she mused that it would be strange seeing Marj again. What would she be like now? *Smart and sophisticated, I'll bet, what with her new life, bopping all over Europe, sopping up culture.*

Nikki was first to arrive. Her car seemed to be the only one in the lot, as she'd made an early reservation to avoid the evening crowd. As she walked up the ramp that had been recently constructed for wheelchair access, a small gray cat with tiger markings ran to meet her and rubbed against her ankle. "Hi, kitty. You're new here, aren't you?" The cat followed her to the door and slipped inside. "Are you sure you're allowed in here?"

The hostess, Josie, met Nikki at the door, intercepted the cat and scooped it up. "She knows she's not supposed to be in the dining room but she keeps trying. Out you go, Stormy!"

"What happened to Mitzi?"

"Old age. Mitzi's gone to the Heavyside Layer. This one showed up one night when there was a thunderstorm, and never left." Josie put the cat out and led Nikki to her table in the non-smoking area, a cheery room at a lower level that had been added some years ago.

Nikki settled herself in one of the ornate enameled iron peacock chairs and observed the view of the gardens where herbs grew and rhododendrons bloomed. It had been some time since she'd been to the Mahle. Nothing much had changed except some of the paintings on the walls, works by local artists. Mitzi the cat who, like Old Deuteronomy, had spent her senior years dozing on the garden wall, was gone as well, replaced now by an orphan of a storm.

Nikki well remembered the night of her own big storm. She had not chosen to forget it, as Boston Charlie had told her she might do. She carried the memory of it like an unappraised diamond in her pocket, not certain of its value, but sensing that it was worth a great deal. From that time, her life had taken a new direction. For one thing, she was no longer a designer of crossword puzzles. Her series of children's books, *The Adventures of Charlie Two*, illustrated with her own drawings, had started out modestly, but gained in popularity. While no threat to *Harry Potter*, her success had been enough to provide her with a comfortable living and a house of her own in Cedar by the Sea. *Charlie Two and the Pink Sandbox* would be coming out in time for Christmas gifting.

The Boston Charlie episode had also initiated in Nikki a keen interest in the paranormal. She'd begun a self-directed study of spiritual and natural law, and her eclectic reading always seemed to be accompanied by "teacher plant" dreams that offered additional information. Nikki sensed that she was undergoing a systematic education. Was Boston Charlie still guiding her? He had said they would meet again, but in a different way. Nikki didn't know.

Nor did Nikki know *what* had happened to Boston Charlie. Had he been successful in undoing the damage? It certainly seemed so; Nikki's world was still afloat. If, indeed, Boston Charlie was, in some way, still influencing her life, then Boston Charlie must have also survived. Yet, there was one thing that sometimes haunted Nikki's waking hours and gave her the odd nightmare. Had Adelaide's appearance—and disappearance—thrown a major monkeywrench into Boston Charlie's plan? In spite of their efforts, was there, somewhere, in the cosmic melange of planes, one in which the—what was it Boston Charlie had called it?—the "negative principle" was doing its worst? That was something Nikki Leino would never know.

Now she saw that Josie was guiding a woman to her table. Nikki jumped up. She and Marj squealed, hugged, laughed, talked at the same time in that incoherent ritual of greeting between two women friends who haven't seen each other in ages. Josie discreetly withdrew to fetch the bottle of Carta de Plata that Nikki had pre-ordered.

Now Nikki and Marj just sat looking at each other, smiling. "Well, Mrs. Byrd, you *do* look marvelous. I love your hair that way. And your *clothes!* Travel in Switzerland obviously agrees with you."

"Oh, just making an effort," Marj laughed, using a favorite *Coronation Street* phrase. "You look fantastic too, Nikki. And you're becoming so successful! When is you next book coming out?"

"September. And you? How long are you going to be on the island?"

"Only a couple of days. Jonah is here for a seminar so I left the twins with their nanny and came along so I could see you."

"Josh and Gabe! How old are they now?"

"They're ten."

"Okay, it's time I said it. I was dead wrong. I couldn't believe you'd ever go back to Jonah, but obviously it's worked out."

Josie brought the wine, uncorked it and went through the formality of having Nikki taste it, then poured two glasses. Marj raised hers: "To the good ship Independence and all who sail in her and to dear old friends met *again.*"

Nikki smiled. "That seems so long ago now—and yet it doesn't." She picked up the menu. "The food here is great. When Phil and I were together we used to come here a lot. You've been here before, haven't you?"

"No." Marj sipped her wine. "This is really *good.* Interesting bouquet. Makes me think of a cranberry bog." She grinned, harking back to their playful wine critiques. "It has a fresh, engaging boldness, although I sense a hint of stage fright."

"Bodegas Berberana Rioja Carta de Plata. Yes, I find it resplendent but a little lacking in confidence, like a novice bullfighter."

"It's delicious. This place is lovely—and a bit of a discovery, way out here on the edge of town."

"It started out modestly, but by now has an international reputation. The Mahle has the best wine selection in town, and wait till you try the food!" Nikki studied the menu. "You have a treat in store. The fresh Chinook salmon with prawns and scallops in Pernod sauce is delicious; the New York steak is always done to perfection—but today I think I'll have the mixed grill: lamb chop, chicken with orange wasabi glaze and kataifi prawns. I'll hike it off later. Of course," Nikki added, slowly raising her eyes, "they also have *local rabbit* with fresh exotic mushrooms."

Marj looked up, startled, met Nikki's gaze, then they both burst out laughing. "I'll have what you're having," Marj said and put down her menu. "Oh god, the rabbits of Eagle Lake Park! I wonder if they're still there. You know, we never talked about it much . . . afterwards."

"No, we never did. It was like having this monstrous secret, so secret that we couldn't even discuss it with each other."

"Do you ever go back there?"

"When you called that you were coming, I took a drive into Eagle Lake Park for the first time since I left. It's all changed. Clark and Shelley Moon run the campground now. Hector and Ida are dead and gone. There are still a few rabbits around, but none of the residents of the trailer park are there anymore. All the mobile homes have been removed except the one Clark and Shelley lived in when they first got married. I didn't see him, but I think George Moon is living in his parents' old house now. Clark and Shelley are in Adelaide's old place. They have a two children."

"I wonder what happened to all the rest of them."

"I ran into Fred Crushill at the Safeway. He seemed to be having trouble remembering things, and didn't recognize me at first. But when I prodded his memory a bit, it seemed to bring back the old days. He told me they'd bought a condo in Nanaimo, and that Paulette died three years ago of heart trouble. He rakishly confided that he's living with a young woman now, no doubt a caregiver. I asked about the other residents of Eagle Lake Park, and he told me that the Hatches had moved to Gabriola Island to be near their family, and that Justin and Emily Laderheim bought a small house in town not far from the hospital. After Emily's stroke, she wanted to be near medical help in case she needed it. Fred lost touch with them so we don't know if any of them are still living. He didn't seem to even remember Janet and Bob Lindsey."

"It all sounds so hideously normal—like nothing unusual ever happened there."

"Fred said he still remembered the night of the big storm—the night Adelaide Moon disappeared. Seeing me again must have brought it back."

"*I* certainly remember it. I *still* have the occasional nightmare!"

"Me too! It's not the sort of thing you ever forget. I could've—maybe—called it hallucination if they'd ever found her body. I remember she went over the bank with the picnic table—and that's *all* I remember."

"I thought you were dead. You were lying there on the edge in the rain and the mud and I thought you were dead."

"Adelaide must have stunned me, or I hit my head when I fell. I still don't know how you managed to drag me back."

"It wasn't easy, but somehow I did it. That part is fuzzy to me too. There was the storm and everything going on. I guess my adrenaline was pumping. You were a soaking wet dead weight!"

"All I remember is waking up in my own bed."

"Yelling for someone to stop."

"Adelaide. I was trying to keep her from going into the light."

"When I found you there wasn't any light."

"Adelaide went into it."

"Over the edge, you mean."

"I suppose. I was sure they'd find her body at the bottom—or on top of Justin's camper."

"The camper *was* totaled by the picnic table. Everybody blamed it on the storm—as if any storm could've blown that thing."

"They never did find a body, did they? Didn't they even drag Eagle Lake after I left?"

"Yes. They found nothing. And all that was left of Boston Charlie was an empty plant pot with hanging wires, and *nobody* attached any significance to that."

"Boston Charlie. He must have been thrown out of his pot. Well, I told you. For me, plants die. I guess we *were* the last ones then to ever see Adelaide Moon."

"George told the police that she'd been despondent after Raymond Cantwell died, and further upset by Prince being put down, and then Emily Laderheim's stroke."

"The queen bee was affected by disturbances in the hive."

"George said she'd been irrational. She couldn't sleep. She kept raving about seeing her half-brother's ghost. That night, George had gotten up to get her something to quiet her down and when he came back she was gone. That was the last he ever saw of her."

"So I guess George knew that Raymond was Adelaide's brother."

"Yes. It all came out after Adelaide vanished—and after you'd left. The story was that while Adelaide's mother was an unmarried teenager, she gave birth to Raymond. She placed him in an institution where he spent most of his life. Adelaide didn't know about him until her mother told her on her death bed. To her credit, Adelaide made it a point to find Raymond, visit him, and eventually she and George brought him home. In their own way, Adelaide and Raymond were very close."

"Maybe that's why Adelaide could see what we saw that night. She was probably psychic too. She may have been a synesthete, like her brother."

"Whatever she was, she just vanished off the face of the earth. Nobody knows what happened to her and no trace of her was ever found."

Off the face of the earth is right. I wonder where she ended up. Was Adelaide now an alien in Boston Charlie's world–the way Charlie had been in this one? "I can't believe we didn't talk more about all this at the time!"

"Me neither. It became a time capsule—not to be opened till now."

"I'd have probably blabbered to anyone who would have listened if it hadn't been for you. You're the one who shut me up."

"What could you have said that wouldn't have landed you in a psych ward? You were pretty freaked."

"All I knew was that I had to get out of there. I grabbed the first vacant apartment in town and I don't even remember the name of the people who bought the mobile home."

"Elderly couple. They were still there when I left . . ."

"—to go back to Jonah."

Marj smiled. "Yes, to go back to Jonah."

"I never could understand that at the time."

"I know it sounds strange. We did have out troubles—what with Jonah's financial shenanigans. I thought for a while he'd wind up in prison, but that's all over now. You know, he's changed. It's hard to picture, but he's become almost saintly. *Too* saintly sometimes. Anything I do is fine with him. And he's wonderful with the twins— and there are times I just don't *believe* the man. He used to be such a son-of-a-bitch. What could've happened?"

We saw his form that night. Boston Charlie pulled in Jonah's replica. I don't know why, unless Jonah had a virus contamination passed on by you. Whatever the reason, Charlie pulled him in—and maybe a little more than just the virus was removed from Jonah Byrd. Maybe Boston Charlie removed more than one negative principle in Jonah's case. Oh hell, I can't tell you that! "I've no idea. Sometimes people change. Probably the love of a good woman."

"Well, whatever. Guess I should be grateful. But I'll tell this to you and only you. I sometimes miss the old hell-raiser."

Nikki laughed. "We women are never satisfied."

"And what about you? You're not still seeing Phil, are you?"

"No. Phil isn't even on the island anymore. She was always socially conscious, a champion of the oppressed, and I always thought she might get into politics, but that's not what happened. Last I heard, she and Susan had joined the Global Volunteer Network and were in Uganda, traveling through native villages, working with children orphaned by the AIDS epidemic. They may still be there."

"Is this the same Phil who was terrified of all creatures great and small, and allergic to everything?"

"Yeah, go figure!"

"But what about you? There must be someone interesting in *your* life."

"Well—no, not really. I've been trying to concentrate on building a career. I haven't had much luck with personal relationships except with my cat! The older I get, the more set in my ways I seem to be."

"As far as career goes, you're doing splendidly. I saw one of your books in a shop in Kajaani. We took the boys to Finland so they could dig around in their Finnish roots, and I saw a translated copy of *The Adventures of Charlie Two.* It was *such* a kick, and I was thrilled for you. I brought one back so you could sign it for me in Finnish." Marj picked up her elegant and expensive leather bag and extracted a slim volume.

Delighted, Nikki took the book: *Kalle Kaksoisen Seikkailut.* There on the jacket, was Charlie Two in his marmalade cartoonishness, riding a magic carpet. Smiling, Marj handed Nikki a pen. Nikki wrote on the flyleaf: *To Marjatta, who was there at the start, with love from Annikki.*

She handed the book back. "I'm sorry I don't read or write Finnish. I wish I did. Do you?"

"A little. My Lapp grandmother's influence. We didn't speak it at home except for my dad who always swore in Finnish. Mummo taught me to read from the *Aapinen*–that's the ABC's. I thought I'd forgotten the language, but was amazed at how much of it came back to me when we were in Kajaani."

"I know a few words but we didn't speak it at home either. My mother could read and write Finnish but my dad couldn't, and he hated it when anyone spoke a language he couldn't understand. He was always convinced they were talking about him."

"Are your parents still living?"

"Vlad and Helga? They'll be going to Florida in November. My grandmother died and left them her house in Lake Worth, so they're snowbirds now. They live in New Brunswick and winter in the tropics."

"So they're still together!

"Proving that marriages really *are* made in heaven. Nobody on *earth* would ever match up those two. Although, age may be mellowing them. Last I heard they're taking ballroom dancing lessons." *And I wonder if Boston Charlie had anything to do with* that. *I don't recall seeing their replicas that night, but there were so many, and I had been in contact with them by phone after Charlie came.*

Marj was looking at her intently. "Your career is really going to be amazing. Yes, you'll be more successful than you ever dreamed."

Nikki grinned. "Really? And will I also meet a tall dark stranger? Of course I'd blow it if I did. I'm not a kid anymore. I'll be forty on my next birthday. I think it would terrify me now to think of actually living with someone."

Marj frowned, seemed to be concentrating. "Nevertheless, I see you with a woman. She *is* tall and she *is* dark—in fact she's black. And she's very, very funny. Has a wild sense of humor. She's teaching you to play a drum!"

"Where would I ever find such an exotic creature on the 49th parallel?" Nikki was playing along, but at the same time not sure whether she should be treating this lightly.

"I don't know, but I see the two of you in what looks like a large, old house. It could be in the Caribbean islands; she has a British accent. Somewhere where's there music and rhythm and a warm climate. I think you may be on vacation there — it could even be Florida. Go visit your folks when they're down there."

"Marj, are you channeling your Lapp grandmother again?"

Marj shook her head slightly. "Oh, I don't know. Ever since that night, I've sometimes been able to see things. I blurt them out, then live to see them come true."

"You mean like your grandmother could? The apparitions of people arriving before they actually get there?"

"No, not those, but I do get . . . I suppose I could call them visions. They never last long. They're more like a flash. Like you, just now, in the tropics. It's a bit like flipping TV stations. I see a scene, then it's gone. It doesn't happen often; I don't have any control over it, and I can't just make it happen. But I'm sure it has something to do with Boston Charlie and that night. Have you noticed anything different in *your* life?"

"With me, it's dreams. I seem to dream everything that happens before it does. I write the Charlie books that way. It's like we actually create our lives in the dream world instead of when we're awake. All the planning is done while we sleep, and we can try out different solutions, then decide which one we want to make real. I know it sounds weird and backwards, but that's what I believe. And I think, in that sense, I'm still in touch with Boson Charlie." Nikki smiled and took a sip of wine. "Of course you're the only person in the world I can tell that to."

The dinner came, beautifully presented on oversized plates and garnished with two fragile filigrees of crisp potato arranged like butterfly wings. "Are these the prawns?" Marj asked, looking at something encased in bristly batter. "They look like they're covered with shredded wheat!"

"That's the kataifi. It's a shredded phyllo dough. Try one, they're delicious."

Marj took a bite. "Oh, *yum!* These are great!"

"The food here never disappoints. And when we get to it, you'll be wanting to try one of their desserts as well."

The meal progressed, and Josie came by to pour the remaining wine and bring dessert menus. "As usual, our compliments to Maureen," Nikki told her. "And yes, we'll have coffee and dessert."

"Oh, Nikki, I don't think I have room . . . "

"In that case, I recommend the small *crème brûlée*. You won't have any trouble handling it and it's a little bit of heaven! Or maybe a single scoop of their lemon sorbet."

They had enjoyed the meal, the quiet atmosphere, and each other. Lingering over coffee they made plans to get together again before Marj had to leave. "Come over tomorrow and see my house. I'll come pick you up."

"That might work. I have the rental car today, and I'm picking up Jonah in about an hour, but he'll be needing it tomorrow to get to his meeting. You could save me from sitting through a seminar on education. Actually, I wouldn't mind cruising by Eagle Lake Park again just out of curiosity."

"Then we'll both go revisit the scene of the crime in my Cherokee."

Marj sipped her coffee. "It's been a lot of years, but we haven't done all that badly, have we? Do you still have Charlie Two?"

"Oh yes. It was because of him I bought the house. He hated being an indoor cat. Now he has the best of both worlds, but he *is* old. I know the day is coming when I'll have to say goodbye to him, and I don't know how I'm going to handle it. He's been my best buddy and my muse for all these years. And you? Do you still have Casimir?"

"No. Sadly, Casimir has passed on. He went on to a surprisingly mellow old age, became almost affectionate, if you can believe it. Then, one day, he just dozed off and never woke up. We don't have any pets now. It's enough of a hassle to travel with two children." Marj raised her coffee cup. "To Casimir!"

"And to Boston Charlie, wherever he is!" As they clinked cups, Nikki smiled as she looked at Marj's right hand, noting that Marj's fingers were long, shapely, manicured and whole—and that one of them was sporting a handsome ruby ring.

www.ingramcontent.com/pod-product-compliance
Lightning Source LLC
Chambersburg PA
CBHW030328200626
46816CB00006BA/1972